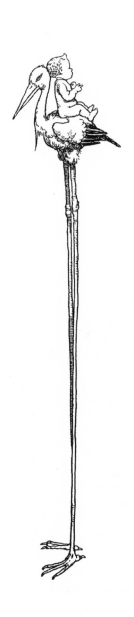

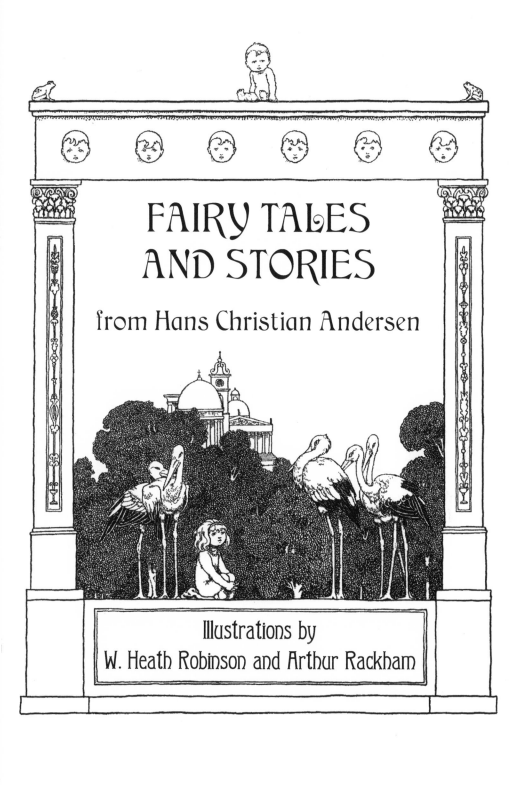

FAIRY TALES AND STORIES

from Hans Christian Andersen

Illustrations by
W. Heath Robinson and Arthur Rackham

Fairy Tales and Stories from Hans Christian Andersen

Illustrations by William Heath Robinson,
Arthur Rackham and Hans Tegner
Translated by H. B. Paull

ISBN 978-1-910880-60-9
Published by Robin Books, 2018
© Marie-Michelle Joy, 2018: book and cover design
www.the-planet-books.com

The Nightingale

IN CHINA, you know, the emperor is a Chinese, and all those about him are Chinamen also. The story I am going to tell you happened a great many years ago, so it is well to hear it now before it is forgotten.

The emperor's palace was the most beautiful in the world. It was built entirely of porcelain, and very costly, but so delicate and brittle that whoever touched it was obliged to be careful. In the garden could be seen the most singular flowers, with pretty silver bells tied to them, which tinkled so that every one who passed could not help noticing the flowers.

Indeed, everything in the emperor's garden was remarkable, and it extended so far that the gardener himself did not know where it ended. Those who travelled beyond its limits knew that there was a noble forest, with lofty trees, sloping down to the deep blue sea, and the great ships sailed under the shadow of its branches.

In one of these trees lived a nightingale, who sang so beautifully that even the poor fishermen, who had so many other things to do, would stop and listen. Sometimes, when they went at night to spread their nets, they would hear her sing and say, "Oh, is not that beautiful?" But when they returned to their fishing, they forgot the bird until the next night. Then they would hear it again and exclaim "Oh, how beautiful is the nightingale's song!"

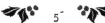

Travellers from every country in the world came to the city of the emperor, which they admired very much, as well as the palace and gardens; but when they heard the nightingale, they all declared it to be the best of all. And the travellers, on their return home, related what they had seen; and learned men wrote books, containing descriptions of the town, the palace, and the gardens; but they did not forget the nightingale, which was really the greatest wonder. And those who could write poetry composed beautiful verses about the nightingale, who lived in a forest near the deep sea.

The books travelled all over the world, and some of them came into the hands of the emperor; and he sat in his golden chair, and, as he read, he nodded his approval every moment, for it pleased him to find such a beautiful description of his city, his palace, and his gardens. But when he came to the words, "the nightingale is the most beautiful of all," he exclaimed, "What is this? I know nothing of any nightingale. Is there such a bird in my empire? and even in my garden? I have never heard of it. Something, it appears, may be learnt from books."

Then he called one of his lords-in-waiting, who was so high-bred, that when any in an inferior rank to himself spoke to him or asked him a question, he would answer, "Pooh," which means nothing.

"There is a very wonderful bird mentioned here, called a nightingale," said the emperor; "they say it is the best thing in my large kingdom. Why have I not been told of it?"

"I have never heard the name," replied the cavalier; "she has not been presented at court."

"It is my pleasure that she shall appear this evening." said the emperor; "the whole world knows what I possess better than I do myself."

"I have never heard of her," said the cavalier; "yet I will endeavour to find her."

But where was the nightingale to be found? The nobleman went up stairs and down, through halls and passages; yet none of those whom he met had heard of the bird. So he returned to the emperor and said that it must be a fable invented by those who had written the book.

"Your imperial majesty," said he, "cannot believe everything contained in books; sometimes they are only fiction, or what is called the black art."

"But the book in which I have read this account," said the emperor, "was sent to me by the great and mighty em-

peror of Japan, and therefore it cannot contain a falsehood. I will hear the nightingale, she must be here this evening; she has my highest favour; and if she does not come, the whole court shall be trampled upon after supper is ended."

"Tsing-pe!" cried the lord-in-waiting, and again he ran up and down stairs, through all the halls and corridors; and half the court ran with him, for they did not like the idea of being trampled upon. There was a great inquiry about this wonderful nightingale, whom all the world knew, but who was unknown to the court.

At last they met with a poor little girl in the kitchen, who said, "Oh, yes, I know the nightingale quite well; indeed, she can sing. Every evening I have permission to take home to my poor sick mother the scraps from the table; she lives down by the sea-shore, and as I come back I feel tired,

and I sit down in the wood to rest and listen to the nightingale's song. Then the tears come into my eyes, and it is just as if my mother kissed me."

"Little maiden," said the lord-in-waiting, "I will obtain for you constant employment in the kitchen, and you shall have permission to see the emperor dine if you will lead us to the nightingale; for she is invited for this evening to the palace."

So she went into the wood where the nightingale sang, and half the court followed her. As they went along, a cow began lowing.

"Oh," said a young courtier, "now we have found her; what wonderful power for such a small creature; I have certainly heard it before."

"No, that is only a cow lowing," said the little girl; "we are a long way from the place yet."

Then some frogs began to croak in the marsh.

"Beautiful," said the young courtier again. "Now I hear it, tinkling like little church bells."

"No, those are frogs," said the little maiden; "but I think we shall soon hear her now," and presently the nightingale began to sing.

"Hark, hark! there she is," said the girl, "and there she sits," she added, pointing to a little gray bird who was perched on a bough.

"Is it possible?" said the lord-in-waiting; "I never imagined it would be a little, plain, simple thing like that. She has certainly changed colour at seeing so many grand people around her."

"Little nightingale," cried the girl, raising her voice, "our most gracious emperor wishes you to sing before him."

"With the greatest pleasure," said the nightingale and began to sing most delightfully.

"It sounds like tiny glass bells," said the lord-in-waiting, "and see how her little throat works. It is surprising that we have never heard this before; she will be a great success at court."

"Shall I sing once more before the emperor?" asked the nightingale, who thought he was present.

"My excellent little nightingale," said the courtier, "I have the great pleasure of inviting you to a court festival this evening, where you will gain imperial favour by your charming song."

"My song sounds best in the green wood," said the bird; but still she came willingly when she heard the emperor's wish.

The palace was elegantly decorated for the occasion. The walls and floors of porcelain glittered in the light of a thousand lamps. Beautiful flowers, round which little bells were tied, stood in the corridors; and there was a running to and fro, which made these bells to tinkle so loudly that no one could speak to be heard.

In the centre of the great hall, a golden perch had been fixed for the nightingale to sit on. The whole court was present, and the little kitchen-maid had received permission to stand by the door. She was now installed as a real court cook.

All were in full dress, and every eye was turned to the little gray bird when the emperor nodded to her to begin. The nightingale sang so sweetly that the tears came into the emperor's eyes, and then rolled down his cheeks, as her song became still more touching and went to every one's heart.

The emperor was so delighted that he declared the nightingale should have his gold slipper to wear round her neck, but she declined the honour with thanks: she had been sufficiently rewarded already. "I have seen tears in the emperor's eyes," she said, "that is my richest reward. Emperor's tears have wonderful power and are quite sufficient honour for me;" and then she sang again more enchantingly than ever.

"That singing is a lovely gift," said the ladies of the court to each other; and then they took water in their mouths to make them utter the gurgling sounds of the nightingale when they spoke to anyone, so that they might fancy themselves nightingales. And the footmen and chambermaids also expressed their satisfaction, which is saying a great deal, for they are very difficult to please.

In fact the nightingale's visit was most successful. She was now to remain at court, to have her own cage, with liberty to go out twice a day and once during the night. Twelve servants were appointed to attend her on these occasions, who each held her by a silken string fastened to her leg. There was certainly not much pleasure in this kind of flying.

The whole city spoke of the wonderful bird, and when two people met, one said "nightin" and the other said "gale," and they understood what was meant, for nothing else was talked of.

Eleven peddlers' children were named after her, but not one of them could sing a note.

One day the emperor received a large packet on which was written "The Nightingale." "Here is no doubt a new book about our celebrated bird," said the emperor. But instead of a book, it was a work of art contained in a casket, an artificial nightingale made to look like a living one and covered all over with diamonds, rubies, and sapphires.

As soon as the artificial bird was wound up, it could sing like the real one and could move its tail up and down, which sparkled with silver and gold. Round its neck hung a piece of ribbon, on which was written "The Emperor of Japan's nightingale is poor compared with that of the Emperor of China's."

"This is very beautiful," exclaimed all who saw it, and he who had brought the artificial bird received the title of "Imperial nightingale-bringer-in-chief."

"Now they must sing together," said the court, "and what a duet it will be." But they did not get on well, for the real nightingale sang in its own natural way, but the artificial bird sang only waltzes.

"That is not a fault," said the music-master, "it is quite perfect to my taste." So the artificial bird must now sing alone and was as successful as the real bird; besides, it was so much prettier to look at, for it sparkled like bracelets and breast-pins. Three and thirty times did it sing the same

tunes without being tired; the people would gladly have heard it again, but the emperor said the living nightingale ought to sing something. But where was she? No one had noticed her when she flew out at the open window, back to her own green woods.

"What strange conduct," said the emperor, when her flight had been discovered; and all the courtiers blamed her and said she was a very ungrateful creature.

"But we have the best bird after all," said one, and then they would have the bird sing again, although it was the thirty-fourth time they had listened to the same piece, and even then they had not learnt it, for it was rather difficult. But the music-master praised the bird in the highest degree and even asserted that it was better than a real nightingale, not only in its dress and the beautiful diamonds, but also in its musical power. "For you must perceive, my chief lord and emperor, that with a real nightingale we can never tell what is going to be sung, but with this bird everything is settled. It can be opened and explained, so that people may understand how the waltzes are formed and why one note follows upon another."

"This is exactly what we think," they all replied, and then the music-master received permission to exhibit the bird to the public on the following Sunday, and the emperor commanded that they should be present to hear it sing.

When they heard it, they were like people intoxicated; however it must have been with drinking tea, which is quite a Chinese custom. They all said "Oh!" and held up their forefingers and nodded, but a poor fisherman, who had heard the real nightingale, said, "it sounds prettily enough, and the melodies are all alike; yet there seems something wanting, I cannot exactly tell what."

And after this the real nightingale was banished from the empire, and the artificial bird placed on a silk cushion close to the emperor's bed. The presents of gold and precious stones which had been received with it were round the bird, and it was now advanced to the title of "Little Imperial Toilet Singer," and to the rank of No. 1 on the left hand; for the emperor considered the left side, on which the heart lies, as the most noble, and the heart of an emperor is in the same place as that of other people.

The music-master wrote a work, in twenty-five volumes, about the artificial bird, which was very learned and very long, and full of the most difficult Chinese words; yet all the people said they had read and understood it, for fear of being thought stupid and having their bodies trampled upon.

So a year passed, and the emperor, the court, and all the other Chinese knew every little turn in the artificial bird's song; and for that same reason it pleased them better. They could sing with the bird, which they often did. The street-boys sang, "Zi-zi-zi, cluck, cluck, cluck," and the emperor himself could sing it also. It was really most amusing.

One evening, when the artificial bird was singing its best and the emperor lay in bed listening to it, something inside the bird sounded "whizz." Then a spring cracked. "Whir-r-r" went all the wheels, running round, and then the music stopped. The emperor immediately sprang out of bed and called for his physician; but what could he do?

Then they sent for a watchmaker; and, after a great deal of talking and examination, the bird was put into something like order; but he said that it must be used very carefully, as the barrels were worn and it would be impossible to put in new ones without injuring the music.

Now there was great sorrow, as the bird could only be allowed to play once a year; and even that was dangerous for the works inside it. Then the music-master made a little speech, full of hard words, and declared that the bird was as good as ever; and, of course, no one contradicted him.

Five years passed, and then a real grief came upon the land. The Chinese really were fond of their emperor, and he now lay so ill that he was not expected to live. Already a new emperor had been chosen, and the people who stood in the street asked the lord-in-waiting how the old emperor was; but he only said, "Pooh!" and shook his head.

Cold and pale, lay the emperor in his royal bed; the whole court thought he was dead, and everyone ran away to pay homage to his successor. The chamberlains went out to have a talk on the matter, and the ladies'-maids invited company to take coffee.

Cloth had been laid down on the halls and passages, so that not a footstep should be heard, and all was silent and still. But the emperor was not yet dead, although he lay white and stiff on his gorgeous bed, with the long velvet curtains and heavy gold tassels. A window stood open, and the moon shone in upon the emperor and the artificial bird.

The poor emperor, finding he could scarcely breathe with a strange weight on his chest, opened his eyes, and saw Death sitting there. He had put on the emperor's golden crown, and held in one hand his sword of state and in the other his beautiful banner. All around the bed and peeping through the long velvet curtains, were a number of strange heads, some very ugly, and others lovely and gentle-looking. These were the emperor's good and bad deeds, which stared him in the face now Death sat at his heart.

"Do you remember this?" "Do you recollect that?" they asked one after another, thus bringing to his remembrance circumstances that made the perspiration stand on his brow.

"I know nothing about it," said the emperor. "Music! music!" he cried; "the large Chinese drum! that I may not hear what they say." But they still went on, and Death nodded like a Chinaman to all they said. "Music! music!" shouted the emperor. "You little precious golden bird, sing, pray sing! I have given you gold and costly presents; I have even hung my golden slipper round your neck. Sing! sing!" But the bird remained silent. There was no one to wind it up, and therefore it could not sing a note.

Death continued to stare at the emperor with his cold, hollow eyes, and the room was fearfully still. Suddenly there came through the open window the sound of sweet music. Outside, on the bough of a tree, sat the living nightingale.

She had heard of the emperor's illness and was therefore come to sing to him of hope and trust. And as she sung, the shadows grew paler and paler; the blood in the emperor's veins flowed more rapidly, and gave life to his weak limbs; and even Death himself listened and said, "Go on, little nightingale, go on."

"Then will you give me the beautiful golden sword and that rich banner? and will you give me the emperor's crown?" said the bird.

So Death gave up each of these treasures for a song; and the nightingale continued her singing. She sung of the quiet churchyard, where the white roses grow, where the elder-tree wafts its perfume on the breeze, and the fresh, sweet grass is moistened by the mourners' tears. Then Death longed to go and see his garden, and floated out through the window in the form of a cold white mist.

"Thanks, thanks, you heavenly little bird. I know you well. I banished you from my kingdom once, and yet you have charmed away the evil faces from my bed and banished Death from my heart, with your sweet song. How can I reward you?"

"You have already rewarded me," said the nightingale. "I shall never forget that I drew tears from your eyes the first time I sang to you. These are the jewels that rejoice a singer's heart. But now sleep, and grow strong and well again. I will sing to you again."

And as she sung, the emperor fell into a sweet sleep; and how mild and refreshing that slumber was! When he awoke, strengthened and restored, the sun shone brightly through the window; but not one of his servants had returned—they all believed he was dead; only the nightingale still sat beside him, and sang.

"You must always remain with me," said the emperor. "You shall sing only when it pleases you; and I will break the artificial bird into a thousand pieces."

"No; do not do that," replied the nightingale; "the bird did very well as long as it could. Keep it here still. I cannot live in the palace and build my nest; let me come when I like. I will sit on a bough outside your window, in the evening and sing to you, so that you may be happy, and have thoughts full of joy. I will sing to you of those who are happy and those who suffer; of the good and the evil, who are hidden around you. The little singing bird flies far from you and your court to the home of the fisherman and the peasant's cot. I love your heart better than your crown; and yet something holy lingers round that also. I will come, I will sing to you; but you must promise me one thing."

"Everything," said the emperor, who, having dressed himself in his imperial robes, stood with the hand that held the heavy golden sword pressed to his heart.

"I only ask one thing," she replied; "let no one know that you have a little bird who tells you everything. It will be best to conceal it." So saying, the nightingale flew away.

The servants now came in to look after the dead emperor; when, lo! there he stood and, to their astonishment, said, "Good morning!"

Little Ida's Flowers

"MY POOR flowers are quite dead," said little Ida, "they were so pretty yesterday evening, and now all the leaves are hanging down quite withered. What do they do that for?" she asked of the student who sat on the sofa. She liked him very much; he could tell the most amusing stories and cut out the prettiest pictures: hearts, and ladies dancing, castles with doors that opened, as well as flowers; he was a delightful student. "Why do the flowers look so faded today?" she asked again and pointed to her nosegay, which was quite withered.

"Don't you know what is the matter with them?" said the student. "The flowers were at a ball last night, and therefore it is no wonder they hang their heads."

"But flowers cannot dance?" cried little Ida.

"Yes, indeed, they can," replied the student. "When it grows dark and everybody is asleep, they jump about quite merrily. They have a ball almost every night."

"Can children go to these balls?"

"Yes," said the student, "little daisies and lilies of the valley."

"Where do the beautiful flowers dance?" asked little Ida.

"Have you not often seen the large castle outside the gates of the town, where the king lives in summer and where the beautiful garden is full of flowers? And have you not fed the swans with bread when they swam towards you? Well, the flowers have capital balls there, believe me."

  17

"I was in the garden out there yesterday with my mother," said Ida, "but all the leaves were off the trees and there was not a single flower left. Where are they? I used to see so many in the summer."

"They are in the castle," replied the student. "You must know that as soon as the king and all the court are gone into the town, the flowers run out of the garden into the castle, and you should see how merry they are. The two most beautiful roses seat themselves on the throne, and are called the king and queen; then all the red cockscombs range themselves on each side and bow: these are the lords-in-waiting. After that the pretty flowers come in, and there is a grand ball. The blue violets represent little naval cadets and dance with hyacinths and crocuses, which they call young ladies. The tulips and tiger-lilies are the old ladies who sit and watch the dancing, so that everything may be conducted with order and propriety."

"But," said little Ida, "is there no one there to hurt the flowers for dancing in the king's castle?"

"No one knows anything about it," said the student. "The old steward of the castle, who has to watch there at night, sometimes comes in; but he carries a great bunch of keys, and as soon as the flowers hear the keys rattle, they run and hide themselves behind the long curtains, and stand quite still, just peeping their heads out. Then the old steward says, 'I smell flowers here,' but he cannot see them."

"Oh how capital," said little Ida, clapping her hands. "Should I be able to see these flowers?"

"Yes," said the student, "mind you think of it the next time you go out, no doubt you will see them if you peep through the window. I did so today, and I saw a long yellow lily lying stretched out on the sofa. She was a court lady."

"Can the flowers from the Botanical Gardens go to these balls?" asked Ida. "It is such a distance!"

"Oh yes," said the student, "whenever they like, for they can fly. Have you not seen those beautiful red, white, and yellow butterflies that look like flowers? They were flowers once. They have flown off their stalks into the air and flap their leaves as if they were little wings to make them fly. Then, if they behave well, they obtain permission to fly about during the day, instead of being obliged to sit still on their stems at home, and so in time their leaves become real wings. It may be, however, that the flowers in the Botanical Gardens have never been to the king's palace, and, therefore, they know nothing of the merry doings at night, which take place there. I will tell you what to do, and the botanical professor, who lives close by here, will be so surprised. You know him very well, do you not? Well, next time you go into his garden, you must tell one of the flowers that there is going to be a grand ball at the castle; then that flower will tell all the others, and they will fly away to the castle as soon as possible. And when the professor walks into his garden, there will not be a single flower left. How he will wonder what has become of them!"

"But how can one flower tell another? Flowers cannot speak?"

"No, certainly not," replied the student; "but they can make signs. Have you not often seen that when the wind blows, they nod at one another and rustle all their green leaves?"

"Can the professor understand the signs?" asked Ida.

"Yes, to be sure he can. He went one morning into his garden and saw a stinging nettle making signs with its leaves to a beautiful red carnation. It was saying, 'You are so pretty, I like you very much.' But the professor did not approve of such nonsense, so he clapped his hands on the nettle to stop it. Then the leaves, which are its fingers, stung him so sharply that he has never ventured to touch a nettle since."

"Oh, how funny!" said Ida, and she laughed.

"How can anyone put such notions into a child's head?" said a tiresome lawyer, who had come to pay a visit and sat on the sofa. He did not like the student and would grumble when he saw him cutting out droll or amusing pictures. Sometimes it would be a man hanging on a gibbet and holding a heart in his hand as if he had been stealing hearts. Sometimes it was an old witch riding through the air on a broom and carrying her husband on her nose. But the lawyer did not like such jokes, and he would say as he had just said, "How can anyone put such nonsense into a child's head? What absurd fancies there are!"

But to little Ida all these stories, which the student told her about the flowers, seemed very droll, and she thought over them a great deal. The flowers did hang their heads, because they had been dancing all night and were very tired, and most likely they were ill. Then she took them into the room where a number of toys lay on a pretty little table, and the whole of the table drawer besides was full of beautiful things.

Her doll Sophy lay in the doll's bed asleep, and little Ida said to her, "You must really get up Sophy and be content to lie in the drawer tonight; the poor flowers are ill, and they must lie in your bed, then perhaps they will get well again." So she took the doll out, who looked quite cross, and said not a single word, for she was angry at being turned out of her bed. Ida placed the flowers in the doll's bed, and drew the quilt over them. Then she told them to lie quite still and be good while she made some tea for them, so that they might be quite well and able to get up the next morning. And she drew the curtains close round the little bed, so that the sun might not shine in their eyes.

During the whole evening she could not help thinking of what the student had told her. And before she went to bed herself, she was obliged to peep behind the curtains into the garden where all her mother's beautiful flowers grew, hyacinths and tulips, and many others. Then she whispered to them quite softly, "I know you are going to a ball tonight." But the flowers appeared as if they did not understand, and not a leaf moved; still Ida felt quite sure she knew all about it. She lay awake a long time after she was in bed, thinking how pretty it must be to see all the beautiful flowers dancing in the king's garden.

"I wonder if my flowers have really been there," she said to herself, and then she fell asleep. In the night she awoke;

she had been dreaming of the flowers and of the student, as well as of the tiresome lawyer who found fault with him. It was quite still in Ida's bedroom; the night-lamp burnt on the table, and her father and mother were asleep. "I wonder if my flowers are still lying in Sophy's bed," she thought to herself; "how much I should like to know." She raised herself a little and glanced at the door of the room where all her flowers and playthings lay; it was partly open, and as she listened, it seemed as if someone in the room was playing the piano, but softly and more prettily than she had ever before heard it. "Now all the flowers are certainly dancing in there," she thought, "oh, how much I should like to see them," but she did not dare move for fear of disturbing her father and mother. "If they would only come in here," she thought; but they did not come, and the music continued to play so beautifully and was so pretty that she could resist no longer. She crept out of her little bed, went softly to the door, and looked into the room.

Oh, what a splendid sight there was to be sure! There was no night-lamp burning, but the room appeared quite light, for the moon shone through the window upon the floor and made it almost like day. All the hyacinths and tulips stood in two long rows down the room, not a single flower remained in the window, and the flower-pots were all empty. The flowers were dancing gracefully on the floor, making turns and holding each other by their long green leaves as they swung round. At the piano sat a large yellow lily which little Ida was sure she had seen in the summer, for she remembered the student saying she was very much like Miss Lina, one of Ida's friends. They all laughed at him then, but now it seemed to little Ida as if the tall yellow flower was really like the young lady. She had just the same manners while playing, bending her long yellow face from side to side and nodding in time to the beautiful music.

Then she saw a large purple crocus jump into the middle of the table where the playthings stood, go up to the doll's bedstead, and draw back the curtains; there lay the sick flowers, but they got up directly and nodded to the others as a sign that they wished to dance with them. The old rough doll, with the broken mouth, stood up and bowed to the pretty flowers. They did not look ill at all now but jumped about and were very merry, yet none of them noticed little Ida.

Presently it seemed as if something fell from the table. Ida looked that way and saw a slight carnival rod jumping down among the flowers as if it belonged to them; it

was, however, very smooth and neat, and a little wax doll with a broad brimmed hat on her head, like the one worn by the lawyer, sat upon it. The carnival rod hopped about among the flowers on its three red stilted feet and stamped quite loud when it danced the Mazurka; the flowers could not perform this dance: they were too light to stamp in that manner.

All at once the wax doll which rode on the carnival rod seemed to grow larger and taller, and it turned round and said to the paper flowers, "How can you put such things in a child's head? they are all foolish fancies;" and then the doll was exactly like the lawyer with the broad brimmed hat and looked as yellow and as cross as he did; but the paper dolls struck him on his thin legs, and he shrunk up again and became quite a little wax doll. This was very amusing, and Ida could not help laughing.

The carnival rod went on dancing, and the lawyer was obliged to dance also. It was no use; he might make himself great and tall, or remain a little wax doll with a large black hat; still he must dance. Then at last the other flowers interceded for him, especially those who had lain in the doll's bed, and the carnival rod gave up his dancing. At the same moment a loud knocking was heard in the drawer, where Ida's doll Sophy lay with many other toys. Then the rough doll ran to the end of the table, laid himself flat down upon it, and began to pull the drawer out a little way.

Then Sophy raised herself and looked round quite astonished.

"There must be a ball here tonight," said Sophy. "Why did not somebody tell me?"

"Will you dance with me?" said the rough doll.

"You are the right sort to dance with, certainly," said she, turning her back upon him.

Then she seated herself on the edge of the drawer and thought that perhaps one of the flowers would ask her to dance; but none of them came. Then she coughed, "Hem, hem, a-hem;" but for all that not one came. The shabby doll now danced quite alone and not very badly, after all. As none of the flowers seemed to notice Sophy, she let herself down from the drawer to the floor, so as to make a very great noise. All the flowers came round her directly and asked if she had hurt herself, especially those who had lain in her bed. But she was not hurt at all, and Ida's flowers thanked her for the use of the nice bed and were very kind to her. They led her into the middle of the room, where the moon shone, and danced with her, while all the other flowers formed a circle round them. Then Sophy was very happy and said they might keep her bed; she did not mind lying in the drawer at all. But the flowers thanked her very much and said:

"We cannot live long. Tomorrow morning we shall be quite dead; and you must tell little Ida to bury us in the garden, near to the grave of the canary; then, in the summer we shall wake up again and be more beautiful than ever."

"No, you must not die," said Sophy, as she kissed the flowers.

Then the door of the room opened, and a number of beautiful flowers danced in. Ida could not imagine where they could come from, unless they were the flowers from the king's garden. First came two lovely roses, with little golden crowns on their heads; these were the king and queen. Beautiful stocks and carnations followed, bowing to every one present. They had also music with them. Large poppies and peonies had pea-shells for instruments, and blew into them till they were quite red in the face. The bunches of blue hyacinths and the little white snowdrops jingled their bell-like flowers, as if they were real bells. Then came many more flowers: blue violets, purple heart's-ease, daisies, and lilies of the valley; they all danced together and kissed each other. It was very beautiful to behold.

At last the flowers wished each other good-night. Then little Ida crept back into her bed again and dreamt of all she had seen. When she arose the next morning, she went quickly to the little table to see if the flowers were still there. She drew aside the curtains of the little bed. There they all lay, but quite faded; much more so than the day before.

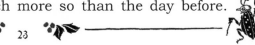

Sophy was lying in the drawer where Ida had placed her; but she looked very sleepy.

"Do you remember what the flowers told you to say to me?" said little Ida. But Sophy looked quite stupid and said not a single word.

"You are not kind at all," said Ida; "and yet they all danced with you."

Then she took a little paper box, on which were painted beautiful birds, and laid the dead flowers in it.

"This shall be your pretty coffin," she said; "and by-and-by, when my cousins come to visit me, they shall help me to bury you out in the garden; so that next summer you may grow up again more beautiful than ever."

Her cousins were two good-tempered boys, whose names were James and Adolphus. Their father had given them each a bow and arrow, and they had brought them to show Ida. She told them about the poor flowers which were dead; and as soon as they obtained permission, they went with her to bury them. The two boys walked first, with their crossbows on their shoulders, and little Ida followed, carrying the pretty box containing the dead flowers. They dug a little grave in the garden. Ida kissed her flowers and then laid them, with the box, in the earth. James and Adolphus then fired their crossbows over the grave, as they had neither guns nor cannons.

The Goblin and the Huckster

THERE was once a regular student, who lived in a garret and had no possessions. And there was also a regular huckster, to whom the house belonged and who occupied the ground floor. A goblin lived with the huckster, because at Christmas he always had a large dish full of jam, with a great piece of butter in the middle. The huckster could afford this; and therefore the goblin remained with the huckster, which was very cunning of him.

One evening the student came into the shop through the back door to buy candles and cheese for himself; he had no one to send, and therefore he came himself; he obtained what he wished, and then the huckster and his wife nodded good evening to him, and she was a woman who could do more than merely nod, for she had usually plenty to say for herself. The student nodded in return as he turned to leave, then suddenly stopped and began reading the piece of paper in which the cheese was wrapped. It was a leaf torn out of an old book, a book that ought not to have been torn up, for it was full of poetry.

"Yonder lies some more of the same sort," said the huckster: "I gave an old woman a few coffee berries for it; you shall have the rest for sixpence, if you will."

"Indeed I will," said the student; "give me the book instead of the cheese; I can eat my bread and butter without cheese. It would be a sin to tear up a book like this. You are

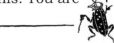

a clever man and a practical man, but you understand no more about poetry than that cask yonder."

This was a very rude speech, especially against the cask; but the huckster and the student both laughed, for it was only said in fun. But the goblin felt very angry that any man should venture to say such things to a huckster who was a householder and sold the best butter. As soon as it was night, and the shop closed, and every one in bed except the student, the goblin stepped softly into the bedroom where the huckster's wife slept and took away her tongue, which, of course, she did not then want.

Whatever object in the room he placed this tongue upon immediately received voice and speech, and was able to express its thoughts and feelings as readily as the lady herself could do. It could only be used by one object at a time, which was a good thing, as a number speaking at once would have caused great confusion. The goblin laid the tongue upon the cask, in which lay a quantity of old newspapers.

"Is it really true," he asked, "that you do not know what poetry is?"

"Of course I know," replied the cask: "poetry is something that always stands in the corner of a newspaper and is sometimes cut out; and I may venture to affirm that I have more of it in me than the student has, and I am only a poor tub of the huckster's."

Then the goblin placed the tongue on the coffee mill; and how it did go to be sure! Then he put it on the butter tub and the cash box, and they all expressed the same opinion as the waste-paper tub; and a majority must always be respected.

"Now I shall go and tell the student," said the goblin; and with these words he went quietly up the back stairs to the garret where the student lived. He had a candle burning still, and the goblin peeped through the keyhole and saw that he was reading in the torn book, which he had brought out of the shop. But how light the room was! From the book shot forth a ray of light which grew broad and full, like the stem of a tree, from which bright rays spread upward and over the student's head. Each leaf was fresh, and each flower was like a beautiful female head; some with dark and sparkling eyes, and others with eyes that were wonderfully blue and clear. The fruit gleamed like stars, and the room was filled with sounds of beautiful music.

The little goblin had never imagined, much less seen or heard of, any sight so glorious as this. He stood still on

tiptoe, peeping in, till the light went out in the garret. The student no doubt had blown out his candle and gone to bed; but the little goblin remained standing there nevertheless and listening to the music, which still sounded on, soft and beautiful, a sweet cradle-song for the student, who had lain down to rest.

"This is a wonderful place," said the goblin; "I never expected such a thing. I should like to stay here with the student;" and the little man thought it over, for he was a sensible little spirit. At last he sighed, "but the student has no jam!" So he went downstairs again into the huckster's shop, and it was a good thing he got back when he did, for the cask had almost worn out the lady's tongue; he had given a description of all that he contained on one side and was just about to turn himself over to the other side to describe what was there, when the goblin entered and restored the tongue to the lady. But from that time forward, the whole shop, from the cash box down to the pinewood logs, formed their opinions from that of the cask; and they all had such confidence in him and treated him with so much respect, that when the huckster read the criticisms on theatricals and art of an evening, they fancied it must all come from the cask.

But after what he had seen, the goblin could no longer sit and listen quietly to the wisdom and understanding downstairs; so, as soon as the evening light glimmered in the garret, he took courage, for it seemed to him as if the rays of light were strong cables, drawing him up and obliging him to go and peep through the keyhole; and, while there, a feeling of vastness came over him such as we experience by the ever-moving sea when the storm breaks forth; and it brought tears into his eyes. He did not himself know why he wept, yet a kind of pleasant feeling mingled with his tears.

"How wonderfully glorious it would be to sit with the student under such a tree;" but that was out of the question, he must be content to look through the keyhole, and be thankful for even that.

There he stood on the cold landing, with the autumn wind blowing down upon him through the trap-door. It was very cold; but the little creature did not really feel it, till the light in the garret went out, and the tones of music died away. Then how he shivered and crept downstairs again to his warm corner, where it felt home-like and comfortable. And when Christmas came again and brought the dish of jam and the great lump of butter, he liked the huckster best of all.

Soon after, in the middle of the night, the goblin was awoke by a terrible noise and knocking against the window shutters and the house doors, and by the sound of the watchman's horn; for a great fire had broken out, and the whole street appeared full of flames. Was it in their house, or a neighbour's? No one could tell, for terror had seized upon all. The huckster's wife was so bewildered that she took her gold ear-rings out of her ears and put them in her pocket, that she might save something at least. The huckster ran to get his business papers, and the servant resolved to save her black silk mantle, which she had managed to buy. Each wished to keep the best things they had. The goblin had the same wish; for, with one spring, he was upstairs and in the student's room, whom he found standing by the open window and looking quite calmly at the fire, which was raging at the house of a neighbour opposite.

The goblin caught up the wonderful book, which lay on the table, and popped it into his red cap, which he held tightly with both hands. The greatest treasure in the house was saved; and he ran away with it to the roof and seated himself on the chimney. The flames of the burning house opposite illuminated him as he sat, both hands pressed tightly over his cap, in which the treasure lay; and then he found out what feelings really reigned in his heart and knew exactly which way they tended. And yet, when the fire was extinguished, and the goblin again began to reflect, he hesitated and said at last, "I must divide myself between the two; I cannot quite give up the huckster because of the jam."

And this is a representation of human nature. We are like the goblin; we all go to visit the huckster "because of the jam."

The Ugly Duckling

IT WAS lovely summer weather in the country, and the golden corn, the green oats, and the haystacks piled up in the meadows looked beautiful. The stork walking about on his long red legs chattered in the Egyptian language, which he had learnt from his mother. The cornfields and meadows were surrounded by large forests, in the midst of which were deep pools. It was, indeed, delightful to walk about in the country.

In a sunny spot stood a pleasant old farm-house close by a deep river, and from the house down to the water side grew great burdock leaves, so high, that under the tallest of them a little child could stand upright. The spot was as wild as the centre of a thick wood.

In this snug retreat sat a duck on her nest, watching for her young brood to hatch; she was beginning to get tired of her task, for the little ones were a long time coming out of their shells, and she seldom had any visitors. The other ducks liked much better to swim about in the river than to climb the slippery banks, and sit under a burdock leaf, to have a gossip with her.

At length one shell cracked, and then another, and from each egg came a living creature that lifted its head and cried, "Peep, peep."

"Quack, quack," said the mother, and then they all quacked as well as they could and looked about them on every side at the large green leaves. Their mother allowed them to look as much as they liked, because green is good for the eyes.

"How large the world is," said the young ducks, when they found how much more room they now had than while they were inside the egg-shell.

"Do you imagine this is the whole world?" asked the mother. "Wait till you have seen the garden; it stretches far beyond that to the parson's field, but I have never ventured to such a distance. Are you all out?" she continued, rising; "No, I declare, the largest egg lies there still. I wonder how long this is to last, I am quite tired of it;" and she seated herself again on the nest.

"Well, how are you getting on?" asked an old duck, who paid her a visit.

"One egg is not hatched yet," said the duck, "it will not break. But just look at all the others, are they not the prettiest little ducklings you ever saw? They are the image of their father, who is so unkind; he never comes to see me."

"Let me see the egg that will not break," said the old duck. "I have no doubt it is a turkey's egg. I was persuaded to hatch some once, and after all my care and trouble with the young ones, they were afraid of the water. I quacked and clucked, but all to no purpose. I could not get them to venture in. Let me look at the egg. Yes, that is a turkey's egg; take my advice, leave it where it is and teach the other children to swim."

"I think I will sit on it a little while longer," said the duck; "as I have sat so long already, a few days will be nothing."

"Please yourself," said the old duck, and she went away.

At last the large egg broke, and a young one crept forth crying, "Peep, peep." It was very large and ugly. The duck stared at it and exclaimed, "It is very large and not at all like the others. I wonder if it really is a turkey. We shall soon find it out, however, when we go to the water. It must go in, if I have to push it in myself."

On the next day the weather was delightful, and the sun shone brightly on the green burdock leaves, so the mother duck took her young brood down to the water and jumped in with a splash. "Quack, quack," cried she, and one after another the little ducklings jumped in. The water closed over their heads, but they came up again in an instant and swam about quite prettily with their legs paddling under them as easily as possible, and the ugly duckling was also in the water swimming with them.

"Oh," said the mother, "that is not a turkey; how well he uses his legs, and how upright he holds himself! He is my own child, and he is not so very ugly after all if you look at him properly. Quack, quack! come with me now, I will take you into grand society and introduce you to the farmyard, but you must keep close to me or you may be trodden upon; and, above all, beware of the cat."

When they reached the farmyard, there was a great disturbance: two families were fighting for an eel's head, which, after all, was carried off by the cat.

"See, children, that is the way of the world," said the mother duck, whetting her beak, for she would have liked the eel's head herself. "Come, now, use your legs, and let me see how well you can behave. You must bow your heads prettily to that old duck yonder; she is the highest born of them all and has Spanish blood, therefore she is well off. Don't you see she has a red rag tied to her leg, which is something very grand and a great honour for a duck: it shows that everyone is anxious not to lose her, as she can be recognized both by man and beast. Come, now, don't turn your toes, a well-bred duckling spreads his feet wide apart, just like his father and mother, in this way; now bend your neck and say 'quack.'"

The ducklings did as they were bid, but the other ducks stared and said, "Look, here comes another brood, as if there were not enough of us

already! And what a queer-looking object one of them is; we don't want him here," and then one flew out and bit him in the neck.

"Let him alone," said the mother; "he is not doing any harm."

"Yes, but he is so big and ugly," said the spiteful duck, "and therefore he must be turned out."

"The others are very pretty children," said the old duck with the rag on her leg, "all but that one; I wish his mother could improve him a little."

"That is impossible, your grace," replied the mother; "he is not pretty, but he has a very good disposition and swims as well or even better than the others. I think he will grow up pretty and perhaps be smaller; he has remained too long in the egg, and therefore his figure is not properly formed;" and then she stroked his neck and smoothed the feathers, saying, "It is a drake, and therefore not of so much consequence. I think he will grow up strong and able to take care of himself."

"The other ducklings are graceful enough," said the old duck. "Now make yourself at home, and if you can find an eel's head, you can bring it to me."

And so they made themselves comfortable.

But the poor duckling, who had crept out of his shell last of all and looked so ugly, was bitten and pushed and made fun of, not only by the ducks, but by all the poultry.

"He is too big," they all said, and the turkey cock, who had been born into the world with spurs, and fancied himself really an emperor, puffed himself out like a vessel in full sail, and flew at the duckling, and became quite red in the head with passion, so that the poor little thing did not know where to go and was quite miserable because he was so ugly and laughed at by the whole farmyard.

So it went on from day to day till it got worse and worse. The poor duckling was driven about by everyone; even his brothers and sisters were unkind to him and would say, "Ah, you ugly creature, I wish the cat would get you," and his mother said she wished he had never been born. The ducks pecked him, the chickens beat him, and the girl who fed the poultry kicked him with her feet.

So at last he ran away, frightening the little birds in the hedge as he flew over the palings. "They are afraid of me because I am so ugly," he said. So he closed his eyes, and flew still farther, until he came out on a large moor inhabited by wild ducks. Here he remained the whole night, feeling very tired and sorrowful.

 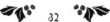

In the morning, when the wild ducks rose in the air, they stared at their new comrade. "What sort of a duck are you?" they all said, coming round him. He bowed to them, and was as polite as he could be, but he did not reply to their question.

"You are exceedingly ugly," said the wild ducks, "but that will not matter if you do not want to marry one of our family." Poor thing! he had no thoughts of marriage; all he wanted was permission to lie among the rushes and drink some of the water on the moor.

After he had been on the moor two days, there came two wild geese, or rather goslings, for they had not been out of the egg long and were very saucy.

"Listen, friend," said one of them to the duckling, "you are so ugly that we like you very well. Will you go with us and become a bird of passage? Not far from here is another moor, in which there are some pretty wild geese, all unmarried. It is a chance for you to get a wife; you may be lucky, ugly as you are."

"Pop, pop," sounded in the air, and the two wild geese fell dead among the rushes, and the water was tinged with blood. "Pop, pop," echoed far and wide in the distance, and whole flocks of wild geese rose up from the rushes.

The sound continued from every direction, for the sportsmen surrounded the moor, and some were even seated on branches of trees, overlooking the rushes. The blue smoke from the guns rose like clouds over the dark trees, and as it floated away across the water, a number of sporting dogs bounded in among the rushes, which bent beneath them wherever they went.

How they terrified the poor duckling! He turned away his head to hide it under his wing, and at the same moment a large terrible dog passed quite near him. His jaws were open, his tongue hung from his mouth, and his eyes glared fearfully. He thrust his nose close to the duckling, showing his sharp teeth, and then, "splash, splash," he went into the water without touching him.

"Oh," sighed the duckling, "how thankful I am for being so ugly; even a dog will not bite me."

And so he lay quite still, while the shot rattled through the rushes, and gun after gun was fired over him.

It was late in the day before all became quiet, but even then the poor young thing did not dare to move. He waited quietly for several hours, and then, after looking carefully around him, hastened away from the moor as fast as he could. He ran over field and meadow till a storm arose and he could hardly struggle against it.

Towards evening, he reached a poor little cottage that seemed ready to fall, and only remained standing because it could not decide on which side to fall first. The storm continued so violent, that the duckling could go no farther; he sat down by the cottage, and then he noticed that the door was not quite closed in consequence of one of the hinges having given way. There was therefore a narrow opening near the bottom large enough for him to slip through, which he did very quietly, and got a shelter for the night.

A woman, a tom cat, and a hen lived in this cottage. The tom cat, whom his mistress called, "My little son," was a great favourite; he could raise his back and purr, and could even throw out sparks from his fur if it were stroked the wrong way. The hen had very short legs, so she was called "Chickie short legs." She laid good eggs, and her mistress loved her as if she had been her own child.

In the morning, the strange visitor was discovered, and the tom cat began to purr, and the hen to cluck.

"What is that noise about?" said the old woman, looking round the room, but her sight was not very good; therefore, when she saw the duckling she thought it must be a fat duck, that had strayed from home. "Oh what a prize!" she exclaimed, "I hope it is not a drake, for then I shall have some duck's eggs. I must wait and see."

So the duckling was allowed to remain on trial for three weeks, but there were no eggs. Now the tom cat was the master of the house, and the hen was mistress, and they al-

ways said, "We and the world," for they believed themselves to be half the world, and the better half too. The duckling thought that others might hold a different opinion on the subject, but the hen would not listen to such doubts.

"Can you lay eggs?" she asked.

"No."

"Then have the goodness to hold your tongue."

"Can you raise your back, or purr, or throw out sparks?" said the tom cat.

"No."

"Then you have no right to express an opinion when sensible people are speaking."

So the duckling sat in a corner, feeling very low spirited, till the sunshine and the fresh air came into the room through the open door, and then he began to feel such a great longing for a swim on the water, that he could not help telling the hen.

"What an absurd idea," said the hen. "You have nothing else to do, therefore you have foolish fancies. If you could purr or lay eggs, they would pass away."

"But it is so delightful to swim about on the water," said the duckling, "and so refreshing to feel it close over your head, while you dive down to the bottom."

"Delightful, indeed!" said the hen, "why you must be crazy! Ask the cat, he is the cleverest animal I know, ask him how he would like to swim about on the water or to dive under it, for I will not speak of my own opinion; ask our mistress, the old woman—there is no one in the world more clever than she is. Do you think she would like to swim or to let the water close over her head?"

"You don't understand me," said the duckling.

"We don't understand you? Who can understand you, I wonder? Do you consider yourself more clever than the cat, or the old woman? I will say nothing of myself. Don't imagine such nonsense, child, and thank your good fortune that you have been received here. Are you not in a warm room and in society from which you may learn something. But you are a chatterer, and your company is not very agreeable. Believe me, I speak only for your own good. I may tell you unpleasant truths, but that is a proof of my friendship. I advise you, therefore, to lay eggs and learn to purr as quickly as possible."

"I believe I must go out into the world again," said the duckling.

"Yes, do," said the hen.

So the duckling left the cottage and soon found water on which it could swim and dive, but was avoided by all other animals because of its ugly appearance.

Autumn came, and the leaves in the forest turned to orange and gold. Then, as winter approached, the wind caught them as they fell and whirled them in the cold air. The clouds, heavy with hail and snow-flakes, hung low in the sky, and the raven stood on the ferns crying, "Croak, croak." It made one shiver with cold to look at him. All this was very sad for the poor little duckling.

One evening, just as the sun set amid radiant clouds, there came a large flock of beautiful birds out of the bushes. The duckling had never seen any like them before. They were swans, and they curved their graceful necks, while their soft plumage shone with dazzling whiteness. They uttered a singular cry, as they spread their glorious wings and flew away from those cold regions to warmer countries across the sea. As they mounted higher and higher in the air, the ugly little duckling felt quite a strange sensation as he watched them. He whirled himself in the water like a wheel, stretched out his neck towards them, and uttered a cry so strange that it frightened himself.

Could he ever forget those beautiful, happy birds; and when at last they were out of his sight, he dived under the water and rose again almost beside himself with excitement. He knew not the names of these birds, nor where they had flown, but he felt towards them as he had never felt for any other bird in the world. He was not envious of these beautiful creatures, but wished to be as lovely as they. Poor ugly creature, how gladly he would have lived even with the ducks had they only given him encouragement.

The winter grew colder and colder; he was obliged to swim about on the water to keep it from freezing, but every night the space on which he swam became smaller and smaller. At length it froze so hard that the ice in the water crackled as he moved, and the duckling had to paddle with his legs as well as he could, to keep the space from closing up. He became exhausted at last and lay still and helpless, frozen fast in the ice.

Early in the morning, a peasant, who was passing by, saw what had happened. He broke the ice in pieces with his wooden shoe and carried the duckling home to his wife. The warmth revived the poor little creature.

But when the children wanted to play with him, the duckling thought they would do him some harm; so he started up in terror, fluttered into the milk-pan, and splashed the milk about the room. Then the woman clapped her hands, which frightened him still more. He flew first into the butter-cask, then into the meal-tub, and out again. What a condition he was in! The woman screamed and struck at him with the tongs; the children laughed and screamed, and tumbled over each other, in their efforts to catch him; but luckily he escaped. The door stood open; the poor creature could just manage to slip out among the bushes and lie down quite exhausted in the newly fallen snow.

It would be very sad, were I to relate all the misery and privations which the poor little duckling endured during the hard winter; but when it had passed, he found himself lying one morning in a moor, amongst the rushes. He felt the warm sun shining, and heard the lark singing, and saw that all around was beautiful spring.

Then the young bird felt that his wings were strong, as he flapped them against his sides, and rose high into the air. They bore him onwards, until he found himself in a large garden, before he well knew how it had happened. The apple-trees were in full blossom, and the fragrant elders bent their long green branches down to the stream which wound round a smooth lawn. Everything looked beautiful, in the freshness of early spring. From a thicket close by came three beautiful white swans, rustling their feathers, and swimming lightly over the smooth water. The duckling remembered the lovely birds and felt more strangely unhappy than ever.

"I will fly to these royal birds," he exclaimed, "and they will kill me, because I am so ugly and dare to approach them; but it does not matter: better be killed by them than pecked by the ducks, beaten by the hens, pushed about by the maiden who feeds the poultry, or starved with hunger in the winter."

Then he flew to the water, and swam towards the beautiful swans. The moment they espied the stranger, they rushed to meet him with outstretched wings. "Kill me," said the poor bird; and he bent his head down to the surface of the water and awaited death. But what did he see in the clear stream below? His own image; no longer a dark, gray bird, ugly and disagreeable to look at, but a graceful and beautiful swan.

To be born in a duck's nest, in a farmyard, is of no consequence to a bird, if it is hatched from a swan's egg.

He now felt glad at having suffered sorrow and trouble, because it enabled him to enjoy so much better all the pleasure and happiness around him; for the great swans

swam round the new-comer and stroked his neck with their beaks, as a welcome.

Into the garden presently came some little children and threw bread and cake into the water.

"See," cried the youngest, "there is a new one;" and the rest were delighted and ran to their father and mother, dancing and clapping their hands, and shouting joyously, "There is another swan come; a new one has arrived."

Then they threw more bread and cake into the water and said, "The new one is the most beautiful of all; he is so young and pretty." And the old swans bowed their heads before him.

Then he felt quite ashamed and hid his head under his wing, for he did not know what to do. He was so happy and yet not at all proud. He had been persecuted and de-

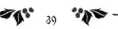

spised for his ugliness, and now he heard them say he was
the most beautiful of all the birds. Even the elder-tree bent
down its boughs into the water before him, and the sun
shone warm and bright.

Then he rustled his feathers, curved his slender neck, and
cried joyfully from the depths of his heart: "I never dreamed
of such happiness as this while I was an ugly duckling!"

The Shepherdess
and the Chimney Sweep

HAVE you ever seen an old wooden cupboard quite black with age and ornamented with carved foliage and curious figures? Well, just such a cupboard stood in a parlour and had been left to the family as a legacy by the great-grandmother. It was covered from top to bottom with carved roses and tulips; the most curious scrolls were drawn upon it, and out of them peeped little stags' heads, with antlers.

In the middle of the cupboard door was the carved figure of a man most ridiculous to look at. He grinned at you, for no one could call it laughing. He had goat's legs, little horns on his head, and a long beard.

The children in the room always called him, "Major-general-field-sergeant-commander Billy-goat's-legs." It was certainly a very difficult name to pronounce, and there are very few who ever receive such a title, but then it seemed wonderful how he

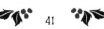

came to be carved at all; yet there he was, always looking at the table under the looking-glass, where stood a very pretty little shepherdess, made of China. Her shoes were gilt, and her dress had a red rose for an orna-ment. She wore a hat, and carried a crook, that were both gild-ed, and looked very bright and pretty.

Close by her side stood a little chimney-sweep, as black as coal, and also made of china. He was, however, quite as clean and neat as any other china figure; he only represent-ed a black chimney-sweep, and the china workers might just as well have made him a prince, had they felt inclined to do so.

He stood holding his ladder quite handily, and his face was as fair and rosy as a girl's; indeed, that was rather a mistake, it should have had some black marks on it. He and the shepherdess had been placed close together, side by side; and, being so placed, they became engaged to each other, for they were very well suited, being both made of the same sort of china and being equally fragile.

Close to them stood another figure, three times as large as they were, and also made of china. He was an old Chinaman, who could nod his head, and used to pretend that he was the grandfather of the shepherdess, although he could not prove it. He however assumed authority over her, and there-fore when "Major-general-field-sergeant-commander Billy-goat's-legs" asked for the little shepherdess to be his wife, he nodded his head to show that he consented.

"You will have a husband," said the old Chinaman to her, "who I really believe is made of mahogany. He will make you the lady of Major-general-field-sergeant-commander Billy-goat's-legs. He has the whole cupboard full of silver plate, which he keeps locked up in secret drawers."

"I won't go into the dark cupboard," said the little shep-herdess. "I have heard that he has eleven china wives there already."

"Then you shall be the twelfth," said the old Chinaman. "Tonight as soon as you hear a rattling in the old cupboard, you shall be married, as true as I am a Chinaman;" and then he nodded his head and fell asleep.

Then the little shepherdess cried and looked at her sweetheart, the china chimney-sweep. "I must entreat you," said she, "to go out with me into the wide world, for we cannot stay here."

"I will do whatever you wish," said the little chimney-sweep; "let us go immediately: I think I shall be able to maintain you with my profession."

"If we were but safely down from the table!" said she; "I shall not be happy till we are really out in the world."

Then he comforted her and showed her how to place her little foot on the carved edge and gilt-leaf ornaments of the table. He brought his little ladder to help her, and so they contrived to reach the floor. But when they looked at the old cupboard, they saw it was all in an uproar. The carved stags pushed out their heads, raised their antlers, and twisted their necks. The major-general sprung up in the air and cried out to the old Chinaman, "They are running away! they are running away!"

The two were rather frightened at this, so they jumped into the drawer of the window-seat.

Here were three or four packs of cards not quite complete, and a doll's theatre, which had been built up very neatly. A comedy was being performed in it, and all the queens of diamonds, clubs, and hearts, and spades, sat in the first row fanning themselves with tulips, and behind them stood all the knaves, showing that they had heads above and below as playing cards generally have. The play was about two lovers, who were not allowed to marry, and the shepherdess wept because it was so like her own story.

"I cannot bear it," said she; "I must get out of the drawer." But when they reached the floor and cast their eyes on the table, there was the old Chinaman awake and shaking his whole body, till all at once down he came on the floor, "plump." "The old Chinaman is coming," cried the little shepherdess in a fright, and down she fell on one knee.

"I have thought of something," said the chimney-sweep; "let us get into the great pot-pourri jar which stands in the corner: there we can lie on rose-leaves and lavender, and throw salt in his eyes if he comes near us."

"No, that will never do," said she, "because I know that the Chinaman and the pot-pourri jar were lovers once, and

43

there always remains behind a feeling of good-will between those who have been so intimate as that. No, there is nothing left for us but to go out into the wide world."

"Have you really courage enough to go out into the wide world with me?" said the chimney-sweep; "have you thought how large it is, and that we can never come back here again?"

"Yes, I have," she replied.

When the chimney-sweep saw that she was quite firm, he said, "My way is through the stove and up the chimney. Have you courage to creep with me through the fire-box and the iron pipe? When we get to the chimney, I shall know how to manage very well. We shall soon climb too high for anyone to reach us, and we shall come through a hole in the top out into the wide world." So he led her to the door of the stove.

"It looks very dark," said she; still she went in with him through the stove and through the pipe, where it was as dark as pitch.

"Now we are in the chimney," said he; "and look, there is a beautiful star shining above it."

It was a real star shining down upon them as if it would show them the way. So they clambered and crept on, and a frightfully steep place it was; but the chimney-sweep helped her and supported her, till they got higher and higher. He showed her the best places on which to set her little china foot, so at last they reached the top of the chimney and sat themselves down, for they were very tired, as may be supposed.

The sky, with all its stars, was over their heads, and below were the roofs of the town. They could see for a very long distance out into the wide world, and the poor little shepherdess leaned her head on her chimney-sweep's shoulder and wept till she washed the gilt off her sash; the world was so different to what she expected.

"This is too much," she said; "I cannot bear it, the world is too large. Oh, I wish I were safe back on the table again, under the looking-glass; I shall never be happy till I am safe back again. Now I have followed you out into the wide world, you will take me back if you love me."

Then the chimney-sweep tried to reason with her and spoke of the old Chinaman and of the Major-general-field-sergeant-commander Billy-goat's-legs; but she sobbed so bitterly and kissed her little chimney-sweep till he was obliged to do all she asked, foolish as it was.

And so, with a great deal of trouble, they climbed down the chimney and then crept through the pipe and stove,

which were certainly not very pleasant places. Then they stood in the dark fire-box and listened behind the door, to hear what was going on in the room. As it was all quiet, they peeped out Alas! there lay the old Chinaman on the floor; he had fallen down from the table, as he attempted to run after them, and was broken into three pieces; his back had separated entirely, and his head had rolled into a corner of the room. The major-general stood in his old place and appeared lost in thought.

"This is terrible," said the little shepherdess. "My poor old grandfather is broken to pieces, and it is our fault. I shall never live after this;" and she wrung her little hands.

"He can be riveted," said the chimney-sweep; "he can be riveted. Do not be so hasty. If they cement his back and put a good rivet in it, he will be as good as new, and be able to say as many disagreeable things to us as ever."

"Do you think so?" said she; and then they climbed up to the table, and stood in their old places.

"As we have done no good," said the chimney-sweep, "we might as well have remained here, instead of taking so much trouble."

"I wish grandfather was riveted," said the shepherdess. "Will it cost much, I wonder?"

And she had her wish. The family had the Chinaman's back mended and a strong rivet put through his neck; he looked as good as new, but he could no longer nod his head.

"You have become proud since your fall broke you to pieces," said Major-general-field-sergeant-commander Billy-goat's-legs. "You have no reason to give yourself such airs. Am I to have her or not?"

The chimney-sweep and the little shepherdess looked piteously at the old Chinaman, for they were afraid he might nod, but he was not able; besides, it was so tiresome to be always telling strangers he had a rivet in the back of his neck.

And so the little china people remained together, and were glad of the grandfather's rivet, and continued to love each other till they were broken to pieces.

The Snow Queen
A Tale in Seven Stories

STORY THE FIRST, WHICH DESCRIBES A LOOKING-GLASS AND THE BROKEN FRAGMENTS

OU must attend to the commencement of this story, for when we get to the end we shall know more than we do now about a very wicked hobgoblin; he was one of the very worst, for he was a real demon.

One day when he was in a merry mood, he made a looking-glass which had the power of making everything good or beautiful that was reflected in it almost shrink to nothing, while everything that was worthless and bad looked increased in size and worse than ever. The most lovely landscapes appeared like boiled spinach, and the people became hideous and looked as if they stood on their heads and had no bodies. Their countenances were so distorted that no one could recognise them, and even one freckle on the face appeared to spread over the whole of the nose and mouth.

The demon said this was very amusing. When a good or pious thought passed through the mind of anyone, it was misrepresented in the glass; and then how the demon laughed at his cunning invention! All who went to the demon's school—for he kept a school—talked everywhere of the wonders they had seen and declared that people could now, for the first time, see what the world and mankind were really like. They carried the glass about everywhere, till at last there was not a land nor a people who had not been looked at through this distorted mirror.

They wanted even to fly with it up to heaven to see the angels; but the higher they flew the more slippery the glass became, and they could scarcely hold it, till at last it slipped from their hands, fell to the earth, and was broken into millions of pieces.

But now the looking-glass caused more unhappiness than ever, for some of the fragments were not as large as a grain of sand, and they flew about the world into every country. When one of these tiny atoms flew into a person's eye, it stuck there unknown to him, and from that moment he saw everything through a distorted medium or could see only the worst side of what he looked at, for even the smallest fragment retained the same power which had belonged to the whole mirror.

Some few persons even got a fragment of the looking-glass in their hearts, and this was very terrible, for their hearts became cold like a lump of ice. A few of the pieces were so large that they could be used as window-panes; it would have been a sad thing to look at our friends through them. Other pieces were made into spectacles; this was dreadful for those who wore them, for they could see nothing either rightly or justly.

At all this the wicked demon laughed till his sides shook—it tickled him so to see the mischief he had done. There were still a number of these little fragments of glass floating about in the air, and now you shall hear what happened with one of them.

Second Story. A Little Boy and a Little Girl

In a large town full of houses and people, there is not room for everybody to have even a little garden; therefore they are obliged to be satisfied with a few flowers in flower-pots. In one of these large towns lived two poor children, who had a garden something larger and better than a few flower-pots. They were not brother and sister, but they loved each other almost as much as if they had been. Their parents lived opposite to each other in two garrets, where the roofs of neighbouring houses projected out towards each other, and the water-pipe ran between them.

In each house was a little window, so that anyone could step across the gutter from one window to the other. The parents of these children had each a large wooden box in which they cultivated kitchen herbs for their own use, and a little rose-bush in each box, which grew splendidly. Now after a while the parents decided to place these two boxes

across the water-pipe, so that they reached from one window to the other and looked like two banks of flowers. Sweet peas dropped over the boxes, and the rose-bushes shot forth long branches, which were trained round the windows and clustered together almost like a triumphal arch of leaves and flowers. The boxes were very high, and the children knew they must not climb upon them without permission, but they were often, however, allowed to step out together and sit upon their little stools under the rose-bushes or play quietly.

In winter all this pleasure came to an end, for the windows were sometimes quite frozen over. But then the children would warm copper pennies on the stove and hold the warm pennies against the frozen pane; there would be very soon a little round hole through which they could peep, and the soft bright eyes of the little boy and girl would beam through the hole at each window as they looked at each other.

Their names were Kay and Gerda. In summer they could be together with one jump from the window, but in winter they had to go up and down the long staircase and out through the snow before they could meet.

"See there are the white bees swarming," said Kay's old grandmother one day when it was snowing.

"Have they a queen bee?" asked the little boy, for he knew that the real bees always had a queen.

"To be sure they have," said the grandmother. "She is flying there where the swarm is thickest. She is the largest of them all, and never remains on the earth, but flies up to the dark clouds. Often at midnight she flies through the streets of the town and looks in at the windows; then the ice freezes on the panes into wonderful shapes, which look like flowers and castles."

"Yes, I have seen them," said both the children, and they knew it must be true.

"Can the Snow Queen come in here?" asked the little girl.

"Only let her come," said the boy, "I'll set her on the stove and then she'll melt."

Then the grandmother smoothed his hair and told him some more tales.

One evening when little Kay was at home, half undressed, he climbed on a chair by the window and peeped out through the little hole. A few flakes of snow were falling, and one of them, rather larger than the rest, alighted on the edge of one of the flower-boxes. This snow-flake grew larger and larger, till at last it became the figure of a woman dressed in garments of white gauze, which looked like millions of starry snow-flakes linked together. She was fair and beautiful, but made of ice—shining and glittering ice. Still she was alive, and her eyes sparkled like bright stars, but there was neither peace nor rest in their glance. She nodded towards the window and waved her hand. The little boy was frightened and sprang from the chair; at the same moment it seemed as if a large bird flew by the window.

On the following day there was a clear frost, and very soon came the spring. The sun shone, the young green leaves burst forth, the swallows built their nests, windows were opened, and the children sat once more in the garden on the roof high above all the other rooms.

How beautifully the roses blossomed this summer! The little girl had learnt a hymn in which roses were spoken of, and then she thought of their own roses, and she sang the hymn to the little boy, and he sang too:

> "Roses bloom and cease to be,
> But we shall the Christ-child see."

Then the little ones held each other by the hand, and kissed the roses, and looked at the bright sunshine, and spoke to it as if the Christ-child were there. Those were splendid summer days. How beautiful and fresh it was out among the rose-bushes, which seemed as if they would never leave off blooming!

One day Kay and Gerda sat looking at a book full of pictures of animals and birds, and then just as the clock in the church tower struck twelve, Kay said, "Oh! something has struck my heart!" and soon after, "There is something in my eye."

The little girl put her arm round his neck and looked into his eye, but she could see nothing.

"I think it is gone," he said. But it was not gone: it was one of those bits of the looking-glass—that magic mirror of which we have spoken—the ugly glass which made everything great and good appear small and ugly, while all that was wicked and bad became more visible, and every little fault could be plainly seen.

Poor little Kay had also received a small grain in his heart, which quickly turned to a lump of ice. He felt no more pain, but the glass was there still.

"Why do you cry?" said he at last; "it makes you look ugly. There is nothing the matter with me now. Oh! see," he cried suddenly, "that rose is worm-eaten, and this one is quite crooked. After all, they are ugly roses, just like the box in which they stand!" And then he kicked the boxes with his foot and pulled off the two roses.

"Kay, what are you doing?" cried the little girl; and then, when he saw how frightened she was, he tore off another rose and jumped through his own window away from sweet little Gerda.

When she afterwards brought out the picture-book, he said, "It is only fit for babies in long clothes." And when the grandmother told stories, he would interrupt her with "but" or, when he could manage it, he would get behind her chair, put on a pair of spectacles, and imitate her very cleverly, to make people laugh. By-and-by he began to mimic the speech and gait of persons in the street. All that was peculiar or disagreeable in a person he would imitate directly, and people said, "That boy will be very clever; he has a remarkable genius!" But it was the piece of glass in his eye and the coldness in his heart that made him act like this. He would even tease little Gerda, who loved him with all her heart.

His games, too, were quite different; they were not so childish. One winter's day, when it snowed, he brought out a burning-glass, then he held out the tail of his blue coat and let the snow-flakes fall upon it. "Look in this glass, Gerda," said he; and she saw how every flake of snow was magnified and looked like a beautiful flower or a glittering star. "Is it not clever?" said Kay, "and much more interesting than looking at real flowers. There is not a single fault in it, and the snow-flakes are quite perfect till they begin to melt."

Soon after, Kay made his appearance in large thick gloves and with his sledge at his back. He called upstairs to Gerda, "I've got leave to go into the great square, where the other boys play and ride." And away he went.

In the great square, the boldest among the boys would often tie their sledges to country people's carts and go with them a good way. This was capital. But while they were all amusing themselves and Kay with them, a great sledge came by. It was painted white, and in it sat someone wrapped in a rough white fur and wearing a white cap.

The sledge drove twice round the square, and Kay fastened his own little sledge to it, so that when it went away he followed with it. It went faster and faster right through the next street, and then the person who drove turned round and nodded pleasantly to Kay, just as if they were acquainted with each other. And whenever Kay wished to loosen his little sledge, the driver nodded again; so Kay sat still, and they drove out through the town gate.

Then the snow began to fall so heavily that the little boy could not see a hand's breadth before him, but still they drove on. Then he suddenly loosened the cord so that the large sledge might go on without him, but it was of no use: his little carriage held fast, and away they went like the wind. Then he called out loudly, but nobody heard him, while the snow beat upon him, and the sledge flew onwards. Every now and then it gave a jump as if they were going over hedges and ditches. The boy was frightened and tried to say a prayer, but he could remember nothing but the multiplication table.

The snow-flakes became larger and larger till they appeared like great white chickens. All at once they sprang on one side, the great sledge stopped, and the person who had driven it rose up. The fur and the cap, which were made entirely of snow, fell off, and Kay saw a lady, tall and white: it was the Snow Queen.

"We have driven well," said she, "but why do you tremble? Here, creep into my warm fur." Then she seated him beside her in the sledge, and as she wrapped the fur round him he felt as if he was sinking into a snow-drift.

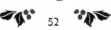

"Are you still cold?" she asked, as she kissed him on the forehead. The kiss was colder than ice; it went quite through to his heart, which was already almost a lump of ice. He felt as if he were going to die, but only for a moment: he soon seemed quite well again and did not notice the cold all around him.

"My sledge! don't forget my sledge," was his first thought, and then he looked and saw that it was bound fast to one of the white chickens, which flew behind him with the sledge at its back. The Snow Queen kissed little Kay again, and by this time he had forgotten little Gerda, his grandmother, and all at home.

"Now you must have no more kisses," she said, "or I should kiss you to death."

Kay looked at her and saw that she was so beautiful; he could not imagine a more intelligent and lovely face; now she did not seem to be made of ice, as when he had seen her through his window and she had nodded to him. In his eyes she was perfect, and he did not feel at all afraid.

He told her he could do mental arithmetic, as far as fractions, and that he knew the number of square miles and the number of inhabitants in the country. And she always smiled so that he thought he did not know enough yet, and looked round the vast expanse as she flew higher and higher with him upon a black cloud, while the storm blew and howled as if it were singing old songs.

They flew over woods and lakes, over sea and land; below them roared the wild wind; the wolves howled and the snow crackled; over them flew the black screaming crows; and above all shone the moon, clear and bright; and so Kay passed through the long winter's night, and by day he slept at the feet of the Snow Queen.

Third Story. The Flower Garden of the Woman Who Could Conjure

But how fared little Gerda during Kay's absence? What had become of him no one knew, nor could anyone give the slightest information excepting the boys who said that he had tied his sledge to another very large one, which had driven through the street and out at the town gate. Nobody knew where it went. Many tears were shed for him, and little Gerda wept bitterly for a long time. She said she knew he must be dead, that he was drowned in the river which flowed close by the school. Oh, indeed, those long winter days were very dreary. But at last spring came with warm sunshine.

"Kay is dead and gone," said little Gerda.

"I don't believe it!" said the sunshine.

"He is dead and gone," she said to the sparrows.

"We don't believe it!" they replied; and at last little Gerda began to doubt it herself.

"I will put on my new red shoes," she said one morning, "those that Kay has never seen, and then I will go down to the river and ask for him."

It was quite early when she kissed her old grandmother, who was still asleep; then she put on her red shoes and went quietly alone out of the town gates towards the river.

"Is it true that you have taken my little playmate away from me?" she asked the river. "I will give you my red shoes if you will give him back to me." And it seemed as if the waves nodded to her in a strange manner. Then she took off her red shoes, which she liked better than anything else, and threw them into the river; but they fell near the bank, and the little waves carried them back to the land, just as if the river would not take from her what she loved best because they could not give her back little Kay.

But she thought the shoes had not been thrown out far enough. And then she crept into a boat that lay among the reeds and threw the shoes again from the farther end of the boat into the water. But the boat was not fastened, and Gerda's movement sent it gliding away from the land.

When she saw this, she hastened to reach the end of the boat, but before she could do so, it was more than a yard from the bank and drifting away faster than ever. Then little Gerda was very much frightened and began to cry, but no one heard her except the sparrows, and they could not carry her to land, but they flew along by the shore and sang, as if to comfort her, "Here we are! Here we are!"

The boat floated with the stream; little Gerda sat quite still with only her stockings on her feet; the red shoes floated after her, but she could not reach them because the boat kept so much in advance.

The banks on each side of the river were very pretty. There were beautiful flowers, old trees, sloping fields, in which cows and sheep were grazing, but not a man to be seen. "Perhaps the river will carry me to little Kay," thought Gerda, and then she became more cheerful, and raised her head, and looked at the beautiful green banks; and so the boat sailed on for hours.

At length she came to a large cherry orchard, in which stood a small house with strange red and blue windows. It had also a thatched roof, and outside were two wooden soldiers, that presented arms to her as she sailed past. Gerda called out to them, for she thought they were alive, but of course they did not answer; and as the boat drifted nearer to the shore, she saw what they really were. Then Gerda called still louder, and there came a very old woman out of the house, leaning on a crutch.

She wore a large hat to shade her from the sun, and on it were painted all sorts of pretty flowers. "You poor little child," said the old woman, "how did you manage to come all this distance into the wide world on such a rapid rolling stream?" And then the old woman walked into the water, seized the boat with her crutch, drew it to land, and lifted little Gerda out. And Gerda was glad to feel herself again on dry ground, although she was rather afraid of the strange old woman. "Come and tell me who you are," said she, "and how you came here."

Then Gerda told her everything, while the old woman shook her head and said, "Hem-hem". And when she had finished, Gerda asked if she had not seen little Kay, and the old woman told her he had not passed by that way but he very likely would come. So she told Gerda not to be sorrowful but to taste the cherries and look at the flowers; they were better than any picture-book, for each of them could tell a story. Then she took Gerda by the hand, led her into the house, and closed the door.

The windows were very high, and as the panes were red, blue, and yellow, the daylight shone through them in all sorts of singular colours. On the table stood some beautiful cherries, and Gerda had permission to eat as many as she would. While she was eating them, the old woman combed out her long flaxen ringlets with a golden comb, and the glossy curls hung down each side of the little round pleasant face, which looked fresh and blooming as a rose.

"I have long been wishing for a dear little maiden like you," said the old woman, "and now you must stay with me and see how happily we shall live together." And while she went on combing little Gerda's hair, the girl thought less and less about her adopted brother Kay, for the old woman could conjure, although she was not a wicked witch; she conjured only a little for her own amusement, and she conjured now because she wanted to keep Gerda. Therefore she went into the garden and stretched out her crutch towards all the rose-trees, beautiful though they were, and they immediately sunk into the dark earth, so that no one could tell where they had once stood. The old woman was afraid that if little Gerda saw roses, she would think of those at home, and then remember little Kay and run away.

Then she took Gerda into the flower-garden. How fragrant and beautiful it was! Every flower that could be thought of for every season of the year was here in full bloom; no picture-book could have more beautiful colours. Gerda jumped for joy and played till the sun went down behind the tall cherry-trees; then she slept in an elegant bed with red silk pillows embroidered with coloured violets; and then she dreamed as pleasantly as a queen on her wedding-day. The next day and for many days after, Gerda played with the flowers in the warm sunshine. She knew every flower, and yet, although there were so many of them, it seemed as if one was missing, but which it was she could not tell. One day, however, as she sat looking at the old woman's hat with the painted flowers on it, she saw that the prettiest of them all was a rose. The old woman had forgotten to take it from her hat when she made all the roses sink into the earth. But it is difficult to keep the thoughts together in everything; one little mistake upsets all our arrangements.

"What, are there no roses here?" cried Gerda; and she ran out into the garden and examined all the beds, and searched and searched. There was not one to be found. Then she sat down and wept, and her tears fell just on the place where one of the rose-trees had sunk down. The warm tears moistened the earth, and the rose-tree sprouted up at once, as blooming as when it had sunk. Gerda embraced it and kissed the roses, and thought of the beautiful roses at home and, with them, of little Kay.

"Oh, how I have been detained!" said the little maiden. "I wanted to seek for little Kay. Do you know where he is?" she asked the roses. "Do you think he is dead?"

And the roses answered, "No, he is not dead. We have been in the ground where all the dead lie; but Kay is not there."

"Thank you," said little Gerda, and then she went to the other flowers, looked into their little cups, and asked, "Do you know where little Kay is?" But each flower, as it stood in the sunshine, dreamed only of its own little fairy tale or history. Not one knew anything of Kay. Gerda heard many stories from the flowers as she asked them one after another about him.

And what said the tiger-lily? "Hark, do you hear the drum?—'tum, tum,'—there are only two notes always, 'tum, tum.' Listen to the women's song of mourning! Hear the cry of the priest! In her long red robe stands the Hindu widow by the funeral pile. The flames rise around her as she places herself on the dead body of her husband; but the Hindu woman is thinking of the living one in that circle; of him, her son, who lighted those flames. Those shining eyes trouble her heart more painfully than the flames which will soon consume her body to ashes. Can the fire of the heart be extinguished in the flames of a funeral pile?"

"I don't understand that at all," said little Gerda.

"That is my story," said the tiger-lily.

What said the convolvulus? "Near yonder narrow road stands an old knight's castle; thick ivy creeps over the old ruined walls, leaf over leaf, even to the balcony, in which stands a beautiful maiden. She bends over the balustrades and looks up the road. No rose on its stem is fresher than she; no apple-blossom, wafted by the wind, floats more lightly than she moves. Her rich silk rustles as she bends over and exclaims, 'Will he not come?'"

"Is it Kay you mean?" asked Gerda.

"I am only speaking of a story of my dream," replied the flower.

What said the little snowdrop? "Between two trees a rope is hanging; there is a piece of board upon it: it is a swing. Two pretty little girls, in dresses white as snow and with long green ribbons fluttering from their hats, are sitting upon it, swinging. Their brother, who is taller than they are, stands in the swing. He has one arm round the rope, to steady himself; in one hand he holds a little bowl and in the other a clay pipe: he is blowing bubbles. As the swing goes on, the bubbles fly upward, reflecting the most beautiful varying colours. The last still hangs from the bowl of the pipe and sways in the wind. On goes the swing; and then a little black

dog comes running up. He is almost as light as the bubble, and he raises himself on his hind legs, and wants to be taken into the swing; but it does not stop, and the dog falls; then he barks and gets angry. The children stoop towards him, and the bubble bursts. A swinging plank, a light sparkling foam picture,—that is my story."

"It may be all very pretty what you are telling me," said little Gerda, "but you speak so mournfully, and you do not mention little Kay at all."

What did the hyacinths say? "There were three beautiful sisters, fair and delicate. The dress of one was red, of the second blue, and of the third pure white. Hand in hand, they danced in the bright moonlight, by the calm lake; but they were human beings, not fairy elves. The sweet fragrance attracted them, and they disappeared in the wood; here the fragrance became stronger. Three coffins, in which lay the three beautiful maidens, glided from the thickest part of the forest across the lake. The fire-flies flew lightly over them, like little floating torches. Do the dancing maidens sleep, or are they dead? The scent of the flowers says that they are corpses. The evening bell tolls their knell."

"You make me quite sorrowful," said little Gerda; "your perfume is so strong; you make me think of the dead maidens. Ah! is little Kay really dead then? The roses have been in the earth, and they say no."

"Cling, clang," tolled the hyacinth bells. "We are not tolling for little Kay; we do not know him. We sing our song, the only one we know."

Then Gerda went to the buttercups that were glittering amongst the bright green leaves.

"You are little bright suns," said Gerda; "tell me if you know where I can find my playfellow."

And the buttercups sparkled up gaily and looked again at Gerda. What song could the buttercups sing? It was not about Kay.

"The bright warm sun shone on a little court, on the first warm day of spring. His bright beams rested on the white walls of the neighbouring house; and close by, bloomed the first yellow flower of the season, glittering like gold in the sun's warm ray. An old woman sat in her arm-chair at the house-door, and her granddaughter, a poor and pretty servant-maid, came to see her for a short visit. When she kissed her grandmother, there was gold everywhere: the gold of the heart in that holy kiss; it was a golden morning; there was gold in the beaming sunlight, gold in the leaves of the lowly flower, and on the lips of the maiden. There, that is my story," said the buttercup.

"My poor old grandmother!" sighed Gerda; "she is longing to see me and grieving for me as she did for little Kay; but I shall soon go home and take little Kay with me. It is no use asking the flowers; they know only their own songs and can give me no information."

And then she tucked up her little dress, that she might run faster, but the narcissus caught her by the leg as she

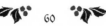

was jumping over it; so she stopped, looked at the tall yellow flower, and said, "Perhaps you may know something."

Then she stooped down quite close to the flower and listened; and what did it say?

"I can see myself, I can see myself," said the narcissus.

"Oh, how sweet is my perfume! Up in a little room with a bow window, stands a little dancing girl, half undressed; she stands sometimes on one leg and sometimes on both, and looks as if she would tread the whole world under her feet. She is nothing but a delusion. She is pouring water out of a tea-pot on a piece of stuff which she holds in her hand; it is her bodice. 'Cleanliness is a good thing,' she says. Her white dress hangs on a peg; it has also been washed in the tea-pot and dried on the roof. She puts it on and ties a saffron-coloured handkerchief round her neck, which makes the dress look whiter. See how she stretches out her legs, as if she were showing off on a stem. I can see myself, I can see myself."

"What do I care for all that," said Gerda, "you need not tell me such stuff." And then she ran to the other end of the garden. The door was fastened, but she pressed against the rusty latch, and it gave way. The door sprang open, and little Gerda ran out with bare feet into the wide world. She looked back three times, but no one seemed to be following her. At last she could run no longer, so she sat down to rest on a great stone; and when she looked round, she saw that the summer was over and autumn very far advanced. She had known nothing of this in the beautiful garden, where the sun shone and the flowers grew all the year round.

"Oh, how I have wasted my time!" said little Gerda; "it is autumn. I must not rest any longer," and she rose up to go on. But her little feet were wounded and sore, and everything around her looked so cold and bleak. The long willow-leaves were quite yellow. The dew-drops fell like water, leaf after leaf dropped from the tree, the sloe-thorn alone still bore fruit, but the sloes were sour and set the teeth on edge. Oh, how dark and weary the whole world appeared!

FOURTH STORY. THE PRINCE AND PRINCESS

Gerda was obliged to rest again, and just opposite the place where she sat, she saw a great crow hopping across the snow towards her. He stood looking at her for some time, and then he wagged his head and said, "Caw, caw; good-day, good-day." He pronounced the words as plainly

as he could because he meant to be kind to the little girl; and then he asked her where she was going all alone in the wide world.

The word "alone" Gerda understood very well and knew how much it expressed. So then she told the crow the whole story of her life and adventures and asked him if he had seen little Kay.

The crow nodded his head very gravely and said, "Perhaps I have—it may be."

"No! Do you think you have?" cried little Gerda, and she kissed the crow and hugged him almost to death with joy.

"Gently, gently," said the crow. "I believe I know. I think it may be little Kay; but he has certainly forgotten you by this time for the princess."

"Does he live with a princess?" asked Gerda.

"Yes, listen," replied the crow; "but it is so difficult to speak your language. If you understand the crows' language, then I can explain it better. Do you?"

"No, I have never learnt it," said Gerda, "but my grandmother understands it, and she used to speak it to me. I wish I had learnt it."

"It does not matter," answered the crow; "I will explain as well as I can, although it will be very badly done;" and he told her what he had heard. "In this kingdom where we now are," said he, "there lives a princess, who is so wonderfully clever that she has read all the newspapers in the world and forgotten them too, although she is so clever.

"A short time ago, as she was sitting on her throne, which people say is not such an agreeable seat as is often supposed, she began to sing a song which commences in these words:

'Why should I not be married?'

"'Why not indeed?' said she, and so she determined to marry if she could find a husband who knew what to say when he is spoken to, and not one who could only look grand, for that was so tiresome. Then she assembled all her court ladies together at the beat of the drum, and when they heard of her intentions, they were very much pleased. 'We are so glad to hear it,' said they, 'we were talking about it ourselves the other day.' You may believe every word I tell you is true," said the crow, "for I have a tame sweetheart who goes freely about the palace, and she told me all this."

Of course his sweetheart was a crow, for "birds of a feather flock together," and one crow always chooses another crow.

"Newspapers were published immediately, with a border of hearts and the initials of the princess among them. They gave notice that every young man who was handsome was free to visit the castle and speak with the princess; and those who could reply loud enough to be heard when spoken to were to make themselves quite at home at the palace; but the one who spoke best would be chosen as a husband for the princess. Yes, yes, you may believe me, it is all as true as

I sit here," said the crow. "The people came in crowds. There was a great deal of crushing and running about, but no one succeeded either on the first or the second day. They could all speak very well while they were outside in the streets, but when they entered the palace gates and saw the guards in silver uniforms, and the footmen in their golden livery on the staircase, and the great halls lighted up, they became quite confused. And when they stood before the throne on which the princess sat, they could do nothing but repeat the last words she had said; and she had no particular wish to hear her own words over again. It was just as if they had all taken something to make them sleepy while they were in the palace, for they did not recover themselves nor speak till they got back again into the street. There was quite a long line of them reaching from the town gate to the palace. I went myself to see them," said the crow. "They were hungry and thirsty, for at the palace they did not even get a glass of water. Some of the wisest had taken a few slices of bread and butter with them, but they did not share it with their neighbours; they thought if others went in to the princess looking hungry, there would be a better chance for themselves."

"But Kay! Tell me about little Kay!" said Gerda, "was he amongst the crowd?"

"Stop a bit; we are just coming to him. It was on the third day; there came marching cheerfully along to the palace a little personage, without horses or carriage, his eyes sparkling like yours; he had beautiful long hair, but his clothes were very poor."

"That was Kay!" said Gerda joyfully. "Oh, then I have found him!" and she clapped her hands.

"He had a little knapsack on his back," added the crow.

"No, it must have been his sledge," said Gerda; "for he went away with it."

"It may have been so," said the crow; "I did not look at it very closely. But I know from my tame sweetheart that he passed through the palace gates, saw the guards in their

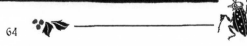

silver uniform and the servants in their liveries of gold on the stairs, but he was not in the least embarrassed. 'It must be very tiresome to stand on the stairs,' he said. 'I prefer to go in.' The rooms were blazing with light. Councillors and ambassadors walked about with bare feet, carrying golden vessels; it was enough to make anyone feel serious. His boots creaked loudly as he walked, and yet he was not at all uneasy."

"It must be Kay," said Gerda, "I know he had new boots on; I have heard them creak in grandmother's room."

"They really did creak," said the crow, "yet he went boldly up to the princess herself, who was sitting on a pearl as large as a spinning wheel, and all the ladies of the court were present with their maids, and all the cavaliers with their servants; and each of the maids had another maid to wait upon her, and the cavaliers' servants had their own servants as well as a page each. They all stood in circles round the princess, and the nearer they stood to the door, the prouder they looked. The servants' pages, who always wore slippers, could hardly be looked at: they held themselves up so proudly by the door."

"It must be quite awful," said little Gerda, "but did Kay win the princess?"

"If I had not been a crow," said he, "I would have married her myself, although I am engaged. He spoke just as well as I do when I speak the crows' language, so I heard from my tame sweetheart. He was quite free and agreeable, and said he had not come to woo the princess but to hear her wisdom; and he was as pleased with her as she was with him."

"Oh, certainly that was Kay," said Gerda, "he was so clever; he could work mental arithmetic and fractions. Oh, will you take me to the palace?"

"It is very easy to ask that," replied the crow, "but how are we to manage it? However, I will speak about it to my tame sweetheart and ask her advice; for I must tell you it will be very difficult to gain permission for a little girl like you to enter the palace."

"Oh, yes; but I shall gain permission easily," said Gerda, "for when Kay hears that I am here, he will come out and fetch me in immediately."

"Wait for me here by the palings," said the crow, wagging his head as he flew away.

It was late in the evening before the crow returned. "Caw, caw," he said, "she sends you greeting, and here is a little roll which she took from the kitchen for you; there is plenty of bread there, and she thinks you must be hungry. It is not possible for you to enter the palace by the front entrance. The guards in silver uniform and the servants in gold livery would not allow it. But do not cry, we will manage to get you in; my sweetheart knows a little back-staircase that leads to the sleeping apartment, and she knows where to find the key."

Then they went into the garden through the great avenue, where the leaves were falling one after another, and they could see the lights in the palace being put out in the

same manner. And the crow led little Gerda to a back door, which stood ajar. Oh! how little Gerda's heart beat with anxiety and longing; it was just as if she were going to do something wrong, and yet she only wanted to know where little Kay was. "It must be he," she thought, "with those clear eyes and that long hair." She could fancy she saw him smiling at her, as he used to at home when they sat among the roses. He would certainly be glad to see her and to hear what a long distance she had come for his sake and to know how sorry they had all been at home because he did not come back. Oh, what joy and yet fear she felt! They were now on the stairs, and in a small closet at the top a lamp was burning. In the middle of the floor stood the tame crow, turning her head from side to side and gazing at Gerda, who curtsied as her grandmother had taught her to do.

"My betrothed has spoken so very highly of you, my little lady," said the tame crow, "your life-history, Vita, as it may be called, is very touching. If you take the lamp, I will walk before you. We will go straight along this way; then we shall meet no one."

"It seems to me as if somebody were behind us," said Gerda, as something rushed by her like a shadow on the wall, and then horses with flying manes and thin legs, hunters, ladies and gentlemen on horseback, glided by her, like shadows on the wall.

"They are only dreams," said the crow; "they are coming to fetch the thoughts of the great people out hunting."

"All the better, for we shall be able to look at them in their beds more safely. I hope that when you rise to honour and favour, you will show a grateful heart."

"You may be quite sure of that," said the crow from the forest.

They now came into the first hall, the walls of which were hung with rose-coloured satin, embroidered with artificial flowers. Here the dreams again flitted by them, but so quickly that Gerda could not distinguish the royal persons. Each hall appeared more splendid than the last; it was enough to bewilder anyone.

At length they reached a bed-room. The ceiling was like a great palm-tree, with glass-leaves of the most costly crystal, and over the centre of the floor two beds, each resembling a lily, hung from a stem of gold. One, in which the princess lay, was white; the other was red, and in this Gerda had to seek for little Kay. She pushed one of the red leaves aside and saw a little brown neck. Oh, that must be Kay! She called his name out quite loud and held the lamp over him. The dreams rushed back into the room on horseback. He woke and turned his head round; it was not little Kay! The prince was only like him in the neck; still he was young and pretty. Then the princess peeped out of her white-lily bed and asked what was the matter. Then little Gerda wept and told her story, and all that the crows had done to help her.

"You poor child," said the prince and princess; then they praised the crows and said they were not angry with them for what they had done, but that it must not happen again, and this time they should be rewarded.

"Would you like to have your freedom?" asked the princess, "or would you prefer to be raised to the position of court crows, with all that is left in the kitchen for yourselves?"

Then both the crows bowed and begged to have a fixed appointment, for they thought of their old age and said it would be so comfortable to feel that they had provision for their old days, as they called it. And then the prince got out of his bed and gave it up to Gerda—he could not do more; and she lay down. She folded her little hands and thought, "How good everybody is to me, men and animals too;" then she closed her eyes and fell into a sweet sleep. All the dreams came flying back again to her, and they looked like angels, and one of them drew a little sledge on which sat Kay and nodded to her. But all this was only a dream and vanished as soon as she awoke.

The following day she was dressed from head to foot in silk and velvet, and they invited her to stay at the palace for a few days and enjoy herself; but she only begged for a pair of boots, a little carriage, and a horse to draw it, so that she might go out into the wide world to seek for Kay. And she obtained, not only boots, but also a muff, and she was neatly dressed. When she was ready to go, there, at the door, she found a coach made of pure gold, with the coat-of-arms of the prince and princess shining upon it like a star, and the coachman, footman, and outriders all wearing golden crowns on their heads.

The prince and princess themselves helped her into the coach and wished her success. The forest crow, who was now married, accompanied her for the first three miles; he sat by Gerda's side as he could not bear riding backwards. The tame crow stood in the doorway flapping her wings.

She could not go with them because she had been suffering from headache ever since the new appointment, no doubt from eating too much. The coach was well stored with sweet cakes, and under the seat were fruit and gingerbread nuts.

"Farewell, farewell!" cried the prince and princess, and little Gerda wept, and the crow wept; and then, after a few miles, the crow also said "Farewell," and this was the saddest parting. However, he flew to a tree and stood flapping his black wings as long as he could see the coach, which glittered in the bright sunshine.

FIFTH STORY. THE LITTLE ROBBER GIRL

The coach drove on through a thick forest, where it lighted up the way like a torch and dazzled the eyes of some robbers, who could not bear to let it pass them unmolested.

"It is gold! It is gold!" cried they, rushing forward and seizing the horses. Then they struck the little jockeys, the coachman, and the footman dead, and pulled little Gerda out of the carriage.

"She is fat and pretty, and she has been fed with the kernels of nuts," said the old robber-woman, who had a long beard and eye-brows that hung over her eyes. "She is as good as a little lamb; how nice she will taste!" and as she said this, she drew forth a shining knife that glittered horribly.

"Oh!" screamed the old woman at the same moment; for her own daughter, who held her back, had bitten her in the ear. She was a wild and naughty girl. The mother called her an ugly thing and had not time to kill Gerda.

"She shall play with me," said the little robber-girl; "she shall give me her muff and her pretty dress, and sleep with me in my bed." And then she bit her mother again, and made her spring in the air and jump about; and all the robbers laughed and said, "See how she is dancing with her young cub!"

"I will have a ride in the coach," said the little robber-girl; and she would have her own way, for she was so self-willed and obstinate.

She and Gerda seated themselves in the coach and drove away, over stumps and stones, into the depths of the forest. The little robber-girl was about the same size as Gerda but stronger; she had broader shoulders and a darker skin; her eyes were quite black, and she had a mournful look. She clasped little Gerda round the waist, and said:

"They shall not kill you as long as you don't make me vexed with you. I suppose you are a princess."

"No," said Gerda; and then she told her all her history and how fond she was of little Kay.

The robber-girl looked earnestly at her, nodded her head slightly, and said, "They sha'n't kill you even if I do get angry with you; for I will do it myself." And then she wiped Gerda's eyes and stuck her own hands in the beautiful muff, which was so soft and warm.

The coach stopped in the courtyard of a robber's castle, the walls of which were cracked from top to bottom. Ravens and crows flew in and out of the holes and crevices while great bulldogs, either of which looked as if it could swallow a man, were jumping about; but they were not allowed to bark. In the large old smoky hall, a bright fire was burning on the stone floor. There was no chimney; so the smoke went up to the ceiling and found a way out for itself. Soup was boiling in a large cauldron.

"You shall sleep with me and all my little animals to-night," said the robber-girl after they had had something to eat and drink. So she took Gerda to a corner of the hall, where some straw and carpets were laid down. Above them, on laths and perches, were more than a hundred pigeons, who all seemed to be asleep, although they moved slightly when the two little girls came near them. "These all belong to me," said the robber-girl; and she seized the nearest to her, held it by the feet, and shook it till it flapped its wings.

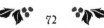

"Kiss it," cried she, flapping it in Gerda's face. "There sit the wood-pigeons," continued she, pointing to a number of laths and a cage which had been fixed into the walls, near one of the openings. "Both rascals would fly away directly if they were not closely locked up. And here is my old sweet-heart 'Ba'," and she dragged out a reindeer by the horn; he wore a bright copper ring round his neck and was tied up. "We are obliged to hold him tight too, or else he would run away from us. I tickle his neck every evening with my sharp knife, which frightens him very much." And then the rob-ber-girl drew a long knife from a chink in the wall and let it slide gently over the reindeer's neck. The poor animal began to kick, and the little robber-girl laughed and pulled down Gerda into bed with her.

"Will you have that knife with you while you are asleep?" asked Gerda, looking at it in great fright.

"I always sleep with the knife by me," said the robber-girl. "No one knows what may happen. But now tell me again all about little Kay and why you went out into the world."

Then Gerda repeated her story over again, while the wood-pigeons in the cage over her cooed, and the other pi-geons slept. The little robber-girl put one arm across Gerda's neck and held the knife in the other, and was soon fast asleep and snoring. But Gerda could not close her eyes at all; she knew not whether she was to live or die. The robbers sat round the fire, singing and drinking, and the old woman stumbled about. It was a terrible sight for a little girl to witness.

Then the wood-pigeons said, "Coo-coo; we have seen lit-tle Kay. A white fowl carried his sledge, and he sat in the carriage of the Snow Queen, which drove through the wood while we were lying in our nest. She blew upon us, and all the young ones died excepting us two. Coo, coo."

"What are you saying up there?" cried Gerda. "Where was the Snow Queen going? Do you know anything about it?"

"She was most likely travelling to Lapland, where there is always snow and ice. Ask the reindeer that is fastened up there with a rope."

"Yes, there is always snow and ice," said the reindeer; "and it is a glorious place; you can leap and run about freely on the sparkling icy plains. The Snow Queen has her sum-mer tent there, but her strong castle is at the North Pole, on an island called Spitsbergen."

"Oh, Kay, little Kay!" sighed Gerda.

"Lie still," said the robber-girl, "or I shall run my knife into your body!"

In the morning Gerda told her all that the wood-pigeons had said; and the little robber-girl looked quite serious, nodded her head, and said, "That is all talk, that is all talk. Do you know where Lapland is?" she asked the reindeer.

"Who should know better than I do?" said the animal, while his eyes sparkled. "I was born and brought up there and used to run about the snow-covered plains."

"Now listen," said the robber-girl; "all our men are gone away,—only my mother is here, and here she will stay; but at noon she always drinks out of a great bottle and afterwards sleeps for a little while; and then I'll do something for you." Then she jumped out of bed, clasped her mother round the neck, and pulled her by the beard, crying, "My own little nanny-goat, good morning." Then her mother filliped her nose till it was quite red, yet she did it all for love.

When the mother had drunk out of the bottle and was gone to sleep, the little robber-maiden went to the reindeer and said, "I should like very much to tickle your neck a few times more with my knife, for it makes you look so funny; but never mind,—I will untie your cord and set you free, so that you may run away to Lapland; but you must make good use of your legs and carry this little maiden to the castle of the Snow Queen where her playfellow is. You have heard what she told me, for she spoke loud enough, and you were listening."

Then the reindeer jumped for joy; and the little robber-girl lifted Gerda on his back, and had the forethought to tie her on, and even to give her her own little cushion to sit on.

"Here are your fur boots for you," said she; "for it will be very cold; but I must keep the muff: it is so pretty. However, you shall not be frozen for the want of it; here are my mother's large warm mittens; they will reach up to your elbows. Let me put them on. There, now your hands look just like my mother's."

But Gerda wept for joy.

"I don't like to see you fret," said the little robber-girl; "you ought to look quite happy now; and here are two loaves, so that you need not starve." These were fastened on the reindeer, and then the little robber-maiden opened the door, coaxed in all the great dogs, and then cut the string with which the reindeer was fastened and said, "Now run, but mind you take good care of the little girl!"

And then Gerda stretched out her hand, with the great mitten on it, towards the little robber-girl and said, "Farewell," and away flew the reindeer, over stumps and stones, through the great forest, over marshes and plains, as quickly as he

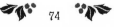

could. The wolves howled, and the ravens screamed; while up in the sky quivered red lights like flames of fire. "There are my old northern lights," said the reindeer; "see how they flash." And he ran on day and night still faster and faster, but the loaves were all eaten by the time they reached Lapland.

Sixth Story. The Lapland Woman and the Finland Woman

They stopped at a little hut; it was very mean looking: the roof sloped nearly down to the ground, and the door was so low that the family had to creep in on their hands and knees when they went in and out. There was no one at home but an old Lapland woman, who was cooking fish by the light of a train-oil lamp. The reindeer told her all about Gerda's story after having first told his own, which seemed to him the most important; and Gerda was so pinched with the cold that she could not speak.

"Oh, you poor things," said the Lapland woman, "you have a long way to go yet. You must travel more than a hundred miles farther, to Finland. The Snow Queen lives there

now, and she burns Bengal lights every evening. I will write a few words on a dried stock-fish, for I have no paper, and you can take it from me to the Finland woman who lives there; she can give you better information than I can."

So when Gerda was warmed and had taken something to eat and drink, the woman wrote a few words on the dried fish and told Gerda to take great care of it. Then she tied her again on the reindeer, and he set off at full speed. Flash, flash, went the beautiful blue northern lights in the air the whole night long. And at length they reached Finland and knocked at the chimney of the Finland woman's hut, for it had no door above the ground.

They crept in, but it was so terribly hot inside that the woman wore scarcely any clothes; she was small and very dirty looking. She loosened little Gerda's dress and took off her fur boots and the mittens, or Gerda would have been unable to bear the heat. Then she placed a piece of ice on the reindeer's head and read what was written on the dried

fish. After she had read it three times, she knew it by heart, so she popped the fish into the soup saucepan, as she knew it was good to eat, and she never wasted anything.

The reindeer told his own story first and then little Gerda's, and the Finlander twinkled with her clever eyes, but she said nothing. "You are so clever," said the reindeer; "I know you can tie all the winds of the world with a piece of twine. If a sailor unties one knot, he has a fair wind; and when he unties the second, it blows hard; but if the third and fourth are loosened, then comes a storm, which will root up whole forests. Cannot you give this little maiden something which will make her as strong as twelve men, to overcome the Snow Queen?"

"The power of twelve men!" said the Finland woman; "that would be of very little use." But she went to a shelf and took down and unrolled a large skin, on which were inscribed wonderful characters, and she read till the perspiration ran down her forehead. But the reindeer begged so hard for little Gerda and Gerda looked at the Finland woman with such beseeching tearful eyes, that her own eyes began to twinkle again; so she drew the reindeer into a corner and whispered to him while she laid a fresh piece of ice on his head, "Little Kay is really with the Snow Queen, but he finds everything there so much to his taste and his liking that he believes it is the finest place in the world; but this is because he has a piece of broken glass in his heart and a little piece of glass in his eye. These must be taken out, or he will never be a human being again, and the Snow Queen will retain her power over him."

"But can you not give little Gerda something to help her to conquer this power?"

"I can give her no greater power than she has already," said the woman; "don't you see how strong she is? How men and animals are obliged to serve her, and how well she has got through the world, barefooted as she is. She cannot receive any power from me greater than she now has, which consists in her own purity and innocence of heart. If she cannot her-self obtain access to the Snow Queen and remove the glass fragments from little Kay, we can do nothing to help her. Two miles from here the Snow Queen's garden begins; you can carry the little girl so far and set her down by the large bush which stands in the snow, covered with red berries. Do not stay gossiping but come back here as quickly as you can." Then the Finland woman lifted little Gerda upon the reindeer, and he ran away with her as quickly as he could.

"Oh, I have forgotten my boots and my mittens," cried little Gerda as soon as she felt the cutting cold, but the rein-deer dared not stop. So he ran on till he reached the bush with the red berries; here he sat Gerda down and kissed her, and the great bright tears trickled over the animal's cheeks. Then he left her and ran back as fast as he could.

There stood poor Gerda, without shoes, without gloves, in the midst of cold, dreary, ice-bound Finland. She ran forwards as quickly as she could, when a whole regiment of snow-flakes came round her; they did not, however, fall from the sky, which was quite clear and glittering with the northern lights. The snow-flakes ran along the ground, and the nearer they came to her, the larger they appeared. Gerda remembered how large and beautiful they looked through the burning glass. But these were really larger and much more terrible, for they were alive, and were the guards of the Snow Queen, and had the strangest shapes. Some were like great porcupines, others like twisted serpents with their heads stretching out, and some few were like little fat bears with hair bristled; but all were dazzlingly white, and all were living snow-flakes.

Then little Gerda repeated the Lord's Prayer, and the cold was so great that she could see her own breath come out of her mouth like steam as she uttered the words. The steam appeared to increase, as she continued her prayer, till it took the shape of little angels, who grew larger the mo-ment they touched the earth. They all wore helmets on their heads and carried spears and shields. Their number contin-

ued to increase more and more; and by the time Gerda had finished her prayers, a whole legion stood around her. They thrust their spears into the terrible snow-flakes, so that they shivered into a hundred pieces, and little Gerda could go forward with courage and safety. The angels stroked her hands and feet, so that she felt the cold less, and she hastened on to the Snow Queen's castle.

But now we must see what Kay is doing. In truth he thought not of little Gerda and never supposed she could be standing in front of the palace.

Seventh Story. Of the Palace of the Snow Queen, and What Happened There at Last

The walls of the palace were formed of drifted snow, and the windows and doors of the cutting winds. There were more than a hundred rooms in it, all as if they had been formed with snow blown together. The largest of them extended for several miles; they were all lighted up by the vivid light of the aurora, and they were so large and empty, so icy cold and glittering! There were no amusements here, not even a little bear's ball, when the storm might have been the music, and the bears could have danced on their hind legs and shown their good manners. There were no pleasant games of snap-dragon, or touch, or even a gossip over the tea-table for the young-lady foxes. Empty, vast, and cold were the halls of the Snow Queen. The flickering flame of

the northern lights could be plainly seen, whether they rose high or low in the heavens, from every part of the castle.

In the midst of this empty, endless hall of snow was a frozen lake, broken on its surface into a thousand forms; each piece resembled another, from being in itself perfect as a work of art, and in the centre of this lake sat the Snow Queen when she was at home. She called the lake "The Mirror of Reason," and said that it was the best and indeed the only one in the world.

Little Kay was quite blue with cold, indeed almost black, but he did not feel it, for the Snow Queen had kissed away the icy shiverings, and his heart was already a lump of ice. He dragged some sharp, flat pieces of ice to and fro and placed them together in all kinds of positions, as if he wished to make something out of them, just as we try to form various figures with little tablets of wood which we call "a Chinese puzzle." Kay's figures were very artistic; it was the icy game of reason at which he played, and in his eyes the figures were very remarkable and of the highest importance; this opinion was owing to the piece of glass still sticking in his eye.

He composed many complete figures, forming different words, but there was one word he never could manage to form, although he wished it very much. It was the word "Eternity." The Snow Queen had said to him, "When you can find out this, you shall be your own master, and I will give you the whole world and a new pair of skates." But he could not accomplish it.

"Now I must hasten away to warmer countries," said the Snow Queen. "I will go and look into the black craters of the tops of the burning mountains, Etna and Vesuvius, as they are called—I shall make them look white, which will be good for them and for the lemons and the grapes." And away flew the Snow Queen, leaving little Kay quite alone in the great hall, which was so many miles in length. So he sat and looked at his pieces of ice, and was thinking so deeply and sat so still that anyone might have supposed he was frozen.

Just at this moment it happened that little Gerda came through the great door of the castle. Cutting winds were raging around her, but she offered up a prayer and the winds

sank down as if they were going to sleep. She went on till she came to the large empty hall and caught sight of Kay. She knew him directly; she flew to him, threw her arms round his neck, and held him fast while she exclaimed, "Kay, dear little Kay, I have found you at last!"

But he sat quite still, stiff, and cold.

Then little Gerda wept hot tears, which fell on his breast, penetrated into his heart, thawed the lump of ice, and washed away the little pieces of glass which had stuck there. Then he looked at her, and she sang:

> "Roses bloom and cease to be,
> But we shall the Christ-child see."

Then Kay burst into tears and wept so that the splinter of glass swam out of his eye. Then he recognised Gerda and said joyfully, "Gerda, dear little Gerda, where have you been all this time, and where have I been?" And he looked all around him and said, "How cold it is, and how large and empty it looks!"

He clung to Gerda, and she laughed and wept for joy. It was so pleasing to see them that the pieces of ice even danced about; and when they were tired and went to lie down, they formed themselves into the letters of the word which the Snow Queen had said he must find out before he could be his own master and have the whole world and a pair of new skates. Then Gerda kissed his cheeks, and they became blooming; she kissed his eyes, and they shone like her own; she kissed his hands and his feet, and then he became quite healthy and cheerful. The Snow Queen might come home now when she pleased, for there stood his certainty of freedom, in the word she wanted, written in shining letters of ice.

Then they took each other by the hand and went forth from the great palace of ice. They spoke of the grandmother and of the roses on the roof; and as they went on, the winds were at rest, and the sun burst forth.

When they arrived at the bush with red berries, there stood the reindeer waiting for them, and he had brought another young reindeer with him, whose udders were full, and the children drank her warm milk and kissed her on the mouth. Then the reindeers carried Kay and Gerda first to the Finland woman, where they warmed themselves thoroughly in the hot room, and she gave them directions about their journey home. Next they went to the Lapland woman, who had made some new clothes for them and put their sleighs in order.

Both the reindeer ran by their side and followed them as far as the boundaries of the country, where the first green leaves were budding. And here they took leave of the two reindeer and the Lapland woman, and all said, "Farewell!"

Then the birds began to twitter, and the forest was full of green young leaves; and out of it came a beautiful horse, which Gerda remembered, for it was the one which had drawn the golden coach. A young girl was riding upon it, with a shining red cap on her head and pistols in her belt. It was the little robber-maiden, who had got tired of staying at home. She was going first to the north, and if that did not suit her, she meant to try some other part of the world. She knew Gerda directly, and Gerda remembered her; it was a joyful meeting.

"You are a fine fellow to go gadding about in this way," said she to little Kay. "I should like to know whether you deserve that anyone should go to the end of the world to find you."

But Gerda patted her cheeks and asked after the prince and princess.

"They are gone to foreign countries," said the robber-girl.

"And the crow?" asked Gerda.

"Oh, the crow is dead," she replied; "his tame sweetheart is now a widow and wears a bit of black worsted round her leg. She mourns very pitifully, but it is all stuff. But now tell me how you managed to get him back."

Then Gerda and Kay told her all about it.

"Snip, snap, snare! it's all right at last," said the robber-girl.

Then she took both their hands and promised that if ever she should pass through the town, she would call and pay them a visit. And then she rode away into the wide world. But Gerda and Kay went hand-in-hand towards home. And as they advanced, spring appeared more lovely with its green verdure and its beautiful flowers.

Very soon they recognised the large town where they lived and the tall steeples of the churches, in which the sweet bells were ringing a merry peal as they entered it, and found their way to their grandmother's door. They went upstairs into the little room, where all looked just as it used to do. The old clock was going "tick, tick," and the hands pointed to the time of day, but as they passed through the door into the room, they perceived that they were both grown up and become a man and woman.

The roses out on the roof were in full bloom and peeped in at the window; and there stood the little chairs, on which they had sat when children; and Kay and Gerda seated themselves each on their own chair and held each other by the hand, while the cold empty grandeur of the Snow Queen's palace vanished from their memories like a painful dream.

The grandmother sat in God's bright sunshine, and she read aloud from the Bible, "Except ye become as little children, ye shall in no wise enter into the kingdom of God." And Kay and Gerda looked into each other's eyes and all at once understood the words of the old song,

> "Roses bloom and cease to be,
> But we shall the Christ-child see."

And they both sat there, grown up, yet children at heart; and it was summer—warm, beautiful summer.

The Swineherd

ONCE upon a time lived a poor prince; his kingdom was very small, but it was large enough to enable him to marry, and marry he would.

It was rather bold of him that he went and asked the emperor's daughter: "Will you marry me?" but he ventured to do so, for his name was known far and wide, and there were hundreds of princesses who would have gladly accepted him, but would she do so? Now we shall see.

On the grave of the prince's father grew a rose-tree, the most beautiful of its kind. It bloomed only once in five years, and then it had only one single rose upon it, but what a rose! It had such a sweet scent that one instantly forgot all sorrow and grief when one smelt it.

He had also a nightingale, which could sing as if every sweet melody was in its throat. This rose and the nightingale he wished to give to the princess; and therefore both were put into big silver cases and sent to her.

The emperor ordered them to be carried into the great hall where the princess was just playing "Visitors are coming" with her ladies-in-waiting; when she saw the large cases with the presents therein, she clapped her hands for joy.

"I wish it were a little pussy cat," she said. But then the rose-tree with the beautiful rose was unpacked.

"Oh, how nicely it is made," exclaimed the ladies.

"It is more than nice," said the emperor, "it is charming."

The princess touched it and nearly began to cry.

"Fie, papa!" she said, "it is not artificial, it is natural!"

"Fie! it is natural!" repeated all her ladies.

"Let us first see what the other case contains before we are angry," said the emperor; then the nightingale was taken out, and it sang so beautifully that no one could possibly say anything unkind about it.

"Superbe! charmant!" said the ladies of the court, for they all prattled French, one worse than the other.

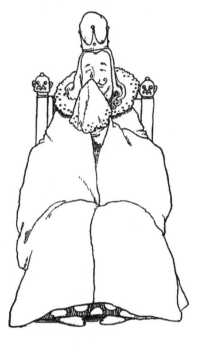

"How much the bird reminds me of the musical box of the late lamented empress!" said an old courtier, "it has exactly the same tone, the same execution."

"You are right," said the emperor and began to cry like a little child.

"I hope it is not natural," said the princess.

"Yes, certainly it is natural," replied those who had brought the presents.

"Then let it fly," said the princess and refused to see the prince.

But the prince was not discouraged. He painted his face, put on common clothes, pulled his cap over his forehead, and came back.

"Good day, emperor," he said, "could you not give me some employment at the court?"

"There are so many," replied the emperor, "who apply for places, that for the present I have no vacancy, but I will remember you. But wait a moment: it just comes into my mind, I require somebody to look after my pigs, for I have a great many."

Thus the prince was appointed imperial swineherd, and as such he lived in a wretchedly small room near the pigsty. There he worked all day long, and when it was night he had

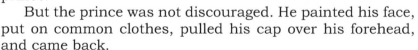

made a pretty little pot. There were little bells round the rim, and when the water began to boil in it, the bells began to play the old tune:

> "Oh, my dear Augustin,
> Everything is gone!"

But more wonderful was that, whoever held his finger in the smoke of the pot, immediately smelt all the dishes that were cooking on every hearth in the town. That was indeed much more remarkable than the rose.

When the princess with her ladies passed by and heard the tune, she stopped and looked quite pleased, for she also could play it—in fact, it was the only tune she could play, and she played it with one finger.

"That is the tune I know," she exclaimed. "He must be a well-educated swineherd. Go and ask him how much the instrument is."

One of the ladies had to go and ask; but she put on pattens.

"What will you take for your pot?" asked the lady.

"I will have ten kisses from the princess," said the swineherd.

"God forbid!" said the lady.

"Well, I cannot sell it for less," replied the swineherd.

"What did he say?" said the princess.

"I really cannot tell you," replied the lady.

"You can whisper it into my ear."

"It is very naughty," said the princess and walked off.

But when she had gone a little distance, the bells rang again so sweetly:

> "Oh, my dear Augustin,
> Everything is gone!"

"Ask him," said the princess, "if he will be satisfied with ten kisses from one of my ladies."

"No, thank you," said the swineherd, "ten kisses from the princess, or I keep my pot."

"That is tiresome," said the princess. "But you must stand before me, so that nobody can see it."

The ladies placed themselves in front of her and spread out their dresses, and she gave the swineherd ten kisses and received the pot.

That was a pleasure! Day and night the water in the pot was boiling; there was not a single fire in the whole town of which they did not know what was preparing on it, the chamberlain's as well as the shoemaker's. The ladies danced and clapped their hands for joy.

"We know who will eat soup and pancakes; we know who will eat porridge and cutlets; oh, how interesting!"

"Very interesting, indeed," said the mistress of the household. "But you must not betray me, for I am the emperor's daughter."

"Of course not," they all said.

The swineherd—that is to say, the prince—but they did not know otherwise than that he was a real swineherd—did not waste a single day without doing something; he made a rattle, which, when turned quickly round, played all the waltzes, galops, and polkas known since the creation of the world.

"But that is superbe!" said the princess passing by. "I have never heard a more beautiful composition. Go down and ask him what the instrument costs; but I shall not kiss him again."

"He will have a hundred kisses from the princess," said the lady, who had gone down to ask him.

"I believe he is mad," said the princess and walked off, but soon she stopped. "One must encourage art," she said. "I am the emperor's daughter. Tell him I will give him ten kisses, as I did the other day; the remainder one of my ladies can give him."

"But we do not like to kiss him," said the ladies.

"That is nonsense," said the princess; "if I can kiss him, you can also do it. Remember that I give you food and employment."

And the lady had to go down once more.

"A hundred kisses from the princess," said the swineherd, "or everybody keeps his own."

"Place yourselves before me," said the princess then. They did as they were bidden, and the princess kissed him.

"I wonder what that crowd near the pigsty means," said the emperor, who had just come out on his balcony. He rubbed his eyes and put his spectacles on.

"The ladies of the court are up to some mischief, I think. I shall have to go down and see." He pulled up his shoes, for they were down at the heels, and he was very quick about it.

When he had come down into the courtyard, he walked quite softly, and the ladies were so busily engaged in counting the kisses, that all should be fair, that they did not notice the emperor. He raised himself on tiptoe.

"What does this mean?" he shouted, when he saw that his daughter was kissing the swineherd, and then he hit their heads with his shoe just as the swineherd received the sixty-eighth kiss.

"Go out of my sight," said the emperor, for he was very angry; and both the princess and the swineherd were banished from the empire.

There she stood and cried, the swineherd scolded her, and the rain came down in torrents.

"Alas, unfortunate creature that I am!" said the princess, "I wish I had accepted the prince. Oh, how wretched I am!"

The swineherd went behind a tree, wiped his face, threw off his poor attire and stepped forth in his princely garments; he looked so beautiful that the princess could not help bowing to him.

"I have now learnt to despise you," he said. "You refused an honest prince; you did not appreciate the rose and the nightingale; but you did not mind kissing a swineherd for his toys; you have no one but yourself to blame!"

And then he returned into his kingdom and left her behind. She could now sing at her leisure:

> "Oh, my dear Augustin,
> Everything is gone!"

The Beetle
Who Went on His Travels

HERE was once an emperor who had a horse shod with gold. He had a golden shoe on each foot, and why was this? He was a beautiful creature, with slender legs, bright, intelligent eyes, and a mane, which hung down over his neck like a veil.

He had carried his master through fire and smoke in the battlefield, with the bullets whistling round him; he had kicked and bitten, and taken part in the fight when the enemy advanced; and, with his master on his back, he had dashed over the fallen foe and saved the golden crown and the emperor's life, which was of more value than the brightest gold. This is the reason of the emperor's horse wearing golden shoes.

A beetle came creeping forth from the stable, where the farrier had been shoeing the horse. "Great ones first, of course," said he, "and then the little ones; but size is not always a proof of greatness." He stretched out his thin leg as he spoke.

"And pray what do you want?" asked the farrier.

"Golden shoes," replied the beetle.

"Why, you must be out of your senses," cried the farrier. "Golden shoes for you, indeed!"

"Yes, certainly; golden shoes," replied the beetle. "Am I not just as good as that great creature yonder, who is waited upon and brushed, and has food and drink placed before him? And don't I belong to the royal stables?"

"But why does the horse have golden shoes?" asked the farrier; "of course you understand the reason?"

"Understand! Well, I understand that it is a personal slight to me," cried the beetle. "It is done to annoy me, so I intend to go out into the world and seek my fortune."

"Go along with you," said the farrier.

"You're a rude fellow," cried the beetle, as he walked out of the stable; and then he flew for a short distance, till he found himself in a beautiful flower-garden, all fragrant with roses and lavender. The lady-birds, with red and black shells on their backs, and delicate wings, were flying about, and one of them said, "Is it not sweet and lovely here? Oh, how beautiful everything is."

"I am accustomed to better things," said the beetle. "Do you call this beautiful? Why, there is not even a dung-heap." Then he went on, and under the shadow of a large haystack he found a caterpillar crawling along.

"How beautiful this world is!" said the caterpillar. "The sun is so warm, I quite enjoy it. And soon I shall go to sleep, and die as they call it, but I shall wake up with beautiful wings to fly with, like a butterfly."

"How conceited you are!" exclaimed the beetle. "Fly about as a butterfly, indeed! what of that. I have come out of the emperor's stable, and no one there, not even the emperor's horse, who, in fact, wears my cast-off golden shoes, has any idea of flying, excepting myself. To have wings and fly! why, I can do that already;" and so saying, he spread his wings and flew away. "I don't want to be disgusted," he said to himself, "and yet I can't help it."

Soon after, he fell down upon an extensive lawn, and for a time pretended to sleep, but at last fell asleep in earnest. Suddenly a heavy shower of rain came falling from the clouds. The beetle woke up with the noise and would have been glad to creep into the earth for shelter, but he could not. He was tumbled over and over with the rain, sometimes swimming on his stomach and sometimes on his back; and as for flying, that was out of the question. He began to doubt whether he should escape with his life, so he remained quietly lying where he was.

After a while the weather cleared up a little, and the beetle was able to rub the water from his eyes and look about him. He saw something gleaming, and he managed to make his way up to it. It was linen which had been laid to bleach on the grass. He crept into a fold of the damp linen, which certainly was not so comfortable a place to lie in as the warm stable, but there was nothing better, so he remained lying there for a whole day and night, and the rain kept on all the time. Towards morning he crept out of his hiding-place, feeling in a very bad temper with the climate. Two frogs were sitting on the linen, and their bright eyes actually glistened with pleasure.

"Wonderful weather this," cried one of them, "and so refreshing. This linen holds the water together so beautifully, that my hind legs quiver as if I were going to swim."

"I should like to know," said another, "if the swallow who flies so far in her many journeys to foreign lands, ever met with a better climate than this. What delicious moisture! It is as pleasant as lying in a wet ditch. I am sure anyone who does not enjoy this has no love for his fatherland."

"Have you ever been in the emperor's stable?" asked the beetle. "There the moisture is warm and refreshing; that's the climate for me, but I could not take it with me on my travels. Is there not even a dunghill here in this garden, where a person of rank, like myself, could take up his abode and feel at home?" But the frogs either did not or would not understand him.

"I never ask a question twice," said the beetle, after he had asked this one three times and received no answer. Then he went on a little farther and stumbled against a piece of broken crockery-ware, which certainly ought not to have been lying there. But as it was there, it formed a good shelter against wind and weather to several families of earwigs who dwelt in it. Their requirements were not many; they were very sociable and full of affection for their children so much that each mother considered her own child the most beautiful and clever of them all.

"Our son has engaged himself," said one mother, "dear innocent boy; his greatest ambition is that he may one day creep into a clergyman's ear. That is a very artless and loveable wish; and being engaged will keep him steady. What happiness for a mother!"

"Our son," said another, "had scarcely crept out of the egg, when he was off on his travels. He is all life and spirits; I expect he will wear out his horns with running. How charming this is for a mother, is it not Mr. Beetle?" for she knew the stranger by his horny coat.

"You are both quite right," said he; so they begged him to walk in, that is to come as far as he could under the broken piece of earthenware.

"Now you shall also see my little earwigs," said a third and a fourth mother, "they are lovely little things and highly amusing. They are never ill-behaved, except when they are uncomfortable in their insides, which unfortunately often happens at their age."

Thus each mother spoke of her baby, and their babies talked after their own fashion, and made use of the little nippers they have in their tails to nip the beard of the beetle.

"They are always busy about something, the little rogues," said the mother, beaming with maternal pride; but the beetle felt it a bore, and he therefore inquired the way to the nearest dung-heap.

"That is quite out in the great world, on the other side of the ditch," answered an earwig, "I hope none of my children will ever go so far, it would be the death of me."

"But I shall try to get so far," said the beetle, and he walked off without taking any formal leave, which is considered a polite thing to do.

When he arrived at the ditch, he met several friends, all of them beetles; "We live here," they said, "and we are very comfortable. May we ask you to step down into this rich mud; you must be fatigued after your journey."

"Certainly," said the beetle, "I shall be most happy; I have been exposed to the rain and have had to lie upon linen, and cleanliness is a thing that greatly exhausts me; I have also pains in one of my wings from standing in the draught under a piece of broken crockery. It is really quite refreshing to be with one's own kindred again."

"Perhaps you came from a dung-heap," observed the oldest of them.

"No, indeed, I came from a much grander place," replied the beetle; "I came from the emperor's stable, where I was born, with golden shoes on my feet. I am travelling on a secret embassy, but you must not ask me any questions, for I cannot betray my secret." Then the beetle stepped down into the rich mud, where sat three young lady beetles, who tittered, because they did not know what to say.

"None of them are engaged yet," said their mother, and the beetle maidens tittered again, this time quite in confusion.

"I have never seen greater beauties, even in the royal stables," exclaimed the beetle, who was now resting himself.

"Don't spoil my girls," said the mother; "and don't talk to them, pray, unless you have serious intentions."

But of course the beetle's intentions were serious, and after a while our friend was engaged. The mother gave them her blessing, and all the other beetles cried "hurrah."

Immediately after the betrothal, came the marriage, for there was no reason to delay. The following day passed very pleasantly, and the next was tolerably comfortable; but on the third it became necessary for him to think of getting food for his wife, and, perhaps, for children.

"I have allowed myself to be taken in," said our beetle to himself, "and now there's nothing to be done but to take them in, in return."

No sooner said than done. Away he went and stayed away all day and all night, and his wife remained behind a forsaken widow.

"Oh," said the other beetles, "this fellow that we have received into our family is nothing but a complete vagabond. He has gone away and left his wife a burden upon our hands."

"Well, she can be unmarried again and remain here with my other daughters," said the mother. "Fie on the villain that forsook her!"

In the meantime the beetle, who had sailed across the ditch on a cabbage leaf, had been journeying on the other side. In the morning two persons came up to the ditch. When they saw him, they took him up and turned him over and over, looking very learned all the time, especially one,

94

who was a boy. "Allah sees the black beetle in the black stone, and the black rock. Is not that written in the Koran?" he asked.

Then he translated the beetle's name into Latin and said a great deal upon the creature's nature and history. The second person, who was older and a scholar, proposed to carry the beetle home, as they wanted just such good specimens as this.

Our beetle considered this speech a great insult, so he flew suddenly out of the speaker's hand. His wings were dry now, so they carried him to a great distance, till at last he reached a hothouse, where a sash of the glass roof was partly open, so he quietly slipped in and buried himself in the warm earth. "It is very comfortable here," he said to himself and soon after fell asleep. Then he dreamed that the emperor's horse was dying, and had left him his golden shoes, and also promised that he should have two more.

All this was very delightful, and when the beetle woke up he crept forth and looked around him. What a splendid place the hothouse was! At the back, large palm-trees were growing, and the sunlight made the leaves look quite glossy; and beneath them what a profusion of luxuriant green, and of flowers red like flame, yellow as amber, or white as new-fallen snow!

"What a wonderful quantity of plants," cried the beetle; "how good they will taste when they are decayed! This is a capital store-room. There must certainly be some relations of mine living here; I will just see if I can find any one with whom I can associate. I'm proud, certainly; but I'm also proud of being so."

Then he prowled about in the earth, and thought what a pleasant dream that was about the dying horse and the golden shoes he had inherited. Suddenly a hand seized the beetle, and squeezed him, and turned him round and round. The gardener's little son and his playfellow had come into the hothouse, and, seeing the beetle, wanted to have some fun with him.

First, he was wrapped in a vine-leaf and put into a warm trousers' pocket. He twisted and turned about with all his might, but he got a good squeeze from the boy's hand, as a hint for him to keep quiet. Then the boy went quickly towards a lake that lay at the end of the garden. Here the beetle was put into an old broken wooden shoe, in which a little stick had been fastened upright for a mast, and to this mast the beetle was bound with a piece of worsted.

Now he was a sailor, and had to sail away. The lake was not very large, but to the beetle it seemed an ocean, and he was so astonished at its size that he fell over on his back, and kicked out his legs. Then the little ship sailed away; sometimes the current of the water seized it, but whenever it went too far from the shore one of the boys turned up his trousers, and went in after it, and brought it back to land. But at last, just as it went merrily out again, the two boys were called, and so angrily, that they hastened to obey and ran away as fast as they could from the pond, so that the little ship was left to its fate. It was carried away farther and farther from the shore, till it reached the open sea. This was a terrible prospect for the beetle, for he could not escape in consequence of being bound to the mast. Then a fly came and paid him a visit. "What beautiful weather," said the fly; "I shall rest here and sun myself. You must have a pleasant time of it."

"You speak without knowing the facts," replied the beetle; "don't you see that I am a prisoner?"

"Ah, but I'm not a prisoner," remarked the fly, and away he flew.

"Well, now I know the world," said the beetle to himself; "it's an abominable world; I'm the only respectable person in it. First, they refuse me my golden shoes; then I have to lie on damp linen and to stand in a draught; and to crown all, they fasten a wife upon me. Then, when I have made a step forward in the world and found out a comfortable position, just as I could wish it to be, one of these human boys comes and ties me up, and leaves me to the mercy of the wild waves, while the emperor's favorite horse goes prancing about proudly on his golden shoes. This vexes me more than anything. But it is useless to look for sympathy in this world. My career has been very interesting, but what's the use of that if nobody knows anything about it? The world does not deserve to be made acquainted with my adventures, for it ought to have given me golden shoes when the emperor's horse was shod, and I stretched out my feet to be shod, too. If I had received golden shoes, I should have been an ornament to the stable; now I am lost to the stable and to the world. It is all over with me."

But all was not yet over. A boat, in which were a few young girls, came rowing up. "Look, yonder is an old wooden shoe sailing along," said one of the young girls.

"And there's a poor little creature bound fast in it," said another.

The boat now came close to our beetle's ship, and the young girls fished it out of the water. One of them drew a small pair of scissors from her pocket, and cut the worsted without hurting the beetle, and when she stepped on shore she placed him on the grass. "There," she said, "creep away, or fly, if thou canst. It is a splendid thing to have thy liberty." Away flew the beetle, straight through the open window of a large building; there he sank down, tired and exhausted, exactly on the mane of the emperor's favorite horse, who was standing in his stable; and the beetle found himself at home again. For some time he clung to the mane, that he might recover himself.

"Well," he said, "here I am, seated on the emperor's favorite horse, sitting upon him as if I were the emperor himself. But what was it the farrier asked me? Ah, I remember now,—that's a good thought,—he asked me why the golden shoes were given to the horse. The answer is quite clear to me, now. They were given to the horse on my account."

And this reflection put the beetle into a good temper. The sun's rays also came streaming into the stable, and shone upon him, and made the place lively and bright. "Travelling expands the mind very much," said the beetle. "The world is not so bad after all if you know how to take things as they come."

Soup from a Sausage Skewer

"WE HAD such an excellent dinner yesterday," said an old mouse of the female sex to another who had not been present at the feast. "I sat number twenty-one below the mouse-king, which was not a bad place. Shall I tell you what we had? Everything was first rate. Mouldy bread, tallow candle, and sausage. And then, when we had finished that course, the same came on all over again; it was as good as two feasts. We were very sociable, and there was as much joking and fun as if we had been all of one family circle. Nothing was left but the sausage skewers, and this formed a subject of conversation, till at last it turned to the proverb, 'Soup from sausage skins;' or, as the people in the neighbouring country call it, 'Soup from a sausage skewer.' Every one had heard the proverb, but no one had ever tasted the soup, much less prepared it. A capital toast was drunk to the inventor of the soup, and some one said he ought to be made a relieving officer to the poor. Was not that witty? Then the old mouse-king rose and promised that the young lady-mouse who should learn how best to prepare this much-admired and savoury soup should be his queen, and a year and a day should be allowed for the purpose."

"That was not at all a bad proposal," said the other mouse; "but how is the soup made?"

"Ah, that is more than I can tell you. All the young lady mice were asking the same question. They wished very much to be queen, but they did not want to take the trouble of going out into the world to learn how to make the soup, which was absolutely necessary to be done first. But it is not everyone who would care to leave her family or her happy corner by the fire-side at home, even to be made queen. It is not always easy to find bacon and cheese-rind in foreign lands every day, and it is not pleasant to have to endure hunger, and be perhaps, after all, eaten up alive by the cat."

Most probably some such thoughts as these discouraged the majority from going out into the world to collect the required information. Only four mice gave notice that they were ready to set out on the journey. They were young and lively, but poor. Each of them wished to visit one of the four divisions of the world, so that it might be seen which was the most favoured by fortune. Every one took a sausage skewer as a traveller's staff, and to remind them of the object of their journey. They left home early in May, and none of them returned till the first of May in the following year, and then only three of them. Nothing was seen or heard of the fourth, although the day of decision was close at hand.

"Ah, yes, there is always some trouble mixed up with the greatest pleasure," said the mouse-king; but he gave orders that all the mice within a circle of many miles should be invited at once. They were to assemble in the kitchen, and the three travelled mice were to stand in a row before them, while a sausage skewer, covered with crape, was to be stuck up instead of the missing mouse. No one dared to express an opinion until the king spoke and desired one of them to go on with her story. And now we shall hear what she said.

What the First Little Mouse
Saw and Heard on Her Travels

"When I first went out into the world," said the little mouse, "I fancied, as so many of my age do, that I already knew everything, but it was not so. It takes years to acquire great knowledge. I went at once to sea in a ship bound for the north. I had been told that the ship's cook must know how to prepare every dish at sea, and it is easy enough to do that with plenty of sides of bacon, and large tubs of salt meat and mouldy flour. There I found plenty of delicate food, but no opportunity for learning how to make soup from a sausage skewer. We sailed on for many days and nights; the ship rocked fearfully, and we did not escape without a wetting.

"As soon as we arrived at the port to which the ship was bound, I left it and went on shore at a place far towards the north. It is a wonderful thing to leave your own little corner at home, to hide yourself in a ship where there are

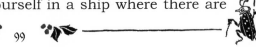

sure to be some nice snug corners for shelter, then suddenly to find yourself thousands of miles away in a foreign land. I saw large pathless forests of pine and birch trees, which smelt so strong that I sneezed and thought of sausage. There were great lakes also which looked as black as ink at a distance, but were quite clear when I came close to them. Large swans were floating upon them, and I thought at first they were only foam, they lay so still; but when I saw them walk and fly, I knew what they were directly. They belong to the goose species; one can see that by their walk. No one can attempt to disguise family descent. I kept with my own kind and associated with the forest and field mice, who, however, knew very little, especially about what I wanted to know, and which had actually made me travel abroad. The idea that soup could be made from a sausage skewer was to them such an out-of-the-way, unlikely thought, that it was repeated from one to another through the whole forest. They declared that the problem would never be solved, that the thing was an impossibility. How little I thought that in this place, on the very first night, I should be initiated into the manner of its preparation.

"It was the height of summer, which the mice told me was the reason that the forest smelt so strong, and that the herbs were so fragrant, and the lakes with the white swimming swans so dark, and yet so clear. On the margin of the wood, near to three or four houses, a pole, as large as the mainmast of a ship, had been erected, and from the summit hung wreaths of flowers and fluttering ribbons; it was the Maypole. Lads and lasses danced round the pole and tried to outdo the violins of the musicians with their singing. They were as merry as ever at sunset and in the moonlight, but I took no part in the merry-making. What has a little mouse to do with a Maypole dance? I sat in the soft moss and held my sausage skewer tight. The moon threw its beams particularly on one spot where stood a tree covered with exceedingly fine moss. I may almost venture to say that it was as fine and soft as the fur of the mouse-king, but it was green, which is a colour very agreeable to the eye. All at once I saw the most charming little people marching towards me. They did not reach higher than my knee; they looked like human beings, but were better proportioned, and they called themselves elves. Their clothes were very delicate and fine, for they were made of the leaves of flowers, trimmed with the wings of flies and gnats, which had not a bad effect. By their manner, it appeared as if they were seeking for something. I knew not what, till at last one of them espied me and came towards me, and the foremost pointed to my sausage skewer, and said, 'There, that is just what we want; see, it is pointed at the top; is it not capital?' and the longer he looked at my pilgrim's staff, the more delighted he became. 'I will lend it to you,' said I, 'but not to keep.'

"'Oh no, we won't keep it!' they all cried; and then they seized the skewer, which I gave up to them, and danced with it to the spot where the delicate moss grew, and set it up in the middle of the green. They wanted a maypole, and the one they now had seemed cut out on purpose for them. Then they decorated it so beautifully that it was quite dazzling to look at. Little spiders spun golden threads around it, and then it was hung with fluttering veils and flags so delicately white that they glittered like snow in the moonshine. After that they took colours from the butterfly's wing and sprinkled them over the white drapery, which gleamed as if covered with flowers and diamonds, so that I could not recognize my sausage skewer at all. Such a maypole had never been seen in all the world as this. Then came a great company of real elves. Nothing could be finer than their clothes, and they invited me to be present at the feast; but I was to keep at a certain distance, because I was too large for them. Then commenced such music that it sounded like a thousand glass bells, and was so full and strong that I thought it must be the song of the swans. I fancied also that I heard the voices of the cuckoo and the blackbird, and it seemed at last as if the whole forest sent forth glorious melodies— the voices of children, the tinkling of bells, and the songs of the birds; and all this wonderful melody came from the elfin maypole. My sausage peg was a complete peal of bells. I could scarcely believe that so much could have been produced from it, till I remembered into what hands it had fallen. I was so much affected that I wept tears such as a little mouse can weep, but they were tears of joy. The night was far too short for me; there are no long nights there in summer, as we often have in this part of the world. When the morning dawned, and the gentle breeze rippled the glassy mirror of the forest lake, all the delicate veils and flags fluttered away into thin air; the waving garlands of the spider's web, the hanging bridges and galleries, or whatever else they may be called, vanished away as if they had never been. Six elves brought me back my sausage skewer and at the same time asked me to make any request, which they would grant

if in their power; so I begged them, if they could, to tell me
how to make soup from a sausage skewer.

"'How do we make it?' said the chief of the elves with a
smile. 'Why you have just seen it; you scarcely knew your
sausage skewer again, I am sure.'

"They think themselves very wise, thought I to myself.
Then I told them all about it, and why I had travelled so
far, and also what promise had been made at home to the
one who should discover the method of preparing this soup.
'What use will it be,' I asked, 'to the mouse-king or to our
whole mighty kingdom that I have seen all these beautiful
things? I cannot shake the sausage peg and say, Look, here
is the skewer, and now the soup will come. That would only
produce a dish to be served when people were keeping a
fast.'

"Then the elf dipped his finger into the cup of a violet and
said to me, 'Look here, I will anoint your pilgrim's staff, so
that when you return to your own home and enter the king's
castle, you have only to touch the king with your staff, and
violets will spring forth and cover the whole of it, even in the
coldest winter time; so I think I have given you really something to carry home, and a little more than something.'"

But before the little mouse explained what this something more was, she stretched her staff out to the king, and
as it touched him the most beautiful bunch of violets sprang
forth and filled the place with perfume. The smell was so
powerful that the mouse-king ordered the mice who stood
nearest the chimney to thrust their tails into the fire, that
there might be a smell of burning, for the perfume of the vi-

olets was overpowering, and not the sort of scent that every
one liked.

"But what was the something more of which you spoke
just now?" asked the mouse-king.

"Why," answered the little mouse, "I think it is what they
call 'effect;'" and thereupon she turned the staff round, and
behold not a single flower was to be seen upon it! She now
only held the naked skewer and lifted it up as a conductor
lifts his baton at a concert. "Violets, the elf told me," continued the mouse, "are for the sight, the smell, and the touch;
so we have only now to produce the effect of hearing and
tasting;" and then, as the little mouse beat time with her
staff, there came sounds of music, not such music as was
heard in the forest, at the elfin feast, but such as is often
heard in the kitchen—the sounds of boiling and roasting. It
came quite suddenly, like wind rushing through the chim-
neys, and seemed as if every pot and kettle were boiling
over. The fire-shovel clattered down on the brass fender;
and then, quite as suddenly, all was still,—nothing could
be heard but the light, vapoury song of the tea-kettle, which
was quite wonderful to hear, for no one could rightly distinguish whether the kettle was just beginning to boil or going
to stop. And the little pot steamed, and the great pot sim-
mered, but without any regard for each; indeed there seemed
no sense in the pots at all. And as the little mouse waved
her baton still more wildly, the pots foamed and threw up
bubbles, and boiled over; while again the wind roared and
whistled through the chimney, and at last there was such a
terrible hubbub, that the little mouse let her stick fall.

"That is a strange sort of soup," said the mouse-king;
"shall we not now hear about the preparation?"

"That is all," answered the little mouse, with a bow.

"That all!" said the mouse-king; "then we shall be glad to
hear what information the next may have to give us."

What the Second Mouse Had to Tell

"I was born in the library, at a castle," said the second
mouse. "Very few members of our family ever had the good
fortune to get into the dining-room, much less the store-
room. On my journey, and here today, are the only times
I have ever seen a kitchen. We were often obliged to suffer
hunger in the library, but then we gained a great deal of
knowledge. The rumour reached us of the royal prize offered
to those who should be able to make soup from a sausage

skewer. Then my old grandmother sought out a manuscript which, however, she could not read, but had heard it read, and in it was written, 'Those who are poets can make soup of sausage skewers.' She then asked me if I was a poet. I felt myself quite innocent of any such pretensions. Then she said I must go out and make myself a poet. I asked again what I should be required to do, for it seemed to me quite as difficult as to find out how to make soup of a sausage skewer. My grandmother had heard a great deal of reading in her day, and she told me three principal qualifications were necessary—understanding, imagination, and feeling. 'If you can manage to acquire these three, you will be a poet, and the sausage-skewer soup will be quite easy to you.'

"So I went forth into the world, and turned my steps towards the west, that I might become a poet. Understanding is the most important matter in everything. I knew that, for the two other qualifications are not thought much of; so I went first to seek for understanding. Where was I to find it? 'Go to the ant and learn wisdom,' said the great Jewish king. I knew that from living in a library. So I went straight on till I came to the first great ant-hill, and then I set myself to watch, that I might become wise. The ants are a very respectable people; they are wisdom itself. All they do is like the working of a sum in arithmetic, which comes right. 'To work and to lay eggs,' say they, 'and to provide for posterity, is to live out your time properly;' and that they truly do. They are divided into the clean and the dirty ants, their rank is pointed out by a number, and the ant-queen is number ONE; and her opinion is the only correct one on everything; she seems to have the whole wisdom of the world in her, which was just the important matter I wished to acquire. She said a great deal which was no doubt very clever; yet to me it sounded like nonsense. She said the ant-hill was the loftiest thing in the world, and yet close to the mound stood a tall tree, which no one could deny was loftier, much loftier, but no mention was made of the tree. One evening an ant lost herself on this tree; she had crept up the stem, not nearly to the top, but higher than any ant had ever ventured; and when at last she returned home, she said that she had found something in her travels much higher than the ant-hill. The rest of the ants considered this an insult to the whole community; so she was condemned to wear a muzzle and to live in perpetual solitude. A short time afterwards another ant got on the tree and made the same journey and the same discovery, but she spoke of it cautiously and indefinitely, and as she was one of the superior ants and very much respected, they believed her, and when she died they erected an eggshell as a monument to her memory, for they cultivated a great respect for science. I saw," said the little mouse, "that the ants were always running to and fro with their burdens on their backs. Once I saw one of them drop her load; she gave herself a great deal of trouble in trying to raise it again, but she could not succeed. Then two others came up and tried with all their strength to help her, till they nearly dropped their own burdens in doing so; then they were obliged to stop for a moment in their help, for every one must think of himself first. And the ant-queen remarked that their conduct that day showed that they possessed kind hearts and good understanding. 'These two qualities,' she continued, 'place us ants in the highest degree above all other reasonable beings. Understanding must therefore be seen among us in the most prominent manner, and my wisdom is greater than all.' And so saying she raised herself on her two hind legs, that no one else might be mistaken for her. I could not therefore make an error, so I ate her up. We are to go to the ants to learn wisdom, and I had got the queen.

"I now turned and went nearer to the lofty tree already mentioned, which was an oak. It had a tall trunk with a wide-spreading top and was very old. I knew that a living being dwelt here, a dryad as she is called, who is born with the tree and dies with it. I had heard this in the library, and here was just such a tree, and in it an oak-maiden. She uttered a terrible scream when she caught sight of me so near to her; like many women, she was very much afraid of mice. And she had more real cause for fear than they have, for I might have gnawed through the tree on which her life depended. I spoke to her in a kind and friendly manner and begged her to take courage. At last she took me up in her delicate hand, and then I told her what had brought me out into the world, and she promised me that perhaps on that very evening she should be able to obtain for me one of the two treasures for which I was seeking. She told me that Phantaesus was her very dear friend, that he was as beautiful as the god of love, that he remained often for many hours with her under the leafy boughs of the tree which then rustled and waved more than ever over them both. He called her his dryad, she said, and the tree his tree; for the grand old oak, with its gnarled trunk, was just to his taste. The root, spreading deep into the earth, the top rising high in the fresh air, knew the value of the drifted snow, the keen wind, and the warm sunshine, as it ought to be known. 'Yes,' continued the dryad, 'the birds sing up above in the branches and talk to each other about the beautiful fields they have visited in foreign lands; and on one of the withered boughs a stork has built his nest,—it is beautifully arranged, and besides it is pleasant to hear a little about the land of the pyramids. All this pleases Phantaesus, but it is not enough for him; I am obliged to relate to him of my life in the woods; and to go back to my childhood, when I was little, and the tree so small and delicate that a sting-ing-nettle could overshadow it, and I have to tell everything that has happened since then till now that the tree is so large and strong. Sit you down now under the green bindwood and pay attention; when Phantaesus comes, I will find an oppor-tunity to lay hold of his wing and to pull out one of the little feathers. That feather you shall have; a better was never giv-en to any poet, it will be quite enough for you.'

"And when Phantaesus came, the feather was plucked, and," said the little mouse, "I seized and put it in water, and kept it there till it was quite soft. It was very heavy and indigestible, but I managed to nibble it up at last. It is not so easy to nibble one's self into a poet: there are so many things to get through. Now, however, I had two of them, understanding and imagination; and through these I knew that the third was to be found in the library. A great man has said and written that there are novels whose sole and only use appeared to be that they might relieve mankind of overflowing tears—a kind of sponge, in fact, for sucking up feelings and emotions. I remembered a few of these books; they had always appeared tempting to the appetite; they had been much read, and were so greasy, that they must have absorbed no end of emotions in themselves. I retraced my steps to the library, and literally devoured a whole novel, that is, properly speaking, the interior or soft part of it; the crust, or binding, I left. When I had digested not only this, but a second, I felt a stirring within me; then I ate a small piece of a third romance, and I felt myself a poet. I said it to myself and told others the same. I had head-ache and back-ache, and I cannot tell what aches besides. I thought over all the stories that may be said to be connected with sausage pegs, and all that has ever been written about skewers, and sticks, and staves, and splinters came to my thoughts; the ant-queen must have had a wonderfully clear understand-ing. I remembered the man who placed a white stick in his mouth by which he could make himself and the stick invis-ible. I thought of sticks as hobby-horses, staves of music or rhyme, of breaking a stick over a man's back, and heaven knows how many more phrases of the same sort relating to sticks, staves, and skewers. All my thoughts ran on skewers, sticks of wood, and staves; and as I am, at last, a poet, and I have worked terribly hard to make myself one, I can of course make poetry on anything. I shall therefore be able to wait upon you every day in the week with a poetical history of a skewer. And that is my soup."

"In that case," said the mouse-king, "we will hear what the third mouse has to say."

"Squeak, squeak," cried a little mouse at the kitchen door; it was the fourth, and not the third, of the four who were contending for the prize, one whom the rest supposed to be dead. She shot in like an arrow, and overturned the sausage peg that had been covered with crape. She had been running day and night. She had watched an opportunity to get into a goods train and had travelled by the railway; and yet she had arrived almost too late. She pressed forward, looking very much ruffled. She had lost her sausage skewer, but not her voice; for she began to speak at once as if they only waited for her, and would hear her only, and as if nothing else in the world

was of the least consequence. She spoke out so clearly and plainly, and she had come in so suddenly, that no one had time to stop her or to say a word while she was speaking. And now let us hear what she said.

What the Fourth Mouse, Who Spoke Before the Third, Had to Tell

"I started off at once to the largest town," said she, "but the name of it has escaped me. I have a very bad memory for names. I was carried from the railway, with some forfeited goods, to the jail, and on arriving I made my escape and ran into the house of the turnkey. The turnkey was speaking of his prisoners, especially of one who had uttered thoughtless words. These words had given rise to other words, and at length they were written down and registered: 'The whole affair is like making soup of sausage skewers,' said he, 'but the soup may cost him his neck.'

"Now this raised in me an interest for the prisoner," continued the little mouse, "and I watched my opportunity, and slipped into his apartment, for there is a mouse-hole to be found behind every closed door. The prisoner looked pale; he had a great beard and large sparkling eyes. There was a lamp burning, but the walls were so black that they only looked the blacker for it. The prisoner scratched pictures and verses with white chalk on the black walls, but I did not read the verses. I think he found his confinement wearisome, so that I was a welcome guest. He enticed me with bread-crumbs, with whistling, and with gentle words, and seemed so friendly towards me, that by degrees I gained confidence in him, and we became friends; he divided his bread and water with me, gave me cheese and sausage, and I really began to love him. Altogether, I must own that it was a very pleasant intimacy. He let me run about on his hand, and on his arm, and into his sleeve; and I even crept into his beard, and he called me his little friend. I forgot what I had come out into the world for; forgot my sausage skewer which I had laid in a crack in the floor—it is lying there still. I wished to stay with him always where I was, for I knew that if I went away, the poor prisoner would have no one to be his friend, which is a sad thing. I stayed, but he did not. He spoke to me so mournfully for the last time, gave me double as much bread and cheese as usual, and kissed his hand to me. Then he went away and never came back. I know nothing more of his history.

"The jailer took possession of me now. He said something about soup from a sausage skewer, but I could not trust him. He took me in his hand certainly, but it was to place me in a cage like a tread-mill. Oh, how dreadful it was! I had to run round and round without getting any farther in advance, and only to make everybody laugh.

"The jailer's grand-daughter was a charming little thing. She had curly hair like the brightest gold, merry eyes, and such a smiling mouth.

"'You poor little mouse,' said she one day as she peeped into my cage, 'I will set you free.' She then drew forth the iron fastening, and I sprang out on the window-sill, and from thence to the roof. Free! free! that was all I could think of; not of the object of my journey. It grew dark, and as night was coming on I found a lodging in an old tower, where dwelt

a watchman and an owl. I had no confidence in either of
them, least of all in the owl, which is like a cat and has a
great failing, for she eats mice. One may however be mistak-
en sometimes; and so was I, for this was a respectable and
well-educated old owl, who knew more than the watchman,
and even as much as I did myself. The young owls made a
great fuss about everything, but the only rough words she
would say to them were, 'You had better go and make some
soup from sausage skewers.' She was very indulgent and
loving to her children. Her conduct gave me such confidence
in her, that from the crack where I sat I called out 'squeak.'
This confidence of mine pleased her so much that she as-
sured me she would take me under her own protection, and
that not a creature should do me harm. The fact was, she
wickedly meant to keep me in reserve for her own eating in
winter, when food would be scarce. Yet she was a very clever
lady-owl; she explained to me that the watchman could only
hoot with the horn that hung loose at his side; and then
she said he is so terribly proud of it, that he imagines himself an owl in the tower;—wants to do great things, but only
succeeds in small;—all soup on a sausage skewer. Then I
begged the owl to give me the recipe for this soup. 'Soup from
a sausage skewer,' said she, 'is only a proverb amongst mankind and may be understood in many ways. Each believes
his own way the best, and, after all, the proverb signifies
nothing.' 'Nothing!' I exclaimed. I was quite struck. Truth is
not always agreeable, but truth is above everything else, as
the old owl said. I thought over all this, and saw quite plainly
that if truth was really so far above everything else, it must
be much more valuable than soup from a sausage skewer.
So I hastened to get away, that I might be home in time and
bring what was highest and best, and above everything—
namely, the truth. The mice are an enlightened people, and
the mouse-king is above them all. He is therefore capable of
making me queen for the sake of truth."

"Your truth is a falsehood," said the mouse who had not
yet spoken; "I can prepare the soup, and I mean to do so."

How It Was Prepared

"I did not travel," said the third mouse; "I stayed in this
country: that was the right way. One gains nothing by travelling—everything can be acquired here quite as easily; so
I stayed at home. I have not obtained what I know from
supernatural beings. I have neither swallowed it, nor learnt

it from conversing with owls. I have got it all from my reflections and thoughts. Will you now set the kettle on the fire—so? Now pour the water in—quite full—up to the brim; place it on the fire; make up a good blaze; keep it burning, that the water may boil; it must boil over and over. There, now I throw in the skewer. Will the mouse-king be pleased now to dip his tail into the boiling water and stir it round with the tail? The longer the king stirs it, the stronger the soup will become. Nothing more is necessary, only to stir it."

"Can no one else do this?" asked the king.

"No," said the mouse; "only in the tail of the mouse-king is this power contained."

And the water boiled and bubbled, as the mouse-king stood close beside the kettle. It seemed rather a dangerous performance; but he turned round, and put out his tail, as mice do in a dairy, when they wish to skim the cream from a pan of milk with their tails and afterwards lick it off. But the mouse-king's tail had only just touched the hot steam, when he sprang away from the chimney in a great hurry, exclaiming, "Oh, certainly, by all means, you must be my queen; and we will let the soup question rest till our golden wedding, fifty years hence; so that the poor in my kingdom, who are then to have plenty of food, will have something to look forward to for a long time, with great joy."

And very soon the wedding took place. But many of the mice, as they were returning home, said that the soup could not be properly called "soup from a sausage skewer," but "soup from a mouse's tail." They acknowledged also that some of the stories were very well told; but that the whole could have been managed differently. "I should have told it so—and so—and so." These were the critics who are always so clever afterwards.

When this story was circulated all over the world, the opinions upon it were divided; but the story remained the same. And, after all, the best way in everything you undertake, great as well as small, is to expect no thanks for anything you may do, even when it refers to "soup from a sausage skewer."

The Elfin Hill

A FEW large lizards were running nimbly about in the clefts of an old tree; they could understand one another very well, for they spoke the lizard language.

"What a buzzing and a rumbling there is in the elfin hill," said one of the lizards. "I have not been able to close my eyes for two nights on account of the noise. I might just as well have had the toothache, for that always keeps me awake."

"There is something going on within there," said the other lizard; "they propped up the top of the hill with four red posts, till cock-crow this morning, so that it is thoroughly aired, and the elfin girls have learnt new dances; there is something."

"I spoke about it to an earth-worm, of my acquaintance," said a third lizard; "the earth-worm had just come from the elfin hill, where he has been groping about in the earth day and night. He has heard a great deal; although he cannot see, poor miserable creature, yet he understands very well how to wriggle and lurk about. They expect friends in the elfin hill, grand company, too; but who they are the earth-worm would not say, or, perhaps, he really did not know. All the will-o'-the-wisps are ordered to be there to hold a torch dance, as it is called. The silver and gold which is plentiful in the hill will be polished and placed out in the moonlight."

"Who can the strangers be?" asked the lizards; "what can be the matter? Hark, what a buzzing and humming there is!"

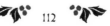

Just at this moment the elfin hill opened, and an old elfin maiden, hollow behind,[1] came tripping out. She was the old elf king's housekeeper and a distant relative of the family; therefore she wore an amber heart on the middle of her forehead. Her feet moved very fast, "trip, trip;" good

---

[1] There is a superstition respecting these elfin maidens, that they are only to be looked at in front, and are therefore made hollow, like the inside of a mask.

 113

gracious, how she could trip right down to the sea to the night-raven![2]

---

[2] In former times, when a ghost appeared, the priest condemned it to enter the earth; when this was done, a stake was driven into the spot to which it had been banished. At midnight a cry was heard, "Let me out!" The stake was then pulled out, and the excommunicated spirit flew away, in the form of a raven, with a hole in its left wing. This ghost-like bird was called the night-raven.

"You are invited to the elf hill for this evening," said she; "but will you do me a great favour and undertake the invitations? you ought to do something, for you have no housekeeping to attend to as I have. We are going to have some very grand people, conjurors, who have always something to say; and therefore the old elf king wishes to make a great display."

"Who is to be invited?" asked the raven.

"All the world may come to the great ball, even human beings, if they can only talk in their sleep or do something after our fashion. But for the feast the company must be carefully selected; we can only admit persons of high rank. I have had a dispute myself with the elf king, as he thought we could not admit ghosts. The merman and his daughter must be invited first, although it may not be agreeable to them to remain so long on dry land, but they shall have a wet stone to sit on, or perhaps something better; so I think they will not refuse this time. We must have all the old demons of the first class, with tails, and the hobgoblins and imps; and then I think we ought not to leave out the death-horse,[3] or the grave-pig, or even the church dwarf, although they do belong to the clergy and are not reckoned among our people; but that is merely their office, they are nearly related to us and visit us very frequently."

"Croak," said the night-raven as he flew away with the invitations.

The elfin maidens were already dancing on the elf hill, and they danced in shawls woven from moonshine and mist, which look very pretty to those who like such things. The large hall within the elf hill was splendidly decorated: the floor had been washed with moonshine and the walls had been rubbed with magic ointment, so that they glowed like tulip-leaves in the light. In the kitchen were frogs roasting on the spit, and dishes preparing of snail skins, with children's fingers in them, salad of mushroom seed, hemlock, noses and marrow of mice, beer from the marsh woman's brewery, and sparkling saltpetre wine from the grave cellars. These were all substantial food. Rusty nails and church-window glass formed the dessert.

---

[3] It is a popular superstition in Denmark that a living horse or a living pig has been buried under every church that is built. The ghost of the dead horse is supposed to limp upon three legs every night to some house, in which someone was going to die. The ghost of the pig was called a grave-pig.

The old elf king had his gold crown polished up with powdered slate-pencil; it was like that used by the first form, and very difficult for an elf king to obtain. In the bedrooms, curtains were hung up and fastened with the slime of snails; there was, indeed, a buzzing and humming everywhere.

"Now we must fumigate the place with burnt horse-hair and pig's bristles, and then I think I shall have done my part," said the elf man-servant.

"Father, dear," said the youngest daughter, "may I now hear who our high-born visitors are?"

"Well, I suppose I must tell you now," he replied; "two of my daughters must prepare themselves to be married, for marriages certainly will take place. The old goblin from Norway, who lives in the ancient Dovre mountains and who possesses many castles built of rock and freestone—besides a gold mine, which is better than all, so it is thought—is coming with his two sons, who are both seeking a wife. The old goblin is a true-hearted, honest, old Norwegian grey-beard; cheerful and straightforward. I knew him formerly, when we used to drink together to our good fellowship; he came here once to fetch his wife, but she is dead now. She was the daughter of the king of the chalk-hills at Moen. They say he took his wife from chalk; I shall be delighted to see him again. It is said that the boys are ill-bred, forward lads, but perhaps that is not quite correct, and they will become better as they grow older. Let me see that you know how to teach them good manners."

"And when are they coming?" asked the daughter.

"That depends upon wind and weather," said the elf king; "they travel economically. They will come when there is the chance of a ship. I wanted them to come over Sweden, but the old man was not inclined to take my advice. He does not go forward with the times, and that I do not like."

Two will-o'-the-wisps came jumping in, one quicker than the other, so of course one arrived first. "They are coming! they are coming!" he cried.

"Give me my crown," said the elf king, "and let me stand in the moonshine."

The daughters drew on their shawls and bowed down to the ground. There stood the old goblin from the Dovre mountains, with his crown of hardened ice and polished fir-cones. Besides this, he wore a bearskin and great, warm boots, while his sons went with their throats bare and wore no braces, for they were strong men.

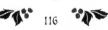

"Is that a hill?" said the youngest of the boys, pointing to the elf hill, "we should call it a hole in Norway."

"Boys," said the old man, "a hole goes in, and a hill stands out; have you no eyes in your heads?"

Another thing they wondered at was, that they were able without trouble to understand the language.

"Take care," said the old man, "or people will think you have not been well brought up."

Then they entered the elfin hill, where the select and grand company was assembled, and so quickly had they appeared that they seemed to have been blown together. But for each guest the neatest and pleasantest arrangement had been made. The sea folks sat at table in great water-tubs, and they said it was just like being at home. All behaved themselves properly excepting the two young northern goblins; they put their legs on the table and thought they were all right.

"Take your legs away from the plates!" said their father. They obeyed, but not immediately. Then they tickled the ladies who waited at table, with the fir-cones, which they carried in their pockets. They took off their boots, that they might be more at ease, and gave them to the ladies to hold. But their father, the old goblin, was very different: he talked pleasantly about the stately Norwegian rocks and told fine

tales of the waterfalls which dashed over them with a clattering noise like thunder or the sound of an organ, spreading their white foam on every side. He told of the salmon that leaps in the rushing waters, while the water-god plays on his golden harp. He spoke of the bright winter nights, when the sledge bells are ringing and the boys run with burning torches across the smooth ice, which is so transparent that they can see the fishes dart forward beneath their feet. He described everything so clearly, that those who listened could see it all; they could see the saw-mills going, the men-servants and the maidens singing songs, and dancing a rattling dance,—when all at once the old goblin gave the old elfin maiden a kiss, such a tremendous kiss, and yet they were almost strangers to each other.

Then the elfin girls had to dance, first in the usual way, and then with stamping feet, which they performed very well; then followed the artistic and solo dance. Dear me, how they did throw their legs about! No one could tell where the dance begun or where it ended, nor indeed which were legs and which were arms, for they were all flying about together, like the shavings in a saw-pit! And then they spun round so quickly that the death-horse and the grave-pig became sick and giddy and were obliged to leave the table.

"Stop!" cried the old goblin, "is that the only housekeeping they can perform? Can they do anything more than dance and throw about their legs, and make a whirlwind?"

"You shall soon see what they can do," said the elf king. And then he called his youngest daughter to him. She was slender and fair as moonlight, and the most graceful of all the sisters. She took a white chip in her mouth and vanished instantly: this was her accomplishment. But the old goblin said he should not like his wife to have such an accomplishment, and thought his boys would have the same objection. Another daughter could make a figure like herself follow her, as if she had a shadow, which none of the goblin folk ever had. The third was of quite a different sort; she had learnt in the brew-house of the moor witch how to lard elfin puddings with glow-worms.

"She will make a good housewife," said the old goblin and then saluted her with his eyes instead of drinking her health; for he did not drink much.

Now came the fourth daughter, with a large harp to play upon; and when she struck the first chord, everyone lifted up the left leg (for the goblins are left-legged), and at the

second chord they found they must all do just what she wanted.

"That is a dangerous woman," said the old goblin; and the two sons walked out of the hill; they had had enough of it. "And what can the next daughter do?" asked the old goblin.

"I have learnt everything that is Norwegian," said she; "and I will never marry, unless I can go to Norway."

Then her younger sister whispered to the old goblin, "That is only because she has heard, in a Norwegian song, that when the world shall decay, the cliffs of Norway will re-

 119

main standing like monuments; and she wants to get there, that she may be safe; for she is so afraid of sinking."

"Ho! ho!" said the old goblin, "is that what she means? Well, what can the seventh and last do?"

"The sixth comes before the seventh," said the elf king, for he could reckon; but the sixth would not come forward.

"I can only tell people the truth," said she. "No one cares for me, nor troubles himself about me; and I have enough to do to sew my grave-clothes."

So the seventh and last came; and what could she do? Why, she could tell stories, as many as you liked, on any subject.

"Here are my five fingers," said the old goblin; "now tell me a story for each of them."

So she took him by the wrist, and he laughed till he nearly choked; and when she came to the fourth finger, there was a gold ring on it, as if it knew there was to be a betrothal. Then the old goblin said, "Hold fast what you have: this hand is yours; for I will have you for a wife myself."

Then the elfin girl said that the stories about the ring-finger and little Peter Playman had not yet been told.

"We will hear them in the winter," said the old goblin, "and also about the fir and the birch-trees, and the ghost stories, and of the tingling frost. You shall tell your tales, for no one over there can do it so well; and we will sit in the stone rooms, where the pine logs are burning, and drink mead out of the golden drinking-horn of the old Norwegian kings. The water-god has given me two; and when we sit there, Nix comes to pay us a visit and will sing you all the songs of the mountain shepherdesses. How merry we shall be! The salmon will be leaping in the waterfalls and dashing against the stone walls, but he will not be able to come in. It is indeed very pleasant to live in old Norway. But where are the lads?"

Where indeed were they? Why, running about the fields and blowing out the poor will-o'-the-wisps, who so good-naturedly came and brought their torches.

"What tricks have you been playing?" said the old goblin. "I have taken a mother for you, and now you may take one of your aunts."

But the youngsters said they would rather make a speech and drink to their good fellowship; they had no wish to marry. Then they made speeches and drank toasts, and tipped their glasses, to show that they were empty. Then they took off their coats and lay down on the table

to sleep; for they made themselves quite at home. But the old goblin danced about the room with his young bride and exchanged boots with her, which is more fashionable than exchanging rings.

"The cock is crowing," said the old elfin maiden who acted as housekeeper; "now we must close the shutters, that the sun may not scorch us."

Then the hill closed up. But the lizards continued to run up and down the riven tree; and one said to the other, "Oh, how much I was pleased with the old goblin!"

"The boys pleased me better," said the earth-worm; but he, poor wretch, could see nothing either of them or of their father, so his opinion was not worth much.

The Steadfast Tin Soldier

HERE were once five-and-twenty tin soldiers, who were all brothers, for they had been made out of the same old tin spoon. They shouldered arms and looked straight before them, and wore a splendid uniform, red and blue.

The first thing in the world they ever heard were the words, "Tin soldiers!" uttered by a little boy, who clapped his hands with delight when the lid of the box, in which they lay, was taken off. They were given him for a birthday present, and he stood at the table to set them up. The soldiers were all exactly alike, excepting one, who had only one leg; he had been left to the last, and then there was not enough of the melted tin to finish him, so they made him to stand firmly on one leg, and this caused him to be very remarkable.

The table on which the tin soldiers stood, was covered with other playthings, but the most attractive to the eye was a pretty little paper castle. Through the small windows the rooms could be seen. In front of the castle a number of little trees surrounded a piece of looking-glass, which was intended to represent a transparent lake. Swans, made of wax swam on the lake and were reflected in it.

All this was very pretty, but the prettiest of all was a tiny little lady, who stood at the open door of the castle;

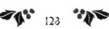

she, also, was made of paper, and she wore a dress of clear muslin, with a narrow blue ribbon over her shoulders just like a scarf. In front of it, was fixed a glittering tinsel rose, as large as her whole face. The little lady was a dancer, and she stretched out both her arms, and raised one of her legs so high, that the tin soldier could not see it at all, and he thought that she, like himself, had only one leg.

"That is the wife for me," he thought; "but she is too grand and lives in a castle, while I have only a box to live in, five-and-twenty of us altogether, that is no place for her. Still I must try and make her acquaintance." Then he laid himself at full length on the table behind a snuff-box that stood upon it, so that he could peep at the little delicate lady, who continued to stand on one leg without losing her balance.

When evening came, the other tin soldiers were all placed in the box, and the people of the house went to bed. Then the playthings began to have their own games together, to pay visits, to have sham fights, and to give balls. The tin soldiers rattled in their box; they wanted to get out and join the amusements, but they could not open the lid. The nut-crackers played at leap-frog, and the pencil jumped about the table. There was such a noise that the canary woke up and began to talk, and in poetry too.

Only the tin soldier and the dancer remained in their places. She stood on tiptoe, with her arms stretched out, as firmly as he did on his one leg. He never took his eyes from her for even a moment. The clock struck twelve, and, with a bounce, up sprang the lid of the snuff-box; but, instead of snuff, there jumped up a little black goblin; for the snuff-box was a toy puzzle.

"Tin soldier," said the goblin, "don't wish for what does not belong to you."

But the tin soldier pretended not to hear.

"Very well; wait till tomorrow, then," said the goblin.

When the children came in the next morning, they placed

the tin soldier in the window. Now, whether it was the goblin who did it or the draught is not known, but the window flew open, and out fell the tin soldier, heels over head, from the third story into the street beneath.

It was a terrible fall; for he came head downwards, his helmet and his bayonet stuck in between the flagstones, and his one leg up in the air. The servant maid and the little boy went downstairs directly to look for him; but he was nowhere to be seen, although once they nearly trod upon him. If he had called out, "Here I am," it would have been all right; but he was too proud to cry out for help while he wore a uniform.

Presently it began to rain, and the drops fell faster and faster, till there was a heavy shower. When it was over, two boys happened to pass by, and one of them said, "Look, there is a tin soldier. He ought to have a boat to sail in."

So they made a boat out of a newspaper, and placed the tin soldier in it, and sent him sailing down the gutter, while the two boys ran by the side of it and clapped their hands. Good gracious, what large waves arose in that gutter! and how fast the stream rolled on! for the rain had been very heavy. The paper boat rocked up and down, and turned itself round sometimes so quickly that the tin soldier trembled; yet he remained firm; his countenance did not change; he looked straight before him and shouldered his musket. Suddenly the boat shot under a bridge which formed a part of a drain, and then it was as dark as the tin soldier's box.

"Where am I going now?" thought he. "This is the black goblin's fault, I am sure. Ah, well, if the little lady were only here with me in the boat, I should not care for any darkness."

Suddenly there appeared a great water-rat, who lived in the drain.

"Have you a passport?" asked the rat, "give it to me at once."

But the tin soldier remained silent and held his musket tighter than ever. The boat sailed on, and the rat followed it. How he did gnash his teeth and cry out to the bits of wood and straw, "Stop him, stop him; he has not paid toll and has not shown his pass."

But the stream rushed on stronger and stronger. The tin soldier could already see daylight shining where the arch ended. Then he heard a roaring sound quite terrible enough to frighten the bravest man. At the end of the tunnel, the

drain fell into a large canal over a steep place, which made it as dangerous for him as a waterfall would be to us. He was too close to it to stop, so the boat rushed on, and the poor tin soldier could only hold himself as stiffly as possible, without moving an eyelid, to show that he was not afraid.

The boat whirled round three or four times and then filled with water to the very edge; nothing could save it from sinking. He now stood up to his neck in water, while deeper and deeper sank the boat, and the paper became soft and loose with the wet, till at last the water closed over the soldier's head. He thought of the elegant little dancer whom he should never see again, and the words of the song sounded in his ears:

> "Farewell, warrior! ever brave,
> Drifting onward to thy grave."

Then the paper boat fell to pieces, and the soldier sank into the water and immediately afterwards was swallowed up by a great fish. Oh how dark it was inside the fish! A great deal darker than in the tunnel and narrower too, but the tin soldier continued firm and lay at full length, shouldering his musket.

The fish swam to and fro, making the most wonderful movements, but at last he became quite still. After a while, a flash of lightning seemed to pass through him, and then the daylight approached, and a voice cried out, "I declare here is the tin soldier." The fish had been caught, taken to the market and sold to the cook, who took him into the kitchen and cut him open with a large knife. She picked up the soldier and held him by the waist between her finger and thumb, and carried him into the room. They were all anxious to see this wonderful soldier who had travelled about inside a fish; but he was not at all proud. They placed him on the table, and—how many curious things do happen in the world!—there he was in the very same room from the window of which he had fallen, there were the same children, the same playthings standing on the table, and the pretty castle with the elegant little dancer at the door; she still balanced herself on one leg and held up the other, so she was as firm as himself. It touched the tin soldier so much to see her that he almost wept tin tears, but he kept them back. He only looked at her, and they both remained silent.

Presently one of the little boys took up the tin soldier, and threw him into the stove. He had no reason for doing so; therefore it must have been the fault of the black goblin who lived in the snuff-box. The flames lighted up the tin soldier, as he stood, the heat was very terrible, but whether it proceeded from the real fire or from the fire of love he could not tell. Then he could see that the bright colours were faded from his uniform, but whether they had been washed off during his journey or from the effects of his sorrow, no one could say.

He looked at the little lady, and she looked at him. He felt himself melting away, but he still remained firm with his gun on his shoulder. Suddenly the door of the room flew open, and the draught of air caught up the little dancer; she fluttered like a sylph right into the stove by the side of the tin soldier, and was instantly in flames and was gone. The tin soldier melted down into a lump, and the next morning, when the maid servant took the ashes out of the stove, she found him in the shape of a little tin heart. But of the little dancer nothing remained but the tinsel rose, which was burnt black as a cinder.

The Tinder Box

SOLDIER came marching along the high road: "Left, right—left, right." He had his knapsack on his back and a sword at his side; he had been to the wars and was now returning home.

As he walked on, he met a very frightful-looking old witch in the road. Her under-lip hung quite down on her breast, and she stopped and said, "Good evening, soldier; you have a very fine sword and a large knapsack, and you are a real soldier; so you shall have as much money as ever you like."

"Thank you, old witch," said the soldier.

"Do you see that large tree?" said the witch, pointing to a tree which stood beside them. "Well, it is quite hollow inside, and you must climb to the top, when you will see a hole, through which you can let yourself down into the tree to a great depth. I will tie a rope round your body, so that I can pull you up again when you call out to me."

"But what am I to do, down there in the tree?" asked the soldier.

"Get money," she replied; "for you must know that when you reach the ground under the tree, you will find yourself in a large hall, lighted up by three hundred lamps; you will then see three doors, which can be easily opened, for the keys are in all the locks. On entering the first of the chambers, to which these doors lead, you will see a large chest, standing in the middle of the floor, and upon it a dog seated, with a pair of eyes as large as teacups. But you need not be at all afraid of him; I will give you my blue checked apron, which you must spread upon the floor, and then boldly seize hold of the dog and place him upon it. You can then open the chest and take from it as many pence as you please, they are only copper pence; but if you would rather have silver money, you must go into the second chamber. Here you will find another dog, with eyes as big as mill-wheels; but do not let that trouble you. Place him upon my apron and then take what money you please. If, however, you like gold best, enter the third chamber, where there is another chest full of it. The dog who sits on this chest is very dreadful; his eyes are as big as a tower, but do not mind him. If he also is placed upon my apron, he cannot hurt you, and you may take from the chest what gold you will."

"This is not a bad story," said the soldier; "but what am I to give you, you old witch? for, of course, you do not mean to tell me all this for nothing."

"No," said the witch; "but I do not ask for a single penny. Only promise to bring me an old tinder-box, which my grandmother left behind the last time she went down there."

"Very well; I promise. Now tie the rope round my body."

"Here it is," replied the witch; "and here is my blue checked apron."

As soon as the rope was tied, the soldier climbed up the tree and let himself down through the hollow to the ground beneath; and here he found, as the witch had told him, a large hall, in which many hundred lamps were all burning.

Then he opened the first door. "Ah!" there sat the dog, with the eyes as large as teacups, staring at him.

"You're a pretty fellow," said the soldier, seizing him and placing him on the witch's apron, while he filled his pockets from the chest with as many pence as they would hold. Then he closed the lid, seated the dog upon it again, and walked into another chamber. And, sure enough, there sat the dog with eyes as big as mill-wheels.

"You had better not look at me in that way," said the soldier; "you will make your eyes water;" and then he seated him also upon the apron and opened the chest. But when he saw what a quantity of silver money it contained, he very quickly threw away all the coppers he had taken and filled his pockets and his knapsack with nothing but silver.

Then he went into the third room, and there the dog was really hideous; his eyes were, truly, as big as towers, and they turned round and round in his head like wheels.

"Good morning," said the soldier, touching his cap, for he had never seen such a dog in his life. But after looking at him more closely, he thought he had been civil enough, so he placed him on the floor and opened the chest. Good gracious, what a quantity of gold there was! enough to buy all the sugar-sticks of the sweet-stuff women; all the tin soldiers, whips, and rocking-horses in the world, or even the whole town itself. There was, indeed, an immense quantity. So the soldier now threw away all the silver money he had taken and filled his pockets and his knapsack with gold instead; and not only his pockets and his knapsack but even his cap and boots, so that he could scarcely walk.

He was really rich now; so he replaced the dog on the chest, closed the door, and called up through the tree, "Now pull me out, you old witch."

"Have you got the tinder-box?" asked the witch.

"No; I declare I quite forgot it." So he went back and fetched the tinder-box, and then the witch drew him up out of the tree, and he stood again in the high road, with his pockets, his knapsack, his cap, and his boots full of gold.

"What are you going to do with the tinder-box?" asked the soldier.

"That is nothing to you," replied the witch; "you have the money, now give me the tinder-box."

"I tell you what," said the soldier, "if you don't tell me what you are going to do with it, I will draw my sword and cut off your head."

"No," said the witch.

The soldier immediately cut off her head, and there she lay on the ground. Then he tied up all his money in her apron and slung it on his back like a bundle, put the tinder-box in his pocket, and walked off to the nearest town.

It was a very nice town, and he put up at the best inn, and ordered a dinner of all his favourite dishes, for now he was rich and had plenty of money.

The servant, who cleaned his boots, thought they certainly were a shabby pair to be worn by such a rich gentleman, for he had not yet bought any new ones. The next day, however, he procured some good clothes and proper boots, so that our soldier soon became known as a fine gentleman, and the people visited him and told him all the wonders that were to be seen in the town and of the king's beautiful daughter, the princess.

"Where can I see her?" asked the soldier.

"She is not to be seen at all," they said; "she lives in a large copper castle, surrounded by walls and towers. No one but the king himself can pass in or out, for there has been a prophecy that she will marry a common soldier, and the king cannot bear to think of such a marriage."

"I should like very much to see her," thought the soldier; but he could not obtain permission to do so. However, he passed a very pleasant time; went to the theatre, drove in the king's garden, and gave a great deal of money to the poor, which was very good of him; he remembered what it had been in olden times to be without a shilling. Now he was rich, had fine clothes, and many friends, who all declared he was a fine fellow and a real gentleman, and all this gratified him exceedingly. But his money would not last forever; and as he spent and gave away a great deal daily, and received none, he found himself at last with only two shillings left.

So he was obliged to leave his elegant rooms, and live in a little garret under the roof, where he had to clean his own boots and even mend them with a large needle. None of his friends came to see him; there were too many stairs to mount up.

One dark evening, he had not even a penny to buy a candle; then all at once he remembered that there was a piece of candle stuck in the tinder-box, which he had brought from the old tree, into which the witch had helped him.

He found the tinder-box, but no sooner had he struck a few sparks from the flint and steel, than the door flew open and the dog with eyes as big as teacups, whom he had seen while down in the tree, stood before him and said, "What orders, master?"

"Hallo," said the soldier; "well this is a pleasant tinder-box if it brings me all I wish for."

"Bring me some money," said he to the dog.

He was gone in a moment and presently returned, carrying a large bag of coppers in his mouth. The soldier very soon discovered after this the value of the tinder-box. If he struck the flint once, the dog who sat on the chest of copper money made his appearance; if twice, the dog came from the chest of silver; and if three times, the dog with eyes like towers, who watched over the gold.

The soldier had now plenty of money; he returned to his elegant rooms and reappeared in his fine clothes, so that his friends knew him again directly and made as much of him as before.

After a while he began to think it was very strange that no one could get a look at the princess. "Everyone says she is very beautiful," he thought to himself; "but what is the use of that if she is to be shut up in a copper castle surrounded by so many towers. Can I, by any means, get to see her? Stop! where is my tinder-box?" Then he struck a light, and in a moment the dog, with eyes as big as teacups, stood before him.

"It is midnight," said the soldier, "yet I should very much like to see the princess, if only for a moment."

The dog disappeared instantly, and before the soldier could even look round, he returned with the princess. She was lying on the dog's back asleep and looked so lovely, that every one who saw her would know she was a real princess. The soldier could not help kissing her, true soldier as he was. Then the dog ran back with the princess; but in the morning, while at breakfast with the king and queen, she told them what a singular dream she had had during the night, of a dog and a soldier, that she had ridden on the dog's back and been kissed by the soldier.

"That is a very pretty story, indeed," said the queen. So the next night one of the old ladies of the court was set to watch by the princess's bed, to discover whether it really was a dream, or what else it might be.

The soldier longed very much to see the princess once more, so he sent for the dog again in the night to fetch her, and to run with her as fast as ever he could. But the old lady put on water boots and ran after him as quickly as he did, and found that he carried the princess into a large house. She thought it would help her to remember the place if she made a large cross on the door with a piece of chalk. Then she went home to bed, and the dog presently returned with the princess. But when he saw that a cross had been made on the door of the house, where the soldier lived, he took another piece of chalk and made crosses on all the doors in the town, so that the lady-in-waiting might not be able to find out the right door.

Early the next morning the king and queen accompanied the lady and all the officers of the household, to see where the princess had been.

"Here it is," said the king, when they came to the first door with a cross on it.

"No, my dear husband, it must be that one," said the queen, pointing to a second door having a cross also.

"And here is one, and there is another!" they all exclaimed; for there were crosses on all the doors in every direction.

So they felt it would be useless to search any farther. But the queen was a very clever woman; she could do a great deal more than merely ride in a carriage. She took her large gold scissors, cut a piece of silk into squares, and made a neat little bag. This bag she filled with buckwheat flour, and tied it round the princess's neck; and then she cut a small hole in the bag, so that the flour might be scattered on the ground as the princess went along. During the night, the dog came again and carried the princess on his back and ran with her to the soldier, who loved her very much and wished that he had been a prince, so that he might have her for a wife.

The dog did not observe how the flour ran out of the bag all the way from the castle wall to the soldier's house, and even up to the window, where he had climbed with the princess. Therefore in the morning the king and queen found out where their daughter had been, and the soldier was taken up and put in prison.

Oh, how dark and disagreeable it was as he sat there, and the people said to him, "Tomorrow you will be hanged." It was not very pleasant news, and besides, he had left the tinder-box at the inn. In the morning he could see through the iron grating of the little window how the people were hastening out of the town to see him hanged; he heard the drums beating, and saw the soldiers marching. Everyone ran out to look at them, and a shoemaker's boy, with a leather apron and slippers on, galloped by so fast, that one of his slippers flew off and struck against the wall where the soldier sat looking through the iron grating.

"Hallo, you shoemaker's boy, you need not be in such a hurry," cried the soldier to him. "There will be nothing to see till I come; but if you will run to the house where I have been living and bring me my tinder-box, you shall have four shillings, but you must put your best foot foremost."

The shoemaker's boy liked the idea of getting the four shillings, so he ran very fast and fetched the tinder-box, and gave it to the soldier. And now we shall see what happened. Outside the town a large gibbet had been erected, round which stood the soldiers and several thousands of people. The king and the queen sat on splendid thrones opposite to the judges and the whole council. The soldier already stood on the ladder; but as they were about to place the rope around his neck, he said that an innocent request was often granted to a poor criminal before he suffered death. He wished very much to smoke a pipe, as it would be the last pipe he should ever smoke in the world. The king could not refuse this request, so the soldier took his tinder-box, and struck fire, once, twice, thrice,—and there in a moment stood all the dogs;—the one with eyes as big as teacups, the one with eyes as large as mill-wheels, and the third, whose eyes were like towers. "Help me now, that I may not be hanged," cried the soldier.

And the dogs fell upon the judges and all the councillors; seized one by the legs and another by the nose, and tossed

them many feet high in the air, so that they fell down and were dashed to pieces.

"I will not be touched," said the king. But the largest dog seized him, as well as the queen, and threw them after the others. Then the soldiers and all the people were afraid, and cried, "Good soldier, you shall be our king, and you shall marry the beautiful princess."

So they placed the soldier in the king's carriage, and the three dogs ran on in front and cried "Hurrah!" and the little boys whistled through their fingers, and the soldiers presented arms. The princess came out of the copper castle, and became queen, which was very pleasing to her. The wedding festivities lasted a whole week, and the dogs sat at the table and stared with all their eyes.

The Wild Swans

FAR away in the land to which the swallows fly when it is winter, dwelt a king who had eleven sons, and one daughter, named Eliza. The eleven brothers were princes, and each went to school with a star on his breast and a sword by his side. They wrote with diamond pencils on gold slates, and learnt their lessons so quickly and read so easily that everyone might know they were princes. Their sister Eliza sat on a little stool of plate-glass, and had a book full of pictures, which had cost as much as half a kingdom.

Oh, these children were indeed happy, but it was not to remain so always. Their father, who was king of the country, married a very wicked queen, who did not love the poor children at all. They knew this from the very first day after the wedding. In the palace there were great festivities, and the children played at receiving company; but instead of having, as usual, all the cakes and apples that were left, she gave them some sand in a tea-cup and told them to pretend it was cake. The week after, she sent little Eliza into the country to a peasant and his wife, and then she told the king so many untrue things about the young princes, that he gave himself no more trouble respecting them.

"Go out into the world and get your own living," said the queen. "Fly like great birds, who have no voice." But she could not make them ugly as she wished, for they were turned into eleven beautiful wild swans. Then, with a strange cry, they flew through the windows of the palace, over the park, to the forest beyond.

It was early morning when they passed the peasant's cottage, where their sister Eliza lay asleep in her room. They hovered over the roof, twisted their long necks and flapped their wings, but no one heard them or saw them, so they were at last obliged to fly away, high up in the clouds; and over the wide world they flew till they came to a thick, dark wood, which stretched far away to the seashore.

Poor little Eliza was alone in her room playing with a green leaf, for she had no other playthings, and she pierced a hole through the leaf and looked through it at the sun, and it was as if she saw her brothers' clear eyes; and when the warm sun shone on her cheeks, she thought of all the kisses they had given her.

One day passed just like another; sometimes the winds rustled through the leaves of the rose-bush and would whisper to the roses, "Who can be more beautiful than you?" But the roses would shake their heads, and say, "Eliza is." And when the old woman sat at the cottage door on Sunday, and read her hymn-book, the wind would flutter the leaves, and say to the book, "Who can be more pious than you?" and then the hymn-book would answer "Eliza." And the roses and the hymn-book told the real truth.

At fifteen she returned home, but when the queen saw how beautiful she was, she became full of spite and hatred towards her. Willingly would she have turned her into a swan, like her brothers, but she did not dare to do so yet, because the king wished to see his daughter. Early one morning the queen went into the bath-room; it was built of marble and had soft cushions, trimmed with the most beautiful tapestry. She took three toads with her, and kissed them, and said to one, "When Eliza comes to the bath, seat yourself upon her head, that she may become as stupid as you are." Then she said to another, "Place yourself on her forehead, that she may become as ugly as you are, and that her father may not know her." "Rest on her heart," she whispered to the third, "then she will have evil inclinations, and suffer in consequence."

So she put the toads into the clear water, and they turned green immediately. She next called Eliza and helped her to undress and get into the bath. As Eliza dipped her head under the water, one of the toads sat on her hair, a second on her forehead, and a third on her breast, but she did not seem to notice them, and when she rose out of the water, there were three red poppies floating upon it. Had not the creatures been venomous or been kissed by the witch, they would have been changed into red roses. At all events they became flowers, because they had rested on Eliza's head, and on her heart. She was too good and too innocent for witchcraft to have any power over her.

When the wicked queen saw this, she rubbed her face with walnut-juice, so that she was quite brown; then she tangled her beautiful hair and smeared it with disgusting ointment, till it was quite impossible to recognize the beautiful Eliza.

When her father saw her, he was much shocked and declared she was not his daughter. No one but the watch-dog and the swallows knew her; but they were only poor animals and could say nothing.

Then poor Eliza wept, and thought of her eleven brothers, who were all away. Sorrowfully, she stole away from the palace and walked, the whole day, over fields and moors, till she came to the great forest. She knew not in what direction to go; but she was so unhappy and longed so for her brothers, who had been, like herself, driven out into the world, that she was determined to seek them.

She had been but a short time in the wood when night came on, and she quite lost the path; so she laid herself down on the soft moss, offered up her evening prayer, and leaned her head against the stump of a tree.

All nature was still, and the soft, mild air fanned her forehead. The light of hundreds of glow-worms shone amidst the grass and the moss, like green fire; and if she touched a twig with her hand, ever so lightly, the brilliant insects fell down around her, like shooting-stars.

All night long she dreamt of her brothers. She and they were children again, playing together. She saw them writing with their diamond pencils on golden slates, while she looked at the beautiful picture-book which had cost half a kingdom. They were not writing lines and letters, as they used to do; but descriptions of the noble deeds they had performed, and of all they had discovered and seen. In the picture-book, too, everything was living. The birds sang, and the people came out of the book and spoke to Eliza and her brothers; but, as the leaves turned over, they darted back again to their places, that all might be in order.

When she awoke, the sun was high in the heavens; yet she could not see it, for the lofty trees spread their branches thickly over her head; but its beams were glancing through the leaves here and there, like a golden mist. There was a sweet fragrance from the fresh green verdure, and the birds almost perched upon her shoulders. She heard water rippling from a number of springs, all flowing into a lake with golden sands. Bushes grew thickly round the lake, and at one spot an opening had been made by a deer, through which Eliza went down to the water. The lake was so clear that, had not the wind rustled the branches of the trees and the bushes, so that they moved, they would have appeared as if painted in the depths of the lake; for every leaf was reflected in the water, whether it stood in the shade or the sunshine.

As soon as Eliza saw her own face, she was quite terrified at finding it so brown and ugly; but when she wetted her little hand and rubbed her eyes and forehead, the white skin gleamed forth once more; and, after she had undressed and dipped herself in the fresh water, a more beautiful king's daughter could not be found in the wide world.

As soon as she had dressed herself again, and braided her long hair, she went to the bubbling spring and drank some water out of the hollow of her hand. Then she wandered far into the forest, not knowing whither she went. She thought of her brothers and felt sure that God would not forsake her. It is God who makes the wild apples grow in the wood, to satisfy the hungry, and He now led her to one of these trees, which was so loaded with fruit, that the boughs bent beneath the weight.

Here she held her noonday repast, placed props under the boughs, and then went into the gloomiest depths of

the forest. It was so still that she could hear the sound of her own footsteps, as well as the rustling of every withered leaf which she crushed under her feet. Not a bird was to be seen, not a sunbeam could penetrate through the large, dark boughs of the trees. Their lofty trunks stood so close together, that, when she looked before her; it seemed as if she were enclosed within trellis-work. Such solitude she had never known before. The night was very dark. Not a single glow-worm glittered in the moss.

Sorrowfully she laid herself down to sleep; and, after a while, it seemed to her as if the branches of the trees parted over her head and that the mild eyes of angels looked down upon her from heaven. When she awoke in the morning, she knew not whether she had dreamt this or if it had really been so. Then she continued her wandering; but she had not gone many steps forward, when she met an old woman with berries in her basket, and she gave her a few to eat. Then Eliza asked her if she had not seen eleven princes riding through the forest.

"No," replied the old woman, "but I saw yesterday eleven swans, with gold crowns on their heads, swimming on the river close by." Then she led Eliza a little distance farther to a sloping bank, and at the foot of it wound a little river. The trees on its banks stretched their long leafy branches across the water towards each other, and where the growth prevented them from meeting naturally, the roots had torn themselves away from the ground, so that the branches might mingle their foliage as they hung over the water.

Eliza bade the old woman farewell and walked by the flowing river, till she reached the shore of the open sea. And there, before the young maiden's eyes, lay the glorious ocean, but not a sail appeared on its surface, not even a boat could be seen. How was she to go farther? She no-

ticed how the countless pebbles on the sea-shore had been smoothed and rounded by the action of the water. Glass, iron, stones, everything that lay there mingled together, had taken its shape from the same power, and felt as smooth, or even smoother than her own delicate hand.

"The water rolls on without weariness," she said, till all that is hard becomes smooth; so will I be unwearied in my task. Thanks for your lessons, bright rolling waves; my heart tells me you will lead me to my dear brothers."

On the foam-covered sea-weeds, lay eleven white swan feathers, which she gathered up and placed together. Drops of water lay upon them; whether they were dew-drops or tears no one could say.

Lonely as it was on the seashore, she did not observe it, for the ever-moving sea showed more changes in a few hours than the most varying lake could produce during a whole year. If a black heavy cloud arose, it was as if the sea said, "I can look dark and angry too;" and then the wind blew, and the waves turned to white foam as they rolled. When the wind slept and the clouds glowed with the red sunlight, then the sea looked like a rose leaf. But however quietly its white glassy surface rested, there was still a motion on the shore, as its waves rose and fell like the breast of a sleeping child.

When the sun was about to set, Eliza saw eleven white swans with golden crowns on their heads, flying towards the land, one behind the other, like a long white ribbon. Then Eliza went down the slope from the shore and hid herself behind the bushes. The swans alighted quite close to her and flapped their great white wings. As soon as the sun had disappeared under the water, the feathers of the swans fell off, and eleven beautiful princes, Eliza's brothers, stood near her.

She uttered a loud cry, for, although they were very much changed, she knew them immediately. She sprang into their arms and called them each by name. Then, how happy the princes were at meeting their little sister again,

for they recognized her, although she had grown so tall and beautiful. They laughed, and they wept, and very soon understood how wickedly their mother had acted to them all.

"We brothers," said the eldest, "fly about as wild swans, so long as the sun is in the sky; but as soon as it sinks behind the hills, we recover our human shape. Therefore must we always be near a resting place for our feet before sunset; for if we should be flying towards the clouds at the time we recovered our natural form as men, we should sink deep into the sea. We do not dwell here, but in a land just as fair, that lies beyond the ocean, which we have to cross for a long distance; there is no island in our passage upon which we could pass, the night; nothing but a little rock rising out of the sea, upon which we can scarcely stand with safety, even closely crowded together. If the sea is rough, the foam dashes over us, yet we thank God even for this rock; we have passed whole nights upon it, or we should never have reached our beloved fatherland, for our flight across the sea occupies two of the longest days in the year. We have permission to visit our home once in every year and to remain eleven days, during which we fly across the forest to look once more at the palace where our father dwells and where we were born, and at the church where our mother lies buried. Here it seems as if the very trees and bushes were related to us. The wild horses leap over the plains as we have seen them in our childhood. The charcoal burners sing the old songs, to which we have danced as children. This is our fatherland, to which we are drawn by loving ties; and here we have found you, our dear little sister. Two days longer we can remain here, and then must we fly away to a beautiful land which is not our home; and how can we take you with us? We have neither ship nor boat."

"How can I break this spell?" said their sister. And then she talked about it nearly the whole night, only slumbering for a few hours. Eliza was awakened by the rustling of the swans' wings as they soared above. Her brothers were again changed to swans, and they flew in circles wider and wider, till they were far away; but one of them, the youngest swan, remained behind and laid his head in his sister's lap, while she stroked his wings; and they remained together the whole day.

Towards evening, the rest came back, and as the sun went down they resumed their natural forms. "Tomorrow," said one, "we shall fly away, not to return again till a whole year has passed. But we cannot leave you here. Have you

courage to go with us? My arm is strong enough to carry you through the wood; and will not all our wings be strong enough to fly with you over the sea?"

"Yes, take me with you," said Eliza.

Then they spent the whole night in weaving a net with the pliant willow and rushes. It was very large and strong. Eliza laid herself down on the net, and when the sun rose and her brothers again became wild swans, they took up the net with their beaks and flew up to the clouds with their dear sister, who still slept. The sunbeams fell on her face, therefore one of the swans soared over her head, so that his broad wings might shade her.

They were far from the land when Eliza woke. She thought she must still be dreaming, it seemed so strange to her to feel herself being carried so high in the air over the sea. By her side lay a branch full of beautiful ripe berries and a bundle of sweet roots; the youngest of her brothers had gathered them for her, and placed them by her side. She smiled her thanks to him; she knew it was the same who had hovered over her to shade her with his wings.

They were now so high, that a large ship beneath them looked like a white sea-gull skimming the waves. A great cloud floating behind them appeared like a vast mountain, and upon it Eliza saw her own shadow and those of the eleven swans, looking gigantic in size. Altogether it formed a more beautiful picture than she had ever seen; but as the sun rose higher, and the clouds were left behind, the shadowy picture vanished away.

Onward the whole day they flew through the air like a winged arrow, yet more slowly than usual, for they had their sister to carry. The weather seemed inclined to be stormy, and Eliza watched the sinking sun with great anxiety, for the little rock in the ocean was not yet in sight. It appeared to her as if the swans were making great efforts with their wings. Alas! she was the cause of their not advancing more quickly. When the sun set, they would change to men, fall into the sea, and be drowned. Then she offered a prayer from her inmost heart, but still no appearance of the rock. Dark clouds came nearer, the gusts of wind told of a coming storm, while from a thick, heavy mass of clouds the lightning burst forth flash after flash.

The sun had reached the edge of the sea, when the swans darted down so swiftly, that Eliza's head trembled; she believed they were falling, but they again soared onward. Presently she caught sight of the rock just below them, and

by this time the sun was half hidden by the waves. The rock did not appear larger than a seal's head thrust out of the water. They sunk so rapidly, that at the moment their feet touched the rock, it shone only like a star, and at last disappeared like the last spark in a piece of burnt paper. Then she saw her brothers standing closely round her with their arms linked together. There was but just room enough for them, and not the smallest space to spare.

The sea dashed against the rock and covered them with spray. The heavens were lighted up with continual flashes, and peal after peal of thunder rolled. But the sister and brothers sat holding each other's hands and singing hymns, from which they gained hope and courage.

In the early dawn the air became calm and still, and at sunrise the swans flew away from the rock with Eliza. The sea was still rough, and from their high position in the air, the white foam on the dark green waves looked like millions of swans swimming on the water. As the sun rose higher, Eliza saw before her, floating in the air, a range of mountains, with shining masses of ice on their summits. In the centre, rose a castle apparently a mile long, with rows of columns rising one above another, while, around it, palm-trees waved and flowers bloomed as large as mill wheels.

She asked if this was the land to which they were hastening. The swans shook their heads, for what she beheld were the beautiful ever-changing cloud palaces of the "Fata Morgana," into which no mortal can enter. Eliza was still gazing at the scene, when mountains, forests, and castles melted away, and twenty stately churches rose in their stead, with high towers and pointed gothic windows. Eliza even fancied she could hear the tones of the organ, but it was the music of the murmuring sea which she heard. As they drew nearer to the churches, they also changed into a fleet of ships, which seemed to be sailing beneath her; but as she looked again, she found it was only a sea mist gliding over the ocean. So there continued to pass before her eyes a constant change of scene, till at last she saw the real land to which they were bound, with its blue mountains, its cedar forests, and its cities and palaces.

Long before the sun went down, she sat on a rock, in front of a large cave, on the floor of which the over-grown yet delicate green creeping plants looked like an embroidered carpet. "Now we shall expect to hear what you dream of to-night," said the youngest brother, as he showed his sister her bedroom.

"Heaven grant that I may dream how to save you," she replied. And this thought took such hold upon her mind that she prayed earnestly to God for help, and even in her sleep she continued to pray. Then it appeared to her as if she were flying high in the air, towards the cloudy palace of the "Fata Morgana," and a fairy came out to meet her, radiant and beautiful in appearance, and yet very much like the old woman who had given her berries in the wood, and who had told her of the swans with golden crowns on their heads. "Your brothers can be released," said she, "if you have only courage and perseverance. True, water is softer than your own delicate hands, and yet it polishes stones into shapes; it feels no pain as your fingers would feel, it has no soul, and cannot suffer such agony and torment as you will have to endure. Do you see the stinging nettle which I hold in my hand? Quantities of the same sort grow round the cave in which you sleep, but none will be of any use to you unless they grow upon the graves in a churchyard. These you must gather even while they burn blisters on your hands. Break them to pieces with your hands and feet, and they will become flax, from which you must spin and weave eleven coats with long sleeves; if these are then thrown over the eleven swans, the spell will be broken. But remember, that from the moment you commence your task until it is finished, even should it occupy years of your life, you must not speak. The first word you utter will pierce through the hearts of your brothers like a deadly dagger. Their lives hang upon your tongue. Remember all I have told you." And as she finished speaking, she touched her hand lightly with the nettle, and a pain, as of burning fire, awoke Eliza.

It was broad daylight, and close by where she had been sleeping lay a nettle like the one she had seen in her dream. She fell on her knees and offered her thanks to God. Then she went forth from the cave to begin her work with her delicate hands. She groped in amongst the ugly nettles, which burnt great blisters on her hands and arms, but she determined to bear it gladly if she could only release her dear brothers. So she bruised the nettles with her bare feet and spun the flax.

At sunset her brothers returned and were very much frightened when they found her dumb. They believed it to be some new sorcery of their wicked step-mother. But when they saw her hands, they understood what she was doing on their behalf, and the youngest brother wept, and where his tears fell the pain ceased and the burning blisters vanished.

She kept to her work all night, for she could not rest till she had released her dear brothers. During the whole of the following day, while her brothers were absent, she sat in solitude, but never before had the time flown so quickly.

One coat was already finished and she had begun the second, when she heard the huntsman's horn and was struck with fear. The sound came nearer and nearer; she heard the dogs barking and fled with terror into the cave. She hastily bound together the nettles she had gathered into a bundle and sat upon them. Immediately a great dog came bounding towards her out of the ravine, and then another and another; they barked loudly, ran back, and then came again. In a very few minutes all the huntsmen stood before the cave, and the handsomest of them was the king of the country. He advanced towards her, for he had never seen a more beautiful maiden.

"How did you come here, my sweet child?" he asked. But Eliza shook her head. She dared not speak, at the cost of her brothers' lives. And she hid her hands under her apron, so that the king might not see how she must be suffering.

"Come with me," he said; "here you cannot remain. If you are as good as you are beautiful, I will dress you in silk and velvet, I will place a golden crown upon your head, and you shall dwell, and rule, and make your home in my richest castle." And then he lifted her on his horse. She wept and wrung her hands, but the king said, "I wish only for your happiness. A time will come when you will thank me for this." And then he galloped away over the mountains, holding her before him on his horse, and the hunters followed behind them.

As the sun went down, they approached a fair royal city, with churches and cupolas. On arriving at the castle, the king led her into marble halls, where large fountains played and where the walls and the ceilings were covered with rich paintings. But she had no eyes for all these glorious sights; she could only mourn and weep. Patiently she allowed the women to array her in royal robes, to weave pearls in her hair, and draw soft gloves over her blistered fingers.

As she stood before them in all her rich dress, she looked so dazzlingly beautiful that the court bowed low in her presence. Then the king declared his intention of making her his bride, but the archbishop shook his head and whispered that the fair young maiden was only a witch who had blinded the king's eyes and bewitched his heart. But the king would not listen to this; he ordered the music to sound, the

daintiest dishes to be served, and the loveliest maidens to dance.

Afterwards he led her through fragrant gardens and lofty halls, but not a smile appeared on her lips or sparkled in her eyes. She looked the very picture of grief. Then the king opened the door of a little chamber in which she was to sleep; it was adorned with rich green tapestry, and resembled the cave in which he had found her. On the floor lay the bundle of flax which she had spun from the nettles, and under the ceiling hung the coat she had made. These things had been brought away from the cave as curiosities by one of the huntsmen.

"Here you can dream yourself back again in the old home in the cave," said the king; "here is the work with which you employed yourself. It will amuse you now in the midst of all this splendour to think of that time."

When Eliza saw all these things which lay so near her heart, a smile played around her mouth, and the crimson blood rushed to her cheeks. She thought of her brothers, and their release made her so joyful that she kissed the king's hand. Then he pressed her to his heart.

Very soon the joyous church bells announced the marriage feast, and that the beautiful dumb girl out of the wood was to be made the queen of the country. Then the archbishop whispered wicked words in the king's ear, but they did not sink into his heart. The marriage was still to take place, and the archbishop himself had to place the crown on the bride's head; in his wicked spite, he pressed the narrow circlet so tightly on her forehead that it caused her pain.

But a heavier weight encircled her heart—sorrow for her brothers. She felt not bodily pain. Her mouth was closed; a single word would cost her brothers their lives. But she loved the kind, handsome king, who did everything to make her happy more and more each day; she loved him with all her heart, and her eyes beamed with the love she dared not speak. Oh! if she had only been able to confide in him and tell him of her grief. But dumb she must remain till her task was finished.

Therefore at night she crept away into her little chamber, which had been decked out to look like the cave, and quickly wove one coat after another. But when she began the seventh she found she had no more flax. She knew that the nettles she wanted to use grew in the churchyard and that she must pluck them herself. How should she get out there?

"Oh, what is the pain in my fingers to the torment which my heart endures?" said she. "I must venture, I shall not be denied help from heaven." Then with a trembling heart, as if she were about to perform a wicked deed, she crept into the garden in the broad moonlight and passed through the narrow walks and the deserted streets, till she reached the churchyard.

Then she saw on one of the broad tombstones a group of ghouls. These hideous creatures took off their rags, as

if they intended to bathe, and then clawing open the fresh graves with their long, skinny fingers, pulled out the dead bodies and ate the flesh!

Eliza had to pass close by them, and they fixed their wicked glances upon her, but she prayed silently, gathered the burning nettles, and carried them home with her to the castle. One person only had seen her, and that was the archbishop—he was awake while everybody was asleep.

Now he thought his opinion was evidently correct. All was not right with the queen. She was a witch, and had bewitched the king and all the people. Secretly he told the king what he had seen and what he feared, and as the hard words came from his tongue, the carved images of the saints shook their heads as if they would say, "It is not so. Eliza is innocent."

But the archbishop interpreted it in another way; he believed that they witnessed against her, and were shaking their heads at her wickedness. Two large tears rolled down the king's cheeks, and he went home with doubt in his heart. At night he pretended to sleep, but there came no real sleep to his eyes, for he saw Eliza get up every night and disappear in her own chamber. From day to day his brow became darker, and Eliza saw it and did not understand the reason, but it alarmed her and made her heart tremble for her brothers. Her hot tears glittered like pearls on the regal velvet and diamonds, while all who saw her were wishing they could be queens.

In the meantime she had almost finished her task; only one coat of mail was wanting, but she had no flax left and not a single nettle. Once more only, and for the last time, must she venture to the churchyard and pluck a few handfuls. She thought with terror of the solitary walk and of the horrible ghouls, but her will was firm, as well as her trust in Providence.

Eliza went, and the king and the archbishop followed her. They saw her vanish through the wicket gate into the churchyard, and when they came nearer they saw the ghouls sitting on the tombstone, as Eliza had seen them, and the king turned away his head, for he thought she was with them—she whose head had rested on his breast that very evening.

"The people must condemn her," said he, and she was very quickly condemned by everyone to suffer death by fire. Away from the gorgeous regal halls was she led to a dark, dreary cell, where the wind whistled through the iron bars.

Instead of the velvet and silk dresses, they gave her the coats of mail which she had woven to cover her and the bundle of nettles for a pillow; but nothing they could give her would have pleased her more. She continued her task with joy and prayed for help, while the street-boys sang jeering songs about her, and not a soul comforted her with a kind word.

Towards evening, she heard at the grating the flutter of a swan's wing: it was her youngest brother—he had found his sister, and she sobbed for joy, although she knew that very likely this would be the last night she would have to live. But still she could hope, for her task was almost finished and her brothers were come.

Then the archbishop arrived, to be with her during her last hours, as he had promised the king. But she shook her head and begged him, by looks and gestures, not to stay; for in this night she knew she must finish her task, otherwise all her pain and tears and sleepless nights would have been suffered in vain. The archbishop withdrew, uttering bitter words against her; but poor Eliza knew that she was innocent, and diligently continued her work.

The little mice ran about the floor; they dragged the nettles to her feet, to help as well as they could; and the thrush sat outside the grating of the window, and sang to her the whole night long, as sweetly as possible, to keep up her spirits.

It was still twilight and at least an hour before sunrise when the eleven brothers stood at the castle gate and demanded to be brought before the king. They were told it could not be, it was yet almost night, and as the king slept they dared not disturb him. They threatened, they entreated. Then the guard appeared, and even the king himself, inquiring what all the noise meant. At this moment the sun rose. The eleven brothers were seen no more, but eleven wild swans flew away over the castle.

And now all the people came streaming forth from the gates of the city, to see the witch burnt. An old horse drew the cart on which she sat. They had dressed her in a garment of coarse sackcloth. Her lovely hair hung loose on her shoulders, her cheeks were deadly pale, her lips moved silently, while her fingers still worked at the green flax. Even on the way to death, she would not give up her task. The ten coats of mail lay at her feet; she was working hard at the eleventh, while the mob jeered her and said, "See the witch, how she mutters! She has no hymn-book in her hand. She sits there with her ugly sorcery. Let us tear it in a thousand pieces."

And then they pressed towards her and would have destroyed the coats of mail, but at the same moment eleven wild swans flew over her and alighted on the cart. Then they flapped their large wings, and the crowd drew on one side in alarm.

"It is a sign from heaven that she is innocent," whispered many of them; but they ventured not to say it aloud.

As the executioner seized her by the hand, to lift her out of the cart, she hastily threw the eleven coats of mail over the swans, and they immediately became eleven handsome princes; but the youngest had a swan's wing, instead of an arm; for she had not been able to finish the last sleeve of the coat.

"Now I may speak," she exclaimed. "I am innocent."

Then the people, who saw what happened, bowed to her, as before a saint; but she sank lifeless in her brothers' arms, overcome with suspense, anguish, and pain.

"Yes, she is innocent," said the eldest brother; and then he related all that had taken place; and while he spoke there rose in the air a fragrance as from millions of roses. Every piece of faggot in the pile had taken root, and threw out branches, and appeared a thick hedge, large and high, covered with roses; while above all bloomed a white and shining flower, that glittered like a star. This flower the king plucked, and placed in Eliza's bosom, when she awoke from her swoon, with peace and happiness in her heart. And all the church bells rang of themselves, and the birds came in great troops. And a marriage procession returned to the castle, such as no king had ever before seen.

Ole-Luk-Oie

T HERE is nobody in the world who knows so many stories as Ole-Luk-Oie, or who can relate them so nicely.
In the evening, while the children are seated at the
table or in their little chairs, he comes up the stairs very
softly, for he walks in his socks, then he opens the doors
without the slightest noise and throws a small quantity of
very fine dust in their eyes, just enough to prevent them
from keeping them open, and so they do not see him. Then
he creeps behind them and blows softly upon their necks,
till their heads begin to droop. But Ole-Luk-Oie does not
wish to hurt them, for he is very fond of children and only
wants them to be quiet that he may relate to them pretty
stories, and they never are quiet until they are in bed and
asleep.

As soon as they are asleep, Ole-Luk-Oie seats himself
upon the bed. He is nicely dressed; his coat is made of silk-
en stuff; it is impossible to say of what colour, for it changes
from green to red, and from red to blue as he turns from
side to side. Under each arm he carries an umbrella; one

of them, with pictures on the inside, he spreads over the good children, and then they dream the most beautiful stories the whole night. But the other umbrella has no pictures, and this he holds over the naughty children, so that they sleep heavily and wake in the morning without having dreamed at all.

Now we shall hear how Ole-Luk-Oie came every night during a whole week to a little boy named Hjalmar and what he told him. There were seven stories, as there are seven days in the week.

MONDAY

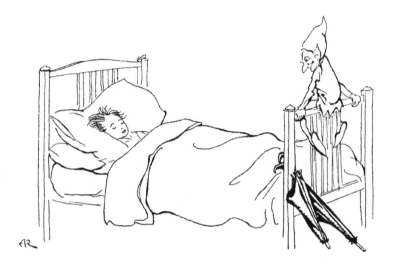

"Now pay attention," said Ole-Luk-Oie, in the evening, when Hjalmar was in bed, "and I will decorate the room."

Immediately all the flowers in the flower-pots became large trees with long branches reaching to the ceiling and stretching along the walls, so that the whole room was like a greenhouse. All the branches were loaded with flowers, each flower as beautiful and as fragrant as a rose; and, had anyone tasted them, he would have found them sweeter even than jam. The fruit glittered like gold, and there were cakes so full of plums that they were nearly bursting. It was incomparably beautiful. At the same time, sounded dismal moans from the table-drawer in which lay Hjalmar's school books.

"What can that be now?" said Ole-Luk-Oie, going to the table and pulling out the drawer.

It was a slate, in such distress because of a false number in the sum that it had almost broken itself to pieces. The pencil pulled and tugged at its string as if it were a little dog that wanted to help but could not.

And then came a moan from Hjalmar's copy-book. Oh, it was quite terrible to hear! On each leaf stood a row of capital letters, every one having a small letter by its side. This formed a copy; under these were other letters, which Hjalmar had written: they fancied they looked like the copy, but they were mistaken; for they were leaning on one side as if they intended to fall over the pencil-lines.

"See, this is the way you should hold yourselves," said the copy. "Look here, you should slope thus, with a graceful curve."

"Oh, we are very willing to do so, but we cannot," said Hjalmar's letters; "we are so wretchedly made."

"You must be scratched out, then," said Ole-Luk-Oie.

"Oh, no!" they cried, and then they stood up so gracefully it was quite a pleasure to look at them.

"Now we must give up our stories and exercise these letters," said Ole-Luk-Oie; "One, two—one, two—" So he drilled them till they stood up gracefully and looked as beautiful as a copy could look. But after Ole-Luk-Oie was gone and Hjalmar looked at them in the morning, they were as wretched and as awkward as ever.

TUESDAY

As soon as Hjalmar was in bed, Ole-Luk-Oie touched, with his little magic wand, all the furniture in the room, which immediately began to chatter, and each article only talked of itself.

Over the chest of drawers hung a large picture in a gilt frame, representing a landscape, with fine old trees, flowers in the grass, and a broad stream, which flowed through the wood, past several castles, far out into the wild ocean. Ole-Luk-Oie touched the picture with his magic wand, and immediately the birds commenced singing, the branches of the trees rustled, and the clouds moved across the sky, casting their shadows on the landscape beneath them.

Then Ole-Luk-Oie lifted little Hjalmar up to the frame and placed his feet in the picture, just on the high grass, and there he stood with the sun shining down upon him through the branches of the trees. He ran to the water and seated himself in a little boat, which lay there and which was painted red and white. The sails glittered like silver, and six swans, each with a golden circlet round its neck and a bright blue star on its forehead, drew the boat past the green wood, where the trees talked of robbers and witches, and the flowers of beautiful little elves and fairies, whose histories the butterflies had related to them. Brilliant fish, with scales like silver and gold, swam after the boat, sometimes making a spring and splashing the water round them, while birds, red and blue, small and great, flew after him in two long lines. The gnats danced round them, and the cockchafers cried "Buz, buz." They all wanted to follow Hjalmar, and all had some story to tell him. It was a most pleasant sail.

Sometimes the forests were thick and dark, sometimes like a beautiful garden, gay with sunshine and flowers; then he passed great palaces of glass and of marble, and on the balconies stood princesses, whose faces were those of little girls whom Hjalmar knew well and had often played with. One of them held out her hand, in which was a heart made of sugar, more beautiful than any confectioner ever sold. As Hjalmar sailed by, he caught hold of one side of the sugar heart and held it fast, and the princess held fast also, so that it broke in two pieces. Hjalmar had one piece, and the princess the other, but Hjalmar's was the largest. At each castle stood little princes acting as sentinels. They presented arms, and had golden swords, and made it rain plums and tin soldiers, so that they must have been real princes.

Hjalmar continued to sail, sometimes through woods, sometimes as it were through large halls, and then by large cities. At last he came to the town where his nurse lived, who had carried him in her arms when he was a very little boy, and had always been kind to him. She nodded and

beckoned to him, and then sang the little verses she had
herself composed and sent to him:

> "How oft my memory turns to thee,
> My own Hjalmar, ever dear!
> When I could watch thy infant glee,
> Or kiss away a pearly tear.
> 'T was in my arms thy lisping tongue
> First spoke the half-remembered word,
> While o'er thy tottering steps I hung,
> My fond protection to afford.
> Farewell! I pray the Heavenly Power
> To keep thee till thy dying hour."

And all the birds sang the same tune, the flowers danced
on their stems, and the old trees nodded as if Ole-Luk-Oie
had been telling them stories as well.

WEDNESDAY

How the rain did pour down! Hjalmar could hear it in his
sleep; and when Ole-Luk-Oie opened the window, the water
flowed quite up to the window-sill. It had the appearance of a
large lake outside, and a beautiful ship lay close to the house.

"Wilt thou sail with me tonight, little Hjalmar?" said
Ole-Luk-Oie; "then we shall see foreign countries, and thou
shalt return here in the morning."

All in a moment, there stood Hjalmar, in his best clothes,
on the deck of the noble ship; and immediately the weather
became fine. They sailed through the streets, round by the
church, and on every side rolled the wide, great sea.

They sailed till the land disappeared, and then they saw
a flock of storks, who had left their own country and were

travelling to warmer climates. The storks flew one behind the other and had already been a long, long time on the wing. One of them seemed so tired that his wings could scarcely carry him. He was the last of the row and was soon left very far behind. At length he sunk lower and lower, with out-stretched wings, flapping them in vain, till his feet touched the rigging of the ship, and he slid from the sails to the deck and stood before them. Then a sailor-boy caught him and put him in the hen-house, with the fowls, the ducks, and the turkeys, while the poor stork stood quite bewildered amongst them.

"Just look at that fellow," said the chickens.

Then the turkey-cock puffed himself out as large as he could and inquired who he was; and the ducks waddled backwards, crying, "Quack, quack."

Then the stork told them all about warm Africa, of the pyramids, and of the ostrich, which, like a wild horse, runs across the desert. But the ducks did not understand what he said and quacked amongst themselves, "We are all of the same opinion; namely, that he is stupid."

"Yes, to be sure, he is stupid," said the turkey-cock and gobbled.

Then the stork remained quite silent and thought of his home in Africa.

"Those are handsome thin legs of yours," said the turkey-cock. "What do they cost a yard?"

"Quack, quack, quack," grinned the ducks; but the stork pretended not to hear.

"You may as well laugh," said the turkey; "for that remark was rather witty, or perhaps it was above you. Ah, ah, is he not clever? He will be a great amusement to us while he remains here." And then he gobbled, and the ducks quacked, "Gobble, gobble; Quack, quack."

What a terrible uproar they made, while they were having such fun among themselves!

Then Hjalmar went to the hen-house and, opening the door, called to the stork. Then he hopped out on the deck. He had rested himself now, and he looked happy, and seemed as if he nodded to Hjalmar, as if to thank him. Then he spread his wings and flew away to warmer countries, while the hens clucked, the ducks quacked, and the turkey-cock turned quite scarlet in the head.

"Tomorrow you shall be made into soup," said Hjalmar to the fowls; and then he awoke and found himself lying in his little bed.

It was a wonderful journey which Ole-Luk-Oie had made him take this night.

Thursday

"What do you think I have got here?" said Ole-Luk-Oie. "Do not be frightened, and you shall see a little mouse." And then he held out his hand to him, in which lay a lovely little creature. "It has come to invite you to a wedding. Two little mice are going to enter into the marriage state tonight. They reside under the floor of your mother's store-room, and that must be a fine dwelling-place."

"But how can I get through the little mouse-hole in the floor?" asked Hjalmar.

"Leave me to manage that," said Ole-Luk-Oie. "I will soon make you small enough." And then he touched Hjalmar with his magic wand, whereupon he became less and less, until at last he was not longer than a little finger. "Now you can borrow the dress of the tin soldier. I think it will just fit you. It looks well to wear a uniform when you go into company."

"Yes, certainly," said Hjalmar, and in a moment he was dressed as neatly as the neatest of all tin soldiers.

"Will you be so good as to seat yourself in your mamma's thimble," said the little mouse, "that I may have the pleasure of drawing you to the wedding."

"Will you really take so much trouble, young lady?" said Hjalmar. And so in this way he rode to the mouse's wedding.

First they went under the floor and then passed through a long passage, which was scarcely high enough to allow the thimble to drive under, and the whole passage was lit up with the phosphorescent light of rotten wood.

"Does it not smell delicious?" asked the mouse, as she drew him along. "The wall and the floor have been smeared with bacon-rind; nothing can be nicer."

Very soon they arrived at the bridal hall. On the right stood all the little lady-mice, whispering and giggling, as if they were making game of each other. To the left were the gentlemen-mice, stroking their whiskers with their fore-paws; and in the centre of the hall could be seen the bridal pair, standing side by side, in a hollow cheese-rind, and kissing each other, while all eyes were upon them; for they had already been betrothed and were soon to be married. More and more friends kept arriving, till the mice were near-ly treading each other to death; for the bridal pair now stood in the doorway, and none could pass in or out.

The room had been rubbed over with bacon-rind, like the passage, which was all the refreshment offered to the guests. But for dessert they produced a pea, on which a mouse belonging to the bridal pair had bitten the first let-ters of their names. This was something quite uncommon. All the mice said it was a very beautiful wedding, and that they had been very agreeably entertained.

After this, Hjalmar returned home. He had certainly been in grand society; but he had been obliged to creep under a room and to make himself small enough to wear the uniform of a tin soldier.

FRIDAY

"It is incredible how many old people there are who would be glad to have me at night," said Ole-Luk-Oie, "es-pecially those who have done something wrong. 'Good little Ole,' say they to me, 'we cannot close our eyes, and we lie

awake the whole night and see all our evil deeds sitting on our beds like little imps and sprinkling us with hot water. Will you come and drive them away, so that we may have a good night's rest?' and then they sigh so deeply and say, 'We would gladly pay you for it. Good-night, Ole-Luk, the money lies on the window.' But I never do anything for gold."

"What shall we do tonight?" asked Hjalmar.

"I do not know whether you would care to go to another wedding," he replied, "although it is quite a different affair to the one we saw last night. Your sister's large doll, that is dressed like a man and is called Herman, intends to marry the doll Bertha. It is also the dolls' birthday, and they will receive many presents."

"Yes, I know that already," said Hjalmar, "my sister always allows her dolls to keep their birthdays or to have a wedding when they require new clothes; that has happened already a hundred times, I am quite sure."

"Yes, so it may; but tonight is the hundred and first wedding, and when that has taken place it must be the last, therefore this is to be extremely beautiful. Only look."

Hjalmar looked at the table, and there stood the little card-board doll's house, with lights in all the windows, and drawn up before it were the tin soldiers presenting arms. The bridal pair were seated on the floor, leaning against the leg of the table, looking very thoughtful, and with good reason. Then Ole-Luk-Oie dressed up in grandmother's black gown married them.

As soon as the ceremony was concluded, all the furniture in the room joined in singing a beautiful song, which had been composed by the lead pencil and which went to the melody of a military tattoo.

> "What merry sounds are on the wind,
> As marriage rites together bind
> A quiet and a loving pair,
> Though formed of kid, yet smooth and fair!
> Hurrah! If they are deaf and blind,
> We'll sing, though weather prove unkind."

And now came the presents; but the bridal pair had nothing to eat, for love was to be their food.

"Shall we go to a country house, or travel?" asked the bridegroom.

Then they consulted the swallow who had travelled so far, and the old hen in the yard, who had brought up five broods of chickens.

And the swallow talked to them of warm countries, where the grapes hang in large clusters on the vines and the air is soft and mild, and about the mountains glowing with colours more beautiful than we can think of.

"But they have no red cabbage like we have," said the hen. "I was once in the country with my chickens for a whole summer; there was a large sand-pit, in which we could walk about and scratch as we liked. Then we got into a garden in which grew red cabbage; oh, how nice it was, I cannot think of anything more delicious."

"But one cabbage stalk is exactly like another," said the swallow; "and here we have often bad weather."

"Yes, but we are accustomed to it," said the hen.

"But it is so cold here and freezes sometimes."

"Cold weather is good for cabbages," said the hen; "besides we do have it warm here sometimes. Four years ago, we had a summer that lasted more than five weeks, and it was so hot one could scarcely breathe. And then in this country we have no poisonous animals, and we are free from robbers. He must be wicked who does not consider our country the finest of all lands. He ought not to be allowed to live here." And then the hen wept very much and said, "I have also travelled. I once went twelve miles in a coop, and it was not pleasant travelling at all."

"The hen is a sensible woman," said the doll Bertha. "I don't care for travelling over mountains, just to go up and come down again. No, let us go to the sand-pit in front of the gate, and then take a walk in the cabbage garden."

And so they settled it.

Saturday

"Am I to hear any more stories?" asked little Hjalmar, as soon as Ole-Luk-Oie had sent him to sleep.

"We shall have no time this evening," said he, spreading out his prettiest umbrella over the child. "Look at these Chinese," and then the whole umbrella appeared like a large china bowl, with blue trees and pointed bridges, upon which stood little Chinamen nodding

their heads. "We must make all the world beautiful for to-morrow morning," said Ole-Luk-Oie, "for it will be a holiday: it is Sunday. I must now go to the church steeple and see if the little sprites who live there have polished the bells, so that they may sound sweetly. Then I must go into the fields and see if the wind has blown the dust from the grass and the leaves, and the most difficult task of all which I have to do is to take down all the stars and brighten them up. I have to number them first before I put them in my apron and also to number the places from which I take them, so that they may go back into the right holes, or else they would not remain, and we should have a number of falling stars, for they would all tumble down one after the other."

"Hark ye! Mr. Luk-Oie," said an old portrait which hung on the wall of Hjalmar's bedroom. "Do you know me? I am Hjalmar's great-grandfather. I thank you for telling the boy stories, but you must not confuse his ideas. The stars cannot be taken down from the sky and polished; they are spheres like our earth, which is a good thing for them."

"Thank you, old great-grandfather," said Ole-Luk-Oie. "I thank you; you may be the head of the family, as no doubt you are, but I am older than you. I am an ancient heathen. The old Romans and Greeks named me the Dream-god. I have visited the noblest houses and continue to do so; still I know how to conduct myself both to high and low, and now you may tell the stories yourself;" and so Ole-Luk-Oie walked off, taking his umbrellas with him.

"Well, well, one is never to give an opinion, I suppose," grumbled the portrait. And it woke Hjalmar.

SUNDAY

"Good evening," said Ole-Luk-Oie.

Hjalmar nodded, and then sprang out of bed, and turned his great-grandfather's portrait to the wall, so that it might not interrupt them as it had done yesterday. "Now," said he, "you must tell me some stories about five green peas that lived in one pod; or of the chickseed that courted the

chickweed; or of the darning needle, who acted so proudly because she fancied herself an embroidery needle."

"You may have too much of a good thing," said Ole-Luk-Oie. "You know that I like best to show you something, so I will show you my brother. He is also called Ole-Luk-Oie, but he never visits any one but once, and when he does come, he takes him away on his horse and tells him stories as they ride along. He knows only two stories. One of these is so wonderfully beautiful, that no one in the world can imagine anything at all like it; but the other is just as ugly and frightful, so that it would be impossible to describe it."

Then Ole-Luk-Oie lifted Hjalmar up to the window. "There now, you can see my brother, the other Ole-Luk-Oie; he is also called Death. You perceive he is not so bad as they represent him in picture books; there he is a skeleton, but now his coat is embroidered with silver, and he wears the splendid uniform of a hussar, and a mantle of black velvet flies behind him, over the horse. Look, how he gallops along."

Hjalmar saw that as this Ole-Luk-Oie rode on, he lifted up old and young and carried them away on his horse. Some he seated in front of him, and some behind, but always inquired first, "How stands the mark-book?"

"Good," they all answered.

"Yes, but let me see for myself," he replied; and they were obliged to give him the books. Then all those who had "Very good," or "Exceedingly good," came in front of the horse and heard the beautiful story; while those who had "Middling," or "Tolerably good," in their books were obliged to sit behind and listen to the frightful tale. They trembled and cried, and wanted to jump down from the horse, but they could not get free, for they seemed fastened to the seat.

"Why, Death is a most splendid Luk-Oie," said Hjalmar. "I am not in the least afraid of him."

"You need have no fear of him," said Ole-Luk-Oie, "if you take care and keep a good conduct book."

"Now I call that very instructive," murmured the great-grandfather's portrait. "It is useful sometimes to express an opinion;" so he was quite satisfied.

These are some of the doings and sayings of Ole-Luk-Oie. I hope he may visit you himself this evening and relate some more.

The Princess and the Pea

ONCE upon a time there was a prince who wanted to marry a princess, but she would have to be a real princess. He travelled far and wide to find one, but nowhere could he get what he wanted. There were princesses enough, but it was difficult to find out whether they were real ones. There was always something about them that was not as it should be. So he came home again and was sad, for he would have liked very much to have a real princess.

One evening a terrible storm came on; there was thunder and lightning, and the rain poured down heavily. Suddenly a knocking was heard at the city gate, and the old king went to open it.

It was a princess standing out there in front of the gate. But, good gracious! what a sight the rain and the wind had made her look. The water ran down from her hair and clothes; it ran down into the toes of her shoes and out again at the heels. And yet she said that she was a real princess.

"Well, we'll soon find that out," thought the old queen. But she said nothing, went into the bed-room, took all the bedding off the bedstead, and laid a pea on the bottom; then she took twenty mattresses and laid them on the pea, and then twenty eider-down beds on top of the mattresses.

On this the princess had to lie all night. In the morning she was asked how she had slept.

"Oh, very badly!" said she. "I hardly closed my eyes all night. God only knows what was in the bed, but I was lying on something hard, so that I am black and blue all over my body. It was horrible!"

Now they knew that she was a real princess because she had felt the pea right through the twenty mattresses and the twenty eider-down beds.

Nobody but a real princess could be as sensitive as that.

So the prince took her for his wife, for now he knew that he had a real princess; and the pea was put in the museum, where it may still be seen, if no one has stolen it.

There, that is a true story.

Thumbelina

THERE was once a woman who wanted to have quite a tiny, little child, but she did not know where to get one from. So one day she went to an old Witch and said to her: "I should so much like to have a tiny, little child; can you tell me where I can get one?"

"Oh, we have just got one ready!" said the Witch. "Here is a barley-corn for you, but it's not the kind the farmer sows in his field or feeds the cocks and hens with, I can tell you. Put it in a flowerpot, and then you will see something happen."

"Oh, thank you!" said the woman and gave the Witch a shilling, for that was what it cost. Then she went home and planted the barley-corn. Immediately there grew out of it a large and beautiful flower, which looked like a tulip, but the petals were tightly closed as if it were still only a bud.

"What a beautiful flower!" exclaimed the woman, and she kissed the red and yellow petals; but as she kissed them the flower burst open. It was a real tulip, such as one can see any day; but in the middle of the blossom, on the green velvety petals, sat a little girl, quite tiny, trim, and pretty.

She was scarcely half a thumb in height; so they called her Thumbelina.

An elegant polished walnut-shell served Thumbelina as a cradle, the blue petals of a violet were her mattress, and a rose-leaf her coverlid. There she lay at night, but in the day-time she used to play about on the table; here the woman had put a bowl, surrounded by a ring of flowers, with their stalks in water, in the middle of which floated a great tulip pedal, and on this Thumbelina sat, and sailed from one side of the bowl to the other, rowing herself with two white horse-hairs for oars. It was such a pretty sight! She could sing, too, with a voice more soft and sweet than had ever been heard before.

One night, when she was lying in her pretty little bed, an old toad crept in through a broken pane in the window. She was very ugly, clumsy, and clammy; she hopped on to the table where Thumbelina lay asleep under the red rose-leaf.

"This would make a beautiful wife for my son," said the toad, taking up the walnut-shell with Thumbelina inside and hopping with it through the window into the garden.

There flowed a great wide stream, with slippery and marshy banks; here the toad lived with her son. Ugh! how ugly and clammy he was, just like his mother! "Croak, croak, croak!" was all he could say when he saw the pretty little girl in the walnut-shell.

"Don't talk so load or you'll wake her," said the old toad. "She might escape us even now; she is as light as a feather. "We will put her at once on a broad water-lily leaf in the stream. That will be quite an island for her; she is so small and light. She can't run away from us there, whilst we are preparing the guest-chamber under the marsh where she shall live."

Outside in the brook grew many water-lilies, with broad green leaves, which looked as if they were swimming about on the water. The leaf farthest away was the largest, and to this the old toad swam with Thumbelina in her walnut-shell.

The tiny Thumbelina woke up very early in the morning, and when she saw where she was she began to cry bitterly; for on every side of the great green leaf was water, and she could not get to the land.

The old toad was down under the marsh, decorating her room with rushes and yellow marigold leaves, to make it very grand for her new daughter-in-law; then she swam out with her ugly son to the leaf where Thumbelina lay. She wanted to fetch the pretty cradle to put it into her room before Thumbelina herself came there. The old toad bowed low in the water before her and said: "Here is my son; you shall marry him and live in great magnificence down under the marsh."

"Croak, croak, croak!" was all that the son could say. Then they took the neat little cradle and swam away with it; but Thumbelina sat alone on the great green leaf and wept, for she did not want to live with the clammy toad or marry her ugly son.

The little fishes swimming about under the water had seen the toad quite plainly and heard what she had said; so they put up their heads to see the little girl. When they saw her, they thought her so pretty that they were very sorry she should go down with the ugly toad to live. No; that must not happen. They assembled in the water round the green stalk which supported the leaf on which she was sitting, and nibbled the stem in two. Away floated the leaf down the stream, bearing Thumbelina far beyond the reach of the toad.

On she sailed past several towns, and the little birds sitting in the bushes saw her and sang, "What a pretty little girl!" The leaf floated farther and farther away; thus Thumbelina left her native land.

A beautiful little white butterfly fluttered above her and at last settled on the leaf. Thumbelina pleased him, and she, too, was delighted, for now the toads could not reach her, and it was so beautiful where she was travelling; the sun shone on the water and made it sparkle like the brightest silver. She took off her sash and tied one end round the butterfly; the other end she fastened to the leaf, so that now it glided along with her faster than ever.

A great cockchafer came flying past; he caught sight of Thumbelina, and in a moment had put his arms round her slender waist, and had flown off with her to a tree. The green leaf floated away down the stream and the butterfly with it, for he was fastened to the leaf and could not get loose from it.

Oh, dear! how terrified poor little Thumbelina was when the cockchafer flew off with her to the tree! But she was especially distressed on the beautiful white butterfly's account, as she had tied him fast, so that if he could not get away he must starve to death.

But the cockchafer did not trouble himself about that; he sat down with her on a large green leaf, gave her the honey out of the flowers to eat, and told her that she was very pretty, although she wasn't in the least like a cockchafer. Later on, all the other cockchafers who lived in the same tree came to pay calls; they examined Thumbelina closely and remarked, "Why, she has only two legs! How very miserable!"

"She has no feelers!" cried another.

"How ugly she is!" said all the lady chafers—and yet Thumbelina was really very pretty.

The cockchafer who had stolen her knew this very well; but when he heard all the ladies saying she was ugly, he began to think so too and would not keep her; she might go wherever she liked. So he flew down from the tree with her and put her on a daisy.

There she sat and wept, because she was so ugly that the cockchafer would have nothing to do with her; and yet she was the most beautiful creature imaginable, so soft and delicate, like the loveliest rose-leaf.

The whole summer poor little Thumbelina lived alone in the great wood. She plaited a bed for herself of blades of grass, and hung it up under a clover-leaf, so that she was protected from the rain. She gathered honey from the flowers for food and drank the dew on the leaves every morning.

Thus the summer and autumn passed, but then came winter—the long, cold winter. All the birds who had sung so sweetly about her had flown away; the trees shed their leaves, the flowers died; the great clover-leaf under which she had lived curled up, and nothing remained of it but the withered stalk.

She was terribly cold, for her clothes were ragged, and she herself was so small and thin. Poor little Thumbelina! she would surely be frozen to death. It began to snow, and every snow-flake that fell on her was to her as a whole shovelful thrown on one of us, for we are so big and she was only an inch high. She wrapt herself round in a dead leaf, but it was torn in the middle and gave her no warmth; she was trembling with cold.

Just outside the wood where she was now living lay a great corn-field. But the corn had been gone a long time; only the dry, bare stubble was left standing in the frozen ground. This made a forest for her to wander about in. All at once she came across the door of a field-mouse, who had a little hole under a corn-stalk. There the mouse lived warm and snug, with a store-room full of corn, a splendid kitchen and dining-room. Poor little Thumbelina went up to the door and begged for a little piece of barley, for she had not had anything to eat for the last two days.

"Poor little creature!" said the field-mouse, for she was a kind-hearted old thing at the bottom. "Come into my warm room and have some dinner with me."

As Thumbelina pleased her, she said: "As far as I am concerned you may spend the winter with me; but you must keep my room clean and tidy, and tell me stories, for I like that very much."

And Thumbelina did all that the kind old field-mouse asked and did it remarkably well too.

"Now I am expecting a visitor," said the field-mouse; "my neighbour comes to call on me once a week. He is in better circumstances than I am, has great, big rooms and wears a fine black-velvet coat. If you could only marry him, you would be well provided for. But he is blind. You must tell him all the prettiest stories you know."

But Thumbelina did not trouble her head about him, for he was only a mole. He came and paid them a visit in his black-velvet coat.

"He is so rich and so accomplished," the field-mouse told her.

"His house is twenty times larger than mine; he possesses great knowledge, but he cannot bear the sun and the beautiful flowers, and speaks slightingly of them, for he has never seen them."

Thumbelina had to sing to him, so she sang "Lady-bird, ladybird, fly away home!" and other songs so prettily that the mole fell in love with her; but he did not say anything, he was a very cautious man.

A short time before, he had dug a long passage through the ground from his own house to that of his neighbour; in this he gave the field-mouse and Thumbelina permission to walk as often as they liked. But he begged them not to be afraid of the dead bird that lay in the passage: it was a real bird with beak and feathers, and must have died a little time ago, and now laid buried just where he had made his tunnel.

The mole took a piece of rotten wood in his mouth, for that glows like fire in the dark, and went in front, lighting them through the long dark passage. When they came to the place where the dead bird lay, the mole put his broad nose against the ceiling and pushed a hole through, so that the daylight could shine down.

In the middle of the path lay a dead swallow, his pretty wings pressed close to his sides, his claws and head drawn under his feathers; the poor bird had evidently died of cold. Thumbelina was very sorry, for she was very fond of all little birds; they had sung and twittered so beautifully to her all through the summer. But the mole kicked him with his bandy legs and said:

"Now he can't sing any more! It must be very miserable to be a little bird! I'm thankful that none of my little children are; birds always starve in winter."

"Yes, you speak like a sensible man," said the field-mouse. "What has a bird, in spite of all his singing, in the winter-time? He must starve and freeze, and that must be very pleasant for him, I must say!"

Thumbelina did not say anything; but when the other two had passed on she bent down to the bird, brushed aside the feathers from his head, and kissed his closed eyes gently. "Perhaps it was he that sang to me so prettily in the summer," she thought. "How much pleasure he did give me, dear little bird!"

The mole closed up the hole again which let in the light and then escorted the ladies home. But Thumbelina could not sleep that night; so she got out of bed, and plaited a great big blanket of straw, and carried it off, and spread it over the dead bird, and piled upon it thistle-down as soft as cotton-wool, which she had found in the field-mouse's room, so that the poor little thing should lie warmly buried.

"Farewell, pretty little bird!" she said. "Farewell, and thank you for your beautiful songs in the summer, when the trees were green, and the sun shone down warmly on us!" Then she laid her head against the bird's heart. But the bird was not dead: he had been frozen, but now that she had warmed him, he was coming to life again.

In autumn the swallows fly away to foreign lands; but there are some who are late in starting, and then they get so cold that they drop down as if dead, and the snow comes and covers them over.

Thumbelina trembled, she was so frightened; for the bird was very large in comparison with herself—only an inch high. But she took courage, piled up the down more closely over the poor swallow, fetched her own coverlid and laid it over his head.

Next night she crept out again to him. There he was alive, but very weak; he could only open his eyes for a moment and look at Thumbelina, who was standing in front of him with a piece of rotten wood in her hand, for she had no other lantern.

"Thank you, pretty little child!" said the swallow to her. "I am so beautifully warm! Soon I shall regain my strength, and then I shall be able to fly out again into the warm sunshine."

"Oh!" she said, "it is very cold outside; it is snowing and freezing! stay in your warm bed; I will take care of you!"

Then she brought him water in a petal, which he drank, after which he related to her how he had torn one of his

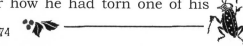

wings on a bramble, so that he could not fly as fast as the other swallows, who had flown far away to warmer lands. So at last he had dropped down exhausted, and then he could remember no more.

The whole winter he remained down there, and Thumbelina looked after him and nursed him tenderly. Neither the mole nor the field-mouse learnt anything of this, for they could not bear the poor swallow.

When the spring came and the sun warmed the earth again, the swallow said farewell to Thumbelina, who opened the hole in the roof for him which the mole had made. The sun shone brightly down upon her, and the swallow asked her if she would go with him; she could sit upon his back. Thumbelina wanted very much to fly far away into the green wood, but she knew that the old field-mouse would be sad if she ran away. "No, I mustn't come!" she said.

"Farewell, dear good little girl!" said the swallow, and flew off into the sunshine. Thumbelina gazed after him with the tears standing in her eyes, for she was very fond of the swallow.

"Tweet, tweet!" sang the bird, and flew into the green wood. Thumbelina was very unhappy. She was not allowed to go out into the warm sunshine. The corn which had been sowed in the field over the field-mouse's home grew up high into the air, and made a thick forest for the poor little girl, who was only an inch high.

"Now you are to be a bride, Thumbelina!" said the field-mouse, "for our neighbour has proposed for you! What a piece of fortune for a poor child like you! Now you must set to work at your linen for your dowry, for nothing must be lacking if you are to become the wife of our neighbour, the mole!"

Thumbelina had to spin all day long, and every evening the mole visited her, and told her that when the summer was over the sun would not shine so hot; now it was burning the earth as hard as a stone. Yes, when the summer had passed, they would keep the wedding.

But she was not at all pleased about it, for she did not like the stupid mole. Every morning when the sun was rising, and every evening when it was setting, she would steal out of the house-door, and when the breeze parted the ears of corn so that she could see the blue sky through them, she thought how bright and beautiful it must be outside, and longed to see her dear swallow again. But he never came; no doubt he had flown away far into the great green wood.

By the autumn Thumbelina had finished the dowry.

"In four weeks you will be married!" said the field-mouse; "don't be obstinate, or I shall bite you with my sharp white teeth! You will get a fine husband! The King himself has not such a velvet coat. His store-room and cellar are full, and you should be thankful for that."

Well, the wedding-day arrived. The mole had come to fetch Thumbelina to live with him deep down under the ground, never to come out into the warm sun again, for that was what he didn't like. The poor little girl was very sad; for now she must say good-bye to the beautiful sun.

"Farewell, bright sun!" she cried, stretching out her arms towards it, and taking another step outside the house; for now the corn had been reaped, and only the dry stubble was left standing. "Farewell, farewell!" she said and put her arms round a little red flower that grew there. "Give my love to the dear swallow when you see him!"

"Tweet, tweet!" sounded in her ear all at once. She looked up. There was the swallow flying past! As soon as he saw Thumbelina, he was very glad. She told him how unwilling she was to marry the ugly mole, as then she had to live underground where the sun never shone, and she could not help bursting into tears.

"The cold winter is coming now," said the swallow. "I must fly away to warmer lands; will you come with me? You can sit on my back, and we will fly far away from the ugly mole and his dark house, over the mountains, to the warm countries where the sun shines more brightly than here, where it is always summer, and there are always beauti-

ful flowers. Do come with me, dear little Thumbelina, who saved my life when I lay frozen in the dark tunnel!"

"Yes, I will go with you," said Thumbelina and got on the swallow's back, with her feet on one of his outstretched wings. Up he flew into the air, over woods and seas, over the great mountains where the snow is always lying. And if she was cold, she crept under his warm feathers, only keeping her little head out to admire all the beautiful things in the world beneath.

At last they came to warm lands; there the sun was brighter, the sky seemed twice as high, and in the hedges hung the finest green and purple grapes; in the woods grew oranges and lemons; the air was scented with myrtle and mint; and on the roads were pretty little children running about and playing with great gorgeous butterflies.

But the swallow flew on farther, and it became more and more beautiful. Under the most splendid green trees besides a blue lake, stood a glittering white-marble castle. Vines hung about the high pillars; there were many swallows' nests, and in one of these lived the swallow who was carrying Thumbelina.

"Here is my house!" said he. "But it won't do for you to live with me; I am not tidy enough to please you. Find a home for yourself in one of the lovely flowers that grow down there; now I will set you down, and you can do whatever you like."

"That will be splendid!" said she, clapping her little hands.

There lay a great white marble column which had fallen to the ground and broken into three pieces, but between these grew the most beautiful white flowers. The swallow flew down with Thumbelina and set her upon one of the broad leaves.

But there, to her astonishment, she found a tiny little man sitting in the middle of the flower, as white and transparent as if he were made of glass; he had the prettiest golden crown on his head and the most beautiful wings on his shoulders; he himself was no bigger than Thumbelina. He was the spirit of the flower. In each blossom there dwelt a tiny man or woman; but this one was the King over the others.

"How handsome he is!" whispered Thumbelina to the swallow.

The little Prince was very much frightened at the swallow, for in comparison with one so tiny as himself he seemed

a giant. But when he saw Thumbelina, he was delighted, for she was the most beautiful girl he had ever seen. So he took his golden crown from off his head and put it on hers, asking her her name, and if she would be his wife, and then she would be Queen of all the flowers. Yes! he was a different kind of husband to the son of the toad and the mole with the black-velvet coat. So she said "Yes" to the noble Prince.

And out of each flower came a lady and gentleman, each so tiny and pretty that it was a pleasure to see them. Each brought Thumbelina a present, but the best of all was a beautiful pair of wings which were fastened on to her back, and now she too could fly from flower to flower. They all wished her joy, and the swallow sat above in his nest and sang the wedding march, and that he did as well as he could; but he was sad, because he was very fond of Thumbelina and did not want to be separated from her.

"You shall not be called Thumbelina!" said the spirit of the flower to her; "that is an ugly name, and you are much too pretty for that. We will call you May Blossom."

"Farewell, farewell!" said the little swallow with a heavy heart and flew away to farther lands, far, far away, right back to Denmark. There he had a little nest above a window, where his wife lived, who can tell fairy-stories. "Tweet, tweet!" he sang to her. And that is the way we learnt the whole story.

What the Old Man Does Is Always Right

I WILL tell you a story that was told me when I was a little boy. Every time I thought of this story, it seemed to me more and more charming; for it is with stories as it is with many people—they become better as they grow older.

I have no doubt that you have been in the country, and seen a very old farmhouse, with a thatched roof, and mosses and small plants growing wild upon it. There is a stork's nest on the ridge of the gable, for we cannot do without the stork. The walls of the house are sloping, and the windows are low, and only one of the latter is made to open. The baking-oven sticks out of the wall like a great knob. An elder-tree hangs over the palings; and beneath its branches, at the foot of the paling, is a pool of water, in which a few ducks are disporting themselves. There is a yard-dog too, who barks at all corners.

Just such a farmhouse as this stood in a country lane; and in it dwelt an old couple, a peasant and his wife. Small as their possessions were; they had one article they could not do without, and that was a horse, which contrived to live upon the grass which it found by the side of the high road. The old peasant rode into the town upon this horse, and his neighbours often borrowed it of him, and paid for the loan of it by rendering some service to the old couple. After a time they thought it would be as well to sell the horse or exchange it for something which might be more useful to them. But what might this something be?

"You'll know best, old man," said the wife. "It is fair-day today; so ride into town and get rid of the horse for money, or make a good exchange; whichever you do will be right to me, so ride to the fair."

And she fastened his neckerchief for him; for she could do that better than he could, and she could also tie it very prettily in a double bow. She also smoothed his hat round and round with the palm of her hand and gave him a kiss. Then he rode away upon the horse that was to be sold or bartered for something else. Yes, the old man knew what he was about.

The sun shone with great heat, and not a cloud was to be seen in the sky. The road was very dusty; for a number of people, all going to the fair, were driving, riding, or walking upon it. There was no shelter anywhere from the hot sunshine. Among the rest, a man came trudging along, and driving a cow to the fair. The cow was as beautiful a creature as any cow could be.

"She gives good milk, I am certain," said the peasant to himself. "That would be a very good exchange: the cow for the horse. Hallo there! you with the cow," he said. "I tell you what; I dare say a horse is of more value than a cow; but I don't care for that,—a cow will be more useful to me; so, if you like, we'll exchange."

"To be sure I will," said the man.

Accordingly the exchange was made; and as the matter was settled, the peasant might have turned back; for he had done the business he came to do. But, having made up his mind to go to the fair, he determined to do so, if only to have a look at it; so on he went to the town with his cow. Leading the animal, he strode on sturdily, and, after a short time, overtook a man who was driving a sheep. It was a good fat sheep, with a fine fleece on its back.

"I should like to have that fellow," said the peasant to himself. "There is plenty of grass for him by our palings, and in the winter we could keep him in the room with us.

Perhaps it would be more profitable to have a sheep than a cow. Shall I exchange?"

The man with the sheep was quite ready, and the bargain was quickly made. And then our peasant continued his way on the high-road with his sheep. Soon after this, he overtook another man, who had come into the road from a field and was carrying a large goose under his arm.

"What a heavy creature you have there!" said the peasant; "it has plenty of feathers and plenty of fat, and would look well tied to a string or paddling in the water at our place. That would be very useful to my old woman; she could make all sorts of profits out of it. How often she has said, 'If now we only had a goose!' Now here is an opportunity, and, if possible, I will get it for her. Shall we exchange? I will give you my sheep for your goose and thanks into the bargain."

The other had not the least objection, and accordingly the exchange was made, and our peasant became possessor of the goose. By this time he had arrived very near the town. The crowd on the high road had been gradually increasing, and there was quite a rush of men and cattle. The cattle walked on the path and by the palings, and at the turnpike-gate they even walked into the toll-keeper's potato-field, where one fowl was strutting about with a string tied to its leg, for fear it should take fright at the crowd, and run away and get lost. The tail-feathers of the fowl were very short, and it winked with both its eyes, and looked very cunning, as it said, "Cluck, cluck."

What were the thoughts of the fowl as it said this I cannot tell you; but directly our good man saw it, he thought, "Why that's the finest fowl I ever saw in my life; it's finer than our parson's brood hen, upon my word. I should like to have that fowl. Fowls can always pick up a few grains that lie about and almost keep themselves. I think it would be a good exchange if I could get it for my goose. Shall we exchange?" he asked the toll-keeper.

"Exchange," repeated the man; "well, it would not be a bad thing."

And so they made an exchange,—the toll-keeper at the turnpike-gate kept the goose, and the peasant carried off the fowl. Now he had really done a great deal of business on his way to the fair, and he was hot and tired. He wanted something to eat and a glass of ale to refresh himself; so he turned his steps to an inn. He was just about to enter when the ostler came out, and they met at the door. The ostler was carrying a sack. "What have you in that sack?" asked the peasant.

"Rotten apples," answered the ostler; "a whole sackful of them. They will do to feed the pigs with."

"Why that will be terrible waste," he replied; "I should like to take them home to my old woman. Last year the old apple-tree by the grass-plot only bore one apple, and we kept it in the cupboard till it was quite withered and rotten. It was always property, my old woman said; and here she would see a great deal of property—a whole sackful; I should like to show them to her."

"What will you give me for the sackful?" asked the ostler.

"What will I give? Well, I will give you my fowl in exchange."

So he gave up the fowl and received the apples, which he carried into the inn parlour. He leaned the sack carefully against the stove and then went to the table. But the stove was hot, and he had not thought of that. Many guests were present—horse dealers, cattle drovers, and two Englishmen. The Englishmen were so rich that their pockets quite bulged out and seemed ready to burst; and they could bet too, as you shall hear. "Hiss-s-s, hiss-s-s." What could that be by the stove? The apples were beginning to roast. "What is that?" asked one.

"Why, do you know"—said our peasant. And then he told them the whole story of the horse, which he had exchanged for a cow, and all the rest of it, down to the apples.

"Well, your old woman will give it you well when you get home," said one of the Englishmen. "Won't there be a noise?"

"What! Give me what?" said the peasant. "Why, she will kiss me, and say, 'what the old man does is always right.'"

"Let us lay a wager on it," said the Englishman. "We'll wager you a ton of coined gold, a hundred pounds to the hundred-weight."

"No; a bushel will be enough," replied the peasant. "I can only set a bushel of apples against it, and I'll throw myself and my old woman into the bargain; that will pile up the measure, I fancy."

"Done! taken!" and so the bet was made.

Then the landlord's coach came to the door, and the two Englishmen and the peasant got in, and away they drove, and soon arrived and stopped at the peasant's hut. "Good evening, old woman." "Good evening, old man." "I've made the exchange."

"Ah, well, you understand what you're about," said the woman. Then she embraced him, and paid no attention to the strangers, nor did she notice the sack.

"I got a cow in exchange for the horse."

"Thank Heaven," said she. "Now we shall have plenty of milk, and butter, and cheese on the table. That was a capital exchange."

"Yes, but I changed the cow for a sheep."

"Ah, better still!" cried the wife. "You always think of everything; we have just enough pasture for a sheep. Ewe's milk and cheese, woollen jackets and stockings! The cow could not give all these, and her hair only falls off. How you think of everything!"

"But I changed away the sheep for a goose."

"Then we shall have roast goose to eat this year. You dear old man, you are always thinking of something to please me. This is delightful. We can let the goose walk about with a string tied to her leg, so she will be fatter still before we roast her."

"But I gave away the goose for a fowl."

"A fowl! Well, that was a good exchange," replied the woman. "The fowl will lay eggs and hatch them, and we shall have chickens; we shall soon have a poultry-yard. Oh, this is just what I was wishing for."

"Yes, but I exchanged the fowl for a sack of shrivelled apples."

"What! I must really give you a kiss for that!" exclaimed the wife. "My dear, good husband, now I'll tell you something. Do you know, almost as soon as you left me this morning, I began to think of what I could give you nice for supper this evening, and then I thought of fried eggs and bacon, with sweet herbs; I had eggs and bacon, but I wanted the herbs; so I went over to the schoolmaster's: I knew they had plenty of herbs, but the schoolmistress is very mean, although she can smile so sweetly. I begged her to lend me a handful of herbs. 'Lend!' she exclaimed, 'I have nothing to lend; nothing at all grows in our garden, not even a shrivelled apple; I could not even lend you a shrivelled apple, my dear woman.' But now I can lend her ten, or a whole sackful, which I'm very glad of; it makes me laugh to think about it;" and then she gave him a hearty kiss.

"Well, I like all this," said both the Englishmen; "always going down the hill and yet always merry; it's worth the money to see it." So they paid a hundred-weight of gold to the peasant, who, whatever he did, was not scolded but kissed.

Yes, it always pays best when the wife sees and maintains that her husband knows best and that whatever he does is right.

This is a story which I heard when I was a child; and now you have heard it too and know that "What the old man does is always right."

The Little Mermaid

AR out in the ocean, where the water is as blue as the prettiest cornflower and as clear as crystal, it is very, very deep; so deep, indeed, that no cable could fathom it: many church steeples, piled one upon another, would not reach from the ground beneath to the surface of the water above. There dwell the Sea King and his subjects.

We must not imagine that there is nothing at the bottom of the sea but bare yellow sand. No, indeed; the most singular flowers and plants grow there; the leaves and stems of which are so pliant that the slightest agitation of the water causes them to stir as if they had life. Fishes, both large and small, glide between the branches, as birds fly among the trees here upon land.

In the deepest spot of all, stands the castle of the Sea King. Its walls are built of coral, and the long, gothic windows are of the clearest amber. The roof is formed of shells, which open and close as the water flows over them. Their appearance is very beautiful, for in each lies a glittering pearl, which would be fit for the diadem of a queen.

The Sea King had been a widower for many years, and his aged mother kept house for him. She was a very wise woman and exceedingly proud of her high birth; on that account she wore twelve oysters on her tail; while others, also of high rank, were only allowed to wear six.

She was, however, deserving of very great praise, especially for her care of the little sea-princesses, her grand-daughters. They were six beautiful children; but the youngest was

the prettiest of them all: her skin was as clear and delicate as a rose-leaf, and her eyes as blue as the deepest sea. But, like all the others, she had no feet, and her body ended in a fish's tail.

All day long they played in the great halls of the castle or among the living flowers that grew out of the walls. The large amber windows were open, and the fish swam in, just as the swallows fly into our houses when we open the windows, excepting that the fishes swam up to the prin-

cesses, ate out of their hands, and allowed themselves to be stroked.

Outside the castle there was a beautiful garden, in which grew bright red and dark blue flowers and blossoms like flames of fire; the fruit glittered like gold, and the leaves and stems waved to and fro continually. The earth itself was the finest sand, but blue as the flame of burning sulphur.

Over everything lay a peculiar blue radiance, as if it were surrounded by the air from above, through which the blue sky shone, instead of the dark depths of the sea. In calm weather the sun could be seen, looking like a purple flower, with the light streaming from the calyx.

Each of the young princesses had a little plot of ground in the garden, where she might dig and plant as she pleased. One arranged her flower-bed into the form of a whale; an-

other thought it better to make hers like the figure of a little mermaid; but that of the youngest was round like the sun, and contained flowers as red as his rays at sunset.

She was a strange child, quiet and thoughtful; and while her sisters would be delighted with the wonderful things which they obtained from the wrecks of vessels, she cared for nothing but her pretty red flowers, like the sun, excepting a beautiful marble statue.

It was the representation of a handsome boy, carved out of pure white stone, which had fallen to the bottom of the sea from a wreck. She planted by the statue a rose-coloured weeping willow. It grew splendidly and very soon hung its fresh branches over the statue, almost down to the blue sands. The shadow had a violet tint and waved to and fro like the branches; it seemed as if the crown of the tree and the root were at play, and trying to kiss each other.

Nothing gave her so much pleasure as to hear about the world above the sea. She made her old grandmother tell her all she knew of the ships and of the towns, the people and the animals. To her it seemed most wonderful and beautiful to hear that the flowers of the land should have fragrance, and not those below the sea; that the trees of the forest should be green; and that the fishes among the trees could sing so sweetly, that it was quite a pleasure to hear them. Her grandmother called the little birds fishes, or she would not have understood her; for she had never seen birds.

"When you have reached your fifteenth year," said the grandmother, "you will have permission to rise up out of the sea, to sit on the rocks in the moonlight, while the great ships are sailing by; and then you will see both forests and towns."

In the following year, one of the sisters would be fifteen; but as each was a year younger than the other, the youngest would have to wait five years before her turn came to rise up from the bottom of the ocean and see the earth as we do.

However, each promised to tell the others what she saw on her first visit and what she thought the most beautiful; for their grandmother could not tell them enough; there were so many things on which they wanted information.

None of them longed so much for her turn to come as the youngest, she who had the longest time to wait and who was so quiet and thoughtful. Many nights she stood by the open window, looking up through the dark blue water and watching the fish as they splashed about with their fins and tails.

She could see the moon and stars shining faintly; but through the water they looked larger than they do to our eyes. When something like a black cloud passed between her and them, she knew that it was either a whale swimming over her head or a ship full of human beings, who never imagined that a pretty little mermaid was standing beneath them, holding out her white hands towards the keel of their ship.

As soon as the eldest was fifteen, she was allowed to rise to the surface of the ocean. When she came back, she had hundreds of things to talk about; but the most beautiful, she said, was to lie in the moonlight, on a sandbank, in the quiet sea, near the coast, and to gaze on a large town nearby, where the lights were twinkling like hundreds of stars; to listen to the sounds of the music, the noise of carriages, and the voices of human beings, and then to hear the merry bells peal out from the church steeples; and because she could not go near to all those wonderful things, she longed for them more than ever.

Oh, did not the youngest sister listen eagerly to all these descriptions? and afterwards, when she stood at the open window looking up through the dark blue water, she thought of the great city, with all its bustle and noise, and even fancied she could hear the sound of the church bells, down in the depths of the sea.

In another year, the second sister received permission to rise to the surface of the water and to swim about where she pleased. She rose just as the sun was setting, and this, she said, was the most beautiful sight of all. The whole sky looked like gold, while violet and rose-coloured clouds, which she could not describe, floated over her; and, still more rapidly than the clouds, flew a large flock of wild swans towards the setting sun, looking like a long white veil across the sea. She also swam towards the sun; but it sunk into the waves, and the rosy tints faded from the clouds and from the sea.

The third sister's turn followed; she was the boldest of them all, and she swam up a broad river that emptied itself into the sea. On the banks she saw green hills covered with beautiful vines; palaces and castles peeped out from amid the proud trees of the forest; she heard the birds singing, and the rays of the sun were so powerful that she was obliged often to dive down under the water to cool her burning face. In a narrow creek she found a whole troop of little human children, quite naked and sporting about in the water; she wanted to play with them, but they fled in a great fright; and then a little black animal came to the water; it was a dog, but she did not know that, for she had never be-

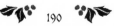

fore seen one. This animal barked at her so terribly that she became frightened and rushed back to the open sea. But she said she should never forget the beautiful forest, the green hills, and the pretty children who could swim in the water, although they had not fish's tails.

The fourth sister was more timid; she remained in the midst of the sea, but she said it was quite as beautiful there as nearer the land. She could see for so many miles around her, and the sky above looked like a bell of glass. She had seen the ships, but at such a great distance that they looked like sea-gulls. The dolphins sported in the waves, and the great whales spouted water from their nostrils till it seemed as if a hundred fountains were playing in every direction.

The fifth sister's birthday occurred in the winter; so when her turn came, she saw what the others had not seen the first time they went up. The sea looked quite green, and large icebergs were floating about, each like a pearl, she said, but larger and loftier than the churches built by men. They were of the most singular shapes and glittered like diamonds. She had seated herself upon one of the largest, and let the wind play with her long hair, and she remarked that all the ships sailed by rapidly and steered as far away as they could from the iceberg, as if they were afraid of it.

Towards evening, as the sun went down, dark clouds covered the sky, the thunder rolled and the lightning flashed, and the red light glowed on the icebergs as they rocked and tossed on the heaving sea. On all the ships the sails were reefed with fear and trembling, while she sat calmly on the floating iceberg, watching the blue lightning, as it darted its forked flashes into the sea.

When first the sisters had permission to rise to the surface, they were each delighted with the new and beautiful sights they saw; but now, as grown-up girls, they could go when they pleased, and they had become indifferent about it. They wished themselves back again in the water, and after a month had passed they said it was much more beautiful down below and pleasanter to be at home.

Yet often, in the evening hours, the five sisters would twine their arms round each other and rise to the surface, in a row. They had more beautiful voices than any human being could have; and before the approach of a storm and when they expected a ship would be lost, they swam before the vessel, and sang sweetly of the delights to be found in the depths of the sea, and begging the sailors not to fear if they sank to the bottom.

But the sailors could not understand the song; they took it for the howling of the storm. And these things were never to be beautiful for them; for if the ship sank, the men were drowned, and their dead bodies alone reached the palace of the Sea King.

When the sisters rose, arm-in-arm, through the water in this way, their youngest sister would stand quite alone, looking after them, ready to cry; only that the mermaids have no tears, and therefore they suffer more. "Oh, were I but fifteen years old," said she; "I know that I shall love the world up there, and all the people who live in it."

At last she reached her fifteenth year. "Well, now, you are grown up," said the old dowager, her grandmother; "so you must let me adorn you like your other sisters;" and she placed a wreath of white lilies in her hair, and every flower leaf was half a pearl. Then the old lady ordered eight great oysters to attach themselves to the tail of the princess to show her high rank.

"But they hurt me so," said the little mermaid.

"Pride must suffer pain," replied the old lady. Oh, how gladly she would have shaken off all this grandeur, and laid aside the heavy wreath! The red flowers in her own garden would have suited her much better, but she could not help herself; so she said, "Farewell," and rose as lightly as a bubble to the surface of the water.

The sun had just set as she raised her head above the waves; but the clouds were tinted with crimson and gold, and through the glimmering twilight beamed the evening star in all its beauty. The sea was calm, and the air mild and fresh. A large ship, with three masts, lay becalmed on the water, with only one sail set; for not a breeze stirred, and the sailors sat idle on deck or amongst the rigging. There was music and song on board; and, as darkness came on, a hundred coloured lanterns were lighted, as if the flags of all nations waved in the air.

The little mermaid swam close to the cabin windows; and now and then, as the waves lifted her up, she could look in through clear glass window-panes and see a number of well-dressed people within. Among them was a young prince, the most beautiful of all, with large black eyes; he was sixteen years of age, and his birthday was being kept with much rejoicing.

The sailors were dancing on deck, but when the prince came out of the cabin, more than a hundred rockets rose in the air, making it as bright as day. The little mermaid

was so startled that she dived under water; and when she again stretched out her head, it appeared as if all the stars of heaven were falling around her, she had never seen such fireworks before. Great suns spurted fire about, splendid fireflies flew into the blue air, and everything was reflected in the clear, calm sea beneath. The ship itself was so brightly illuminated that all the people, and even the smallest rope, could be distinctly and plainly seen. And how handsome the young prince looked, as he pressed the hands of all present and smiled at them, while the music resounded through the clear night air.

It was very late; yet the little mermaid could not take her eyes from the ship or from the beautiful prince. The coloured lanterns had been extinguished, no more rockets rose in the air, and the cannon had ceased firing; but the sea became restless, and a moaning, grumbling sound could be heard beneath the waves; still the little mermaid remained by the cabin window, rocking up and down on the water, which enabled her to look in.

After a while, the sails were quickly unfurled, and the noble ship continued her passage; but soon the waves rose higher, heavy clouds darkened the sky, and lightning appeared in the distance. A dreadful storm was approaching; once more the sails were reefed, and the great ship pursued her flying course over the raging sea.

The waves rose mountains high, as if they would have overtopped the mast; but the ship dived like a swan between them, and then rose again on their lofty, foaming crests.

To the little mermaid this appeared pleasant sport; not so to the sailors. At length the ship groaned and creaked; the thick planks gave way under the lashing of the sea as it broke over the deck; the mainmast snapped asunder like a reed; the ship lay over on her side; and the water rushed in.

The little mermaid now perceived that the crew was in danger; even she herself was obliged to be careful to avoid the beams and planks of the wreck which lay scattered on the water. At one moment it was so pitch dark that she could not see a single object, but a flash of lightning revealed the whole scene; she could see every one who had been on board excepting the prince. When the ship parted, she had seen him sink into the deep waves, and she was glad, for she thought he would now be with her; and then she remembered that human beings could not live in the water, so that when he got down to her father's palace he would be quite dead. But he must not die. So she swam about among the beams and planks which strewed the surface of the sea, forgetting that they could crush her to pieces. Then she dived deeply under the dark waters, rising and falling with the waves, till at length she managed to reach the young prince, who was fast losing the power of swimming in that stormy sea. His limbs were failing him, his beautiful eyes were closed, and he would have died had not the little mermaid come to his assistance. She held his head above the water, and let the waves drift them where they would.

In the morning the storm had ceased; but of the ship not a single fragment could be seen. The sun rose up red and glowing from the water, and its beams brought back the hue of health to the prince's cheeks; but his eyes remained closed. The mermaid kissed his high, smooth forehead, and stroked back his wet hair; he seemed to her like the marble statue in her little garden, and she kissed him again, and wished that he might live.

Presently they came in sight of land; she saw lofty blue mountains, on which the white snow rested as if a flock of swans were lying upon them. Near the coast were beautiful green forests, and close by stood a large building, whether a church or a convent she could not tell. Orange and citron trees grew in the garden, and before the door stood lofty palms. The sea here formed a little bay, in which the water was quite still, but very deep; so she swam with the handsome prince to the beach, which was covered with fine, white sand, and there she laid him in the warm sunshine, taking care to raise his head higher than his body.

Then bells sounded in the large white building, and a number of young girls came into the garden. The little mermaid swam out farther from the shore and placed herself between some high rocks that rose out of the water; then she covered her head and neck with the foam of the sea so that her little face might not be seen and watched to see what would become of the poor prince.

She did not wait long before she saw a young girl approach the spot where he lay. She seemed frightened at first, but only for a moment; then she fetched a number of people, and the mermaid saw that the prince came to life again and smiled upon those who stood round him.

But to her he sent no smile; he knew not that she had saved him. This made her very unhappy, and when he was led away into the great building, she dived down sorrowfully into the water and returned to her father's castle.

She had always been silent and thoughtful, and now she was more so than ever. Her sisters asked her what she had seen during her first visit to the surface of the water; but she would tell them nothing.

Many an evening and morning did she rise to the place where she had left the prince. She saw the fruits in the garden ripen till they were gathered, the snow on the tops of the mountains melt away; but she never saw the prince, and therefore she returned home, always more sorrowful than before.

It was her only comfort to sit in her own little garden and fling her arm round the beautiful marble statue, which was like the prince; but she gave up tending her flowers, and they grew in wild confusion over the paths, twining their long leaves and stems round the branches of the trees, so that the whole place became dark and gloomy.

At length she could bear it no longer, and told one of her sisters all about it. Then the others heard the secret, and very soon it became known to two mermaids whose intimate friend happened to know who the prince was. She had also seen the festival on board ship, and she told them where the prince came from, and where his palace stood.

"Come, little sister," said the other princesses; then they entwined their arms and rose up in a long row to the surface of the water, close by the spot where they knew the prince's palace stood.

It was built of bright yellow shining stone, with long flights of marble steps, one of which reached quite down to the sea. Splendid gilded cupolas rose over the roof, and between the pillars that surrounded the whole building stood life-like statues of marble. Through the clear crystal of the lofty windows could be seen noble rooms, with costly silk curtains and hangings of tapestry; while the walls were covered with

beautiful paintings, which were a pleasure to look at. In the centre of the largest saloon a fountain threw its sparkling jets high up into the glass cupola of the ceiling, through which the sun shone down upon the water and upon the beautiful plants growing round the basin of the fountain.

Now that she knew where he lived, she spent many an evening and many a night on the water near the palace. She would swim much nearer the shore than any of the others ventured to do. Indeed once she went quite up the narrow channel under the marble balcony, which threw a broad shadow on the water. Here she would sit and watch the young prince, who thought himself quite alone in the bright moonlight.

She saw him many times of an evening sailing in a pleasant boat, with music playing and flags waving. She peeped out from among the green rushes, and if the wind caught her long silvery-white veil, those who saw it believed it to be a swan, spreading out its wings.

On many a night, too, when the fishermen, with their torches, were out at sea, she heard them relate so many good things about the doings of the young prince, that she was glad she had saved his life when he had been tossed about half-dead on the waves. And she remembered that his head had rested on her bosom and how heartily she had kissed him; but he knew nothing of all this and could not even dream of her.

She grew more and more fond of human beings and wished more and more to be able to wander about with those whose world seemed to be so much larger than her own. They could fly over the sea in ships and mount the high hills which were far above the clouds; and the lands they possessed, their woods and their fields, stretched far away beyond the reach of her sight.

There was so much that she wished to know, and her sisters were unable to answer all her questions. Then she applied to her old grandmother, who knew all about the upper world, which she very rightly called the lands above the sea.

"If human beings are not drowned," asked the little mermaid, "can they live forever? do they never die as we do here in the sea?"

"Yes," replied the old lady, "they must also die, and their term of life is even shorter than ours. We sometimes live to three hundred years, but when we cease to exist here we only become the foam on the surface of the water, and we have not even a grave down here of those we love. We have not immortal souls, we shall never live again; but, like the green sea-weed, when once it has been cut off, we can never flourish more. Human beings, on the contrary, have a soul which lives forever, lives after the body has been turned to dust. It rises up through the clear, pure air beyond the glittering stars. As we rise out of the water, and behold all the land of the earth, so do they rise to unknown and glorious regions which we shall never see."

"Why have not we an immortal soul?" asked the little mermaid mournfully; "I would give gladly all the hundreds of years that I have to live, to be a human being only for one day, and to have the hope of knowing the happiness of that glorious world above the stars."

"You must not think of that," said the old woman; "we feel ourselves to be much happier and much better off than human beings."

"So I shall die," said the little mermaid, "and as the foam of the sea I shall be driven about never again to hear the music of the waves, or to see the pretty flowers nor the red sun. Is there anything I can do to win an immortal soul?"

"No," said the old woman, "unless a man were to love you so much that you were more to him than his father or mother; and if all his thoughts and all his love were fixed upon you, and the priest placed his right hand in yours, and he promised to be true to you here and hereafter, then his soul would glide into your body and you would obtain a share in the future happiness of mankind. He would give a soul to you and retain his own as well; but this can never happen. Your fish's tail, which amongst us is considered so beautiful, is thought on earth to be quite ugly; they do not know any better, and they think it necessary to have two stout props, which they call legs, in order to be handsome."

Then the little mermaid sighed and looked sorrowfully at her fish's tail. "Let us be happy," said the old lady, "and dart and spring about during the three hundred years that we have to live, which is really quite long enough; after that we can rest ourselves all the better. This evening we are going to have a court ball."

It was one of those splendid sights which we can never see on earth. The walls and the ceiling of the large ball-room were of thick, but transparent crystal. Many hundreds of colossal shells, some of a deep red, others of a grass green, stood on each side in rows, with blue fire in them, which lighted up the whole saloon, and shone through the walls, so that the sea was also illuminated. Innumerable fishes, great and small, swam past the crystal walls; on some of them the scales glowed with a purple brilliancy, and on others they shone like silver and gold.

Through the halls flowed a broad stream, and in it danced the mermen and the mermaids to the music of their own sweet singing. No one on earth has such a lovely voice as theirs. The little mermaid sang more sweetly than them all. The whole court applauded her with hands and tails; and for a moment her heart felt quite gay, for she knew she had the loveliest voice of any on earth or in the sea. But she soon thought again of the world above her, for she could not forget the charming prince, nor her sorrow that she had not an immortal soul like his. Therefore she crept away silently out of her father's palace, and while everything within was gladness and song, she sat in her own little garden sorrowful and alone.

Then she heard the bugle sounding through the water and thought: "He is certainly sailing above, he on whom my wishes depend, and in whose hands I should like to place the happiness of my life. I will venture all for him, and to win an immortal soul; while my sisters are dancing in my father's palace, I will go to the sea witch, of whom I have always been so much afraid, but she can give me counsel and help."

And then the little mermaid went out from her garden and took the road to the foaming whirlpools, behind which the sorceress lived. She had never been that way before: neither flowers nor grass grew there; nothing but bare, gray, sandy ground stretched out to the whirlpool, where the water, like foaming mill-wheels, whirled round everything that it seized, and cast it into the fathomless deep.

Through the midst of these crushing whirlpools the little mermaid was obliged to pass, to reach the dominions of the sea witch; and also for a long distance the only road lay right across a quantity of warm, bubbling mire, called by the witch her turf-moor.

Beyond this stood her house, in the centre of a strange forest, in which all the trees and flowers were polypi, half animals and half plants; they looked like serpents with a hundred heads growing out of the ground. The branches were long slimy arms, with fingers like flexible worms, moving limb after limb from the root to the top. All that could be reached in the sea they seized upon, and held fast, so that it never escaped from their clutches.

The little mermaid was so alarmed at what she saw, that she stood still, and her heart beat with fear, and she was very nearly turning back; but she thought of the prince, and of the human soul for which she longed, and her courage returned.

She fastened her long flowing hair round her head, so that the polypi might not seize hold of it. She laid her hands together across her bosom, and then she darted forward as a fish shoots through the water, between the supple arms and fingers of the ugly polypi, which were stretched out on each side of her.

She saw that each held in its grasp something it had seized with its numerous little arms, as if they were iron bands. The white skeletons of human beings who had perished at sea and had sunk down into the deep waters, skeletons of land animals, oars, rudders, and chests of ships were lying tightly grasped by their clinging arms; even a little mermaid, whom they had caught and strangled; and this seemed the most shocking of all to the little princess.

She now came to a space of marshy ground in the wood, where large, fat water-snakes were rolling in the mire and showing their ugly, drab-coloured bodies. In the midst of this spot stood a house, built with the bones of shipwrecked human beings. There sat the sea witch, allowing a toad to eat from her mouth, just as people sometimes feed a canary with a piece of sugar. She called the ugly water-snakes her little chickens and allowed them to crawl all over her bosom.

"I know what you want," said the sea witch; "it is very stupid of you, but you shall have your way, and it will bring you to sorrow, my pretty princess. You want to get rid of your fish's tail and to have two supports instead of it, like human beings on earth, so that the young prince may fall in love with you and that you may have an immortal soul." And then the witch laughed so loud and disgustingly, that the toad and the snakes fell to the ground and lay there wriggling about.

"You are but just in time," said the witch; "for after sunrise tomorrow I should not be able to help you till the end of another year. I will prepare a draught for you, with which you must swim to land tomorrow before sunrise and sit down on the shore and drink it. Your tail will then disappear and shrink up into what mankind calls legs; and you will feel great pain, as if a sword were passing through you. But all who see you will say that you are the prettiest little human being they ever saw. You will still have the same floating gracefulness of movement, and no dancer will ever tread so lightly; but at every step you take it will feel as if you were treading upon sharp knives, and that the blood must flow. If you will bear all this, I will help you."

"Yes, I will," said the little princess in a trembling voice, as she thought of the prince and the immortal soul.

"But think again," said the witch; "for when once your shape has become like a human being, you can no more be a mermaid. You will never return through the water to your sisters or to your father's palace again; and if you do not win the love of the prince, so that he is willing to forget his father and mother for your sake, and to love you with his whole soul, and allow the priest to join your hands that you may be man and wife, then you will never have an immortal soul. The first morning after he marries another your heart will break, and you will become foam on the crest of the waves."

"I will do it," said the little mermaid, and she became pale as death.

"But I must be paid also," said the witch, "and it is not a trifle that I ask. You have the sweetest voice of any who dwell here in the depths of the sea, and you believe that you will be able to charm the prince with it also, but this voice you must give to me; the best thing you possess will I have for the price of my draught. My own blood must be mixed with it, that it may be as sharp as a two-edged sword."

"But if you take away my voice," said the little mermaid, "what is left for me?"

"Your beautiful form, your graceful walk, and your expressive eyes; surely with these you can enchain a man's heart. Well, have you lost your courage? Put out your little tongue that I may cut it off as my payment; then you shall have the powerful draught."

"It shall be," said the little mermaid.

Then the witch placed her cauldron on the fire, to prepare the magic draught.

"Cleanliness is a good thing," said she, scouring the vessel with snakes, which she had tied together in a large knot; then she pricked herself in the breast, and let the black blood drop into it. The steam that rose formed itself into such horrible shapes that no one could look at them without fear.

Every moment the witch threw something else into the vessel, and when it began to boil, the sound was like the weeping of a crocodile. When at last the magic draught was

ready, it looked like the clearest water. "There it is for you," said the witch.

Then she cut off the mermaid's tongue, so that she became dumb and would never again speak or sing. "If the polypi should seize hold of you as you return through the wood," said the witch, "throw over them a few drops of the potion, and their fingers will be torn into a thousand pieces." But the little mermaid had no occasion to do this, for the polypi sprang back in terror when they caught sight of the glittering draught, which shone in her hand like a twinkling star.

So she passed quickly through the wood and the marsh, and between the rushing whirlpools. She saw that in her father's palace the torches in the ballroom were extinguished and all within asleep; but she did not venture to go in to them, for now she was dumb and going to leave them forever, she felt as if her heart would break. She stole into the garden, took a flower from the flower-beds of each of her sisters, kissed her hand a thousand times towards the palace, and then rose up through the dark blue waters.

The sun had not risen when she came in sight of the prince's palace and approached the beautiful marble steps, but the moon shone clear and bright. Then the little mermaid drank the magic draught, and it seemed as if a two-edged sword went through her delicate body; she fell into a swoon and lay like one dead.

When the sun arose and shone over the sea, she recovered and felt a sharp pain; but just before her stood the handsome young prince. He fixed his coal-black eyes upon her so earnestly that she cast down her own, and then became aware that her fish's tail was gone, and that she had as pretty a pair of white legs and tiny feet as any little maiden could have; but she had no clothes, so she wrapped herself in her long, thick hair.

The prince asked her who she was and where she came from, and she looked at him mildly and sorrowfully with her deep blue eyes; but she could not speak. Then he took her by the hand, and led her to the palace. Every step she took was as the witch had said it would be, she felt as if treading upon the points of needles or sharp knives; but she bore it willingly and stepped as lightly by the prince's side as a soap-bubble, so that he and all who saw her wondered at her graceful, swaying movements. She was very soon arrayed in costly robes of silk and muslin and was the most beautiful creature in the palace; but she was dumb and could neither speak nor sing.

Beautiful female slaves, dressed in silk and gold, stepped forward and sang before the prince and his royal parents. One sang better than all the others, and the prince clapped his hands and smiled at her. This was great sorrow to the little mermaid; she knew how much more sweetly she herself could sing once, and she thought, "Oh if he could only know that! I have given away my voice forever, to be with him."

The slaves next performed some pretty fairy-like dances, to the sound of beautiful music. Then the little mermaid raised her lovely white arms, stood on the tips of her toes, and glided over the floor, and danced as no one yet had been able to dance. At each moment her beauty became more revealed, and her expressive eyes appealed more directly to the heart than the songs of the slaves. Everyone was enchanted, especially the prince, who called her his little foundling; and she danced again quite readily, to please him, though each time her foot touched the floor it seemed as if she trod on sharp knives.

The prince said she should remain with him always, and she received permission to sleep at his door, on a velvet cushion. He had a page's dress made for her, that she might accompany him on horseback. They rode together through the sweet-scented woods, where the green boughs touched their shoulders and the little birds sang among the fresh leaves.

She climbed with the prince to the tops of high mountains; and although her tender feet bled so that even her steps were marked, she only laughed and followed him till they could see the clouds beneath them looking like a flock of birds travelling to distant lands. While at the prince's palace, and when all the household were asleep, she would go and sit on the broad marble steps; for it eased her burning feet to bathe them in the cold sea-water; and then she thought of all those below in the deep.

Once during the night her sisters came up arm-in-arm, singing sorrowfully, as they floated on the water. She beckoned to them, and then they recognized her and told her how she had grieved them. After that, they came to the same place every night; and once she saw in the distance her old grandmother, who had not been to the surface of the sea for many years, and the old Sea King, her father, with his crown on his head. They stretched out their hands towards her, but they did not venture so near the land as her sisters did.

As the days passed, she loved the prince more fondly, and he loved her as he would love a little child, but it never came into his head to make her his wife; yet, unless he married her, she could not receive an immortal soul; and, on the morning after his marriage with another, she would dissolve into the foam of the sea.

"Do you not love me the best of them all?" the eyes of the little mermaid seemed to say, when he took her in his arms and kissed her fair forehead.

"Yes, you are dear to me," said the prince; "for you have the best heart and you are the most devoted to me; you are like a young maiden whom I once saw, but whom I shall never meet again. I was in a ship that was wrecked, and the waves cast me ashore near a holy temple, where several young maidens performed the service. The youngest of them found me on the shore and saved my life. I saw her but twice, and she is the only one in the world whom I could love; but you are like her, and you have almost driven her image out of my mind. She belongs to the holy temple, and my good fortune has sent you to me instead of her; and we will never part."

"Ah, he knows not that it was I who saved his life," thought the little mermaid. "I carried him over the sea to the wood where the temple stands; I sat beneath the foam, and watched till the human beings came to help him. I saw the pretty maiden that he loves better than he loves me;" and the mermaid sighed deeply, but she could not shed tears. "He says the maiden belongs to the holy temple, therefore she will never return to the world. They will meet no more,

while I am by his side and see him every day. I will take care of him, and love him, and give up my life for his sake."

Very soon it was said that the prince must marry and that the beautiful daughter of a neighbouring king would be his wife, for a fine ship was being fitted out. Although the prince gave out that he merely intended to pay a visit to the king, it was generally supposed that he really went to see his daughter. A great company was to go with him. The little mermaid smiled and shook her head. She knew the prince's thoughts better than any of the others.

"I must travel," he had said to her; "I must see this beautiful princess: my parents desire it; but they will not oblige me to bring her home as my bride. I cannot love her; she is not like the beautiful maiden in the temple, whom you resemble. If I were forced to choose a bride, I would rather choose you, my dumb foundling, with those expressive eyes." And then he kissed her rosy mouth, played with her long waving hair, and laid his head on her heart, while she dreamed of human happiness and an immortal soul.

"You are not afraid of the sea, my dumb child," said he, as they stood on the deck of the noble ship which was to carry them to the country of the neighbouring king. And then he told her of storm and of calm, of strange fishes in the deep beneath them, and of what the divers had seen there; and she smiled at his descriptions, for she knew better than anyone what wonders were at the bottom of the sea.

In the moonlight, when all on board were asleep, excepting the man at the helm, who was steering, she sat on the deck, gazing down through the clear water. She thought she could distinguish her father's castle and upon it her aged grandmother, with the silver crown on her head, looking through the rushing tide at the keel of the vessel. Then her sisters came up on the waves and gazed at her mournfully, wringing their white hands. She beckoned to them, and smiled, and wanted to tell them how happy and well off she was; but the cabin-boy approached, and when her sisters dived down he thought it was only the foam of the sea which he saw.

The next morning the ship sailed into the harbour of a beautiful town belonging to the king whom the prince was going to visit. The church bells were ringing, and from the high towers sounded a flourish of trumpets; and soldiers, with flying colours and glittering bayonets, lined the roads through which they passed. Every day was a festival; balls and entertainments followed one another.

But the princess had not yet appeared. People said that she was being brought up and educated in a religious house, where she was learning every royal virtue. At last she came. Then the little mermaid, who was very anxious to see whether she was really beautiful, was obliged to acknowledge that she had never seen a more perfect vision of beauty. Her skin was delicately fair, and beneath her long dark eye-lashes her laughing blue eyes shone with truth and purity.

"It was you," said the prince, "who saved my life when I lay dead on the beach," and he folded his blushing bride in his arms. "Oh, I am too happy," said he to the little mermaid; "my fondest hopes are all fulfilled. You will rejoice at my happiness; for your devotion to me is great and sincere."

The little mermaid kissed his hand and felt as if her heart were already broken. His wedding morning would bring death to her, and she would change into the foam of the sea.

All the church bells rung, and the heralds rode about the town proclaiming the betrothal. Perfumed oil was burning in costly silver lamps on every altar. The priests waved the censers, while the bride and bridegroom joined their hands and received the blessing of the bishop.

The little mermaid, dressed in silk and gold, held up the bride's train; but her ears heard nothing of the festive music, and her eyes saw not the holy ceremony; she thought of the night of death which was coming to her and of all she had lost in the world.

On the same evening the bride and bridegroom went on board ship; cannons were roaring, flags waving, and in the centre of the ship a costly tent of purple and gold had been erected. It contained elegant couches, for the reception of the bridal pair during the night. The ship, with swelling sails and a favourable wind, glided away smoothly and lightly over the calm sea. When it grew dark, a number of coloured lamps were lit and the sailors danced merrily on the deck.

The little mermaid could not help thinking of her first rising out of the sea, when she had seen similar festivities and joys; and she joined in the dance, poised herself in the air as a swallow when he pursues his prey, and all present cheered her with wonder.

She had never danced so elegantly before. Her tender feet felt as if cut with sharp knives, but she cared not for it; a sharper pang had pierced through her heart. She knew this was the last evening she should ever see the prince, for whom she had forsaken her kindred and her home; she had given up her beautiful voice and suffered unheard-of pain daily for him, while he knew nothing of it. This was the last evening that she would breathe the same air with him or gaze on the starry sky and the deep sea; an eternal night, without a thought or a dream, awaited her: she had no soul, and now she could never win one.

All was joy and gayety on board ship till long after midnight; she laughed and danced with the rest, while the thoughts of death were in her heart. The prince kissed his beautiful bride, while she played with his raven hair, till they went arm-in-arm to rest in the splendid tent. Then all became still on board the ship; the helmsman, alone awake, stood at the helm.

The little mermaid leaned her white arms on the edge of the vessel and looked towards the east for the first blush of morning, for that first ray of the dawn that would bring her death. She saw her sisters rising out of the flood: they were as pale as herself; but their long beautiful hair waved no more in the wind: it had been cut off.

"We have given our hair to the witch," said they, "to obtain help for you, that you may not die tonight. She has given us a knife: here it is, see it is very sharp. Before the sun rises you must plunge it into the heart of the prince; when the warm blood falls upon your feet they will grow together again and form into a fish's tail, and you will be once more a mermaid and return to us to live out your three hundred years before you die and change into the salt sea foam. Haste, then; he or you must die before sunrise. Our old grandmother mourns so for you, that her white hair is falling off from sorrow, as ours fell under the witch's scissors. Kill the prince and come back; hasten: do you not see the first red streaks in the sky? In a few minutes the sun will rise, and you must die." And then they sighed deeply and mournfully, and sank down beneath the waves.

The little mermaid drew back the crimson curtain of the tent and beheld the fair bride with her head resting on the prince's breast. She bent down and kissed his fair brow, then looked at the sky on which the rosy dawn grew brighter and brighter; then she glanced at the sharp knife, and again fixed her eyes on the prince, who whispered the name of his bride in his dreams. She was in his thoughts, and the knife trembled in the hand of the little mermaid. Then she flung it far away from her into the waves; the water turned red where it fell, and the drops that spurted up looked like blood. She cast one more lingering, half-fainting glance at

the prince, and then threw herself from the ship into the sea and thought her body was dissolving into foam.

The sun rose above the waves, and his warm rays fell on the cold foam of the little mermaid, who did not feel as if she were dying. She saw the bright sun, and all around her floated hundreds of transparent beautiful beings; she could see through them the white sails of the ship and the red clouds in the sky. Their speech was melodious, but too ethereal to be heard by mortal ears, as they were also unseen by mortal eyes.

The little mermaid perceived that she had a body like theirs and that she continued to rise higher and higher out of the foam. "Where am I?" asked she, and her voice sounded ethereal, as the voice of those who were with her; no earthly music could imitate it.

"Among the daughters of the air," answered one of them. "A mermaid has not an immortal soul, nor can she obtain one unless she wins the love of a human being. On the power of another hangs her eternal destiny. But the daughters of the air, although they do not possess an immortal soul, can, by their good deeds, procure one for themselves. We fly to warm countries and cool the sultry air that destroys mankind with the pestilence. We carry the perfume of the flowers to spread health and restoration. After we have striven for three hundred years to do all the good in our power, we receive an immortal soul and take part in the happiness of mankind. You, poor little mermaid, have tried with your whole heart to do as we are doing; you have suffered and endured and raised yourself to the spirit-world by your good deeds; and now, by striving for three hundred years in the same way, you may obtain an immortal soul."

The little mermaid lifted her glorified eyes towards the sun and felt them, for the first time, filling with tears. On the ship, in which she had left the prince, there were life and noise; she saw him and his beautiful bride searching for her; sorrowfully they gazed at the pearly foam, as if they knew she had thrown herself into the waves. Unseen she kissed the forehead of the bride and fanned the prince, and then mounted with the other children of the air to a rosy cloud that floated through the aether.

The Travelling Companion

POOR John was very sad; for his father was so ill, he
had no hope of his recovery. John sat alone with the
sick man in the little room, and the lamp had nearly
burnt out; for it was late in the night.

"You have been a good son, John," said the sick father,
"and God will help you on in the world." He looked at him,
as he spoke, with mild, earnest eyes, drew a deep sigh, and
died; yet it appeared as if he still slept.

John wept bitterly. He had no one in the wide world now;
neither father, mother, brother, nor sister. Poor John! he
knelt down by the bed, kissed his dead father's hand, and
wept many, many bitter tears. But at last his eyes closed,
and he fell asleep with his head resting against the hard
bedpost. Then he dreamed a strange dream; he thought he
saw the sun shining upon him, and his father alive and
well, and even heard him laughing as he used to do when
he was very happy. A beautiful girl, with a golden crown on
her head, and long shining hair, gave him her hand; and
his father said, "See what a bride you have won. She is the
loveliest maiden on the whole earth." Then he awoke, and all
the beautiful things vanished before his eyes; his father lay
dead on the bed, and he was all alone. Poor John!

During the following week the dead man was buried. The
son walked behind the coffin which contained his father,
whom he so dearly loved and would never again behold. He
heard the earth fall on the coffin-lid and watched it till only a
corner remained in sight, and at last that also disappeared.
He felt as if his heart would break with its weight of sorrow,
till those who stood round the grave sang a psalm, and the
sweet, holy tones brought tears into his eyes, which relieved

him. The sun shone brightly down on the green trees, as if it would say, "You must not be so sorrowful, John. Do you see the beautiful blue sky above you? Your father is up there, and he prays to the loving Father of all, that you may do well in the future."

"I will always be good," said John, "and then I shall go to be with my father in heaven. What joy it will be when we see each other again! How much I shall have to relate to him, and how many things he will be able to explain to me of the delights of heaven, and teach me as he once did on earth. Oh, what joy it will be!"

He pictured it all so plainly to himself that he smiled even while the tears ran down his cheeks.

The little birds in the chestnut-trees twittered, "Tweet, tweet;" they were so happy, although they had seen the funeral; but they seemed as if they knew that the dead man was now in heaven and that he had wings much larger and more beautiful than their own, that he was happy now because he had been good here on earth, and they were glad of it. John saw them fly away out of the green trees into the wide world, and he longed to fly with them; but first he cut out a large wooden cross to place on his father's grave; and when he brought it there in the evening, he found the grave decked out with gravel and flowers. Strangers had done this; they who had known the good old father who was now dead and who had loved him very much.

Early the next morning, John packed up his little bundle of clothes and placed all his money, which consisted of fifty dollars and a few shillings, in his girdle; with this he determined to try his fortune in the world. But first he went into the churchyard; and, by his father's grave, he offered up a prayer and said, "Farewell."

As he passed through the fields, all the flowers looked fresh and beautiful in the warm sunshine and nodded in the wind, as if they wished to say, "Welcome to the green wood, where all is fresh and bright."

Then John turned to have one more look at the old church, in which he had been christened in his infancy and where his father had taken him every Sunday to hear the service and join in singing the psalms. As he looked at the old tower, he espied the ringer standing at one of the narrow openings, with his little pointed red cap on his head and shading his eyes from the sun with his bent arm. John nodded farewell to him, and the little ringer waved his red cap, laid his hand on his heart, and kissed his hand to him

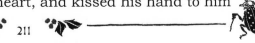

a great many times, to show that he felt kindly towards him and wished him a prosperous journey.

John continued his journey and thought of all the wonderful things he should see in the large beautiful world, till he found himself farther away from home than ever he had been before. He did not even know the names of the places he passed through and could scarcely understand the language of the people he met, for he was far away, in a strange land. The first night he slept on a haystack, out in the fields, for there was no other bed for him; but it seemed to him so nice and comfortable that even a king need not wish for a better. The field, the brook, the haystack, with the blue sky above, formed a beautiful sleeping-room. The green grass, with the little red and white flowers, was the carpet; the elder-bushes and the hedges of wild roses looked like garlands on the walls; and for a bath he could have the clear, fresh water of the brook; while the rushes bowed their heads to him, to wish him good morning and good evening. The moon, like a large lamp, hung high up in the blue ceiling, and he had no fear of its setting fire to his curtains. John slept here quite safely all night; and when he awoke, the sun was up, and all the little birds were singing round him, "Good morning, good morning. Are you not up yet?"

It was Sunday, and the bells were ringing for church. As the people went in, John followed them; he heard God's word, joined in singing the psalms, and listened to the preacher. It seemed to him just as if he were in his own church, where he had been christened and had sung the psalms with his father. Out in the churchyard were several graves, and on some of them the grass had grown very high. John thought of his father's grave, which he knew at last would look like these, as he was not there to weed and attend to it. Then he set to work, pulled up the high grass, raised the wooden crosses which had fallen down, and replaced the wreaths which had been blown away from their places by the wind, thinking all the time, "Perhaps someone is doing the same for my father's grave, as I am not there to do it."

Outside the church door stood an old beggar, leaning on his crutch. John gave him his silver shillings, and then he continued his journey, feeling lighter and happier than ever. Towards evening, the weather became very stormy, and he hastened on, as quickly as he could, to get shelter; but it was quite dark by the time he reached a little lonely church, which stood on a hill. "I will go in here," he said, "and sit down in a corner; for I am quite tired and want rest."

So he went in and seated himself; then he folded his hands and offered up his evening prayer, and was soon fast asleep and dreaming, while the thunder rolled and the lightning flashed without. When he awoke, it was still night; but the storm had ceased, and the moon shone in upon him through the windows. Then he saw an open coffin standing in the centre of the church, which contained a dead man, waiting for burial. John was not at all timid; he had a good conscience, and he knew also that the dead can never injure anyone. It is living wicked men who do harm to others. Two such wicked persons stood now by the dead man, who had been brought to the church to be buried. Their evil intentions were to throw the poor dead body outside the church door, and not leave him to rest in his coffin.

"Why do you do this?" asked John, when he saw what they were going to do; "it is very wicked. Leave him to rest in peace, in Christ's name."

"Nonsense," replied the two dreadful men. "He has cheated us; he owed us money which he could not pay, and now he is dead we shall not get a penny; so we mean to have our revenge, and let him lie like a dog outside the church door."

"I have only fifty dollars," said John, "it is all I possess in the world, but I will give it to you if you will promise me faithfully to leave the dead man in peace. I shall be able to get on without the money; I have strong and healthy limbs, and God will always help me."

"Why, of course," said the horrid men, "if you will pay his debt we will both promise not to touch him. You may depend upon that;" and then they took the money he offered them, laughed at him for his good nature, and went their way.

Then he laid the dead body back in the coffin, folded the hands, and took leave of it; and went away contentedly through the great forest. All around him he could see were the prettiest little elves dancing in the moonlight, which shone through the trees. They were not disturbed by his appearance, for they knew he was good and harmless among men. They are wicked people only who can never obtain a glimpse of fairies. Some of them were not taller than the breadth of a finger, and they wore golden combs in their long yellow hair. They were rocking themselves two together on the large dew-drops with which the leaves and the high grass were sprinkled. Sometimes the dew-drops would roll away, and then they fell down between the stems of the long grass, and caused a great deal of laughing and noise among the other little people. It was quite charming to watch them at play. Then they sang songs, and John remembered that he had learnt those pretty songs when he was a little boy.

Large speckled spiders, with silver crowns on their heads, were employed to spin suspension bridges and palaces from one hedge to another, and when the tiny drops fell upon them, they glittered in the moonlight like shining glass. This continued till sunrise. Then the little elves crept into the flower-buds, and the wind seized the bridges and palaces, and fluttered them in the air like cobwebs.

As John left the wood, a strong man's voice called after him, "Hallo, comrade, where are you travelling?"

"Into the wide world," he replied; "I am only a poor lad, I have neither father nor mother, but God will help me."

"I am going into the wide world also," replied the stranger; "shall we keep each other company?"

"With all my heart," said he, and so they went on together. Soon they began to like each other very much, for they were both good; but John found out that the stranger was much more clever than himself. He had travelled all over the world, and could describe almost everything. The sun was high in the heavens when they seated themselves under a large tree to eat their breakfast, and at the same moment an old woman came towards them. She was very old and almost bent double. She leaned upon a stick and carried on her back a bundle of firewood, which she had collected in the forest; her apron was tied round it, and John saw three great stems of fern and some willow twigs peeping out. Just as she came close up to them, her foot slipped and she fell to the ground screaming loudly: poor old woman, she had broken her leg! John proposed directly that they should carry the old woman home to her cottage; but the stranger opened his knapsack and took out a box, in which he said he had a salve that would quickly make her leg well and strong again, so that she would be able to walk home herself, as if her leg had never been broken. And all that he would ask in return was the three fern stems which she carried in her apron.

"That is rather too high a price," said the old woman, nodding her head quite strangely. She did not seem at all inclined to part with the fern stems. However, it was not very agreeable to lie there with a broken leg, so she gave them to him; and such was the power of the ointment, that no sooner had he rubbed her leg with it than the old mother rose up and walked even better than she had done before. But then this wonderful ointment could not be bought at a chemist's.

"What can you want with those three fern rods?" asked John of his fellow-traveller.

"Oh, they will make capital brooms," said he; "and I like them because I have strange whims sometimes." Then they walked on together for a long distance.

"How dark the sky is becoming," said John; "and look at those thick, heavy clouds."

"Those are not clouds," replied his fellow-traveller; "they are mountains—large lofty mountains—on the tops of which we should be above the clouds, in the pure, free air. Believe me, it is delightful to ascend so high; tomorrow we shall be there." But the mountains were not so near as they appeared; they had to travel a whole day before they reached them and pass through black forests and piles of rock as large as a town.

The journey had been so fatiguing that John and his fellow-traveller stopped to rest at a roadside inn, so that they might gain strength for their journey on the morrow. In the large public room of the inn a great many persons were assembled to see a comedy performed by dolls. The showman had just erected his little theatre, and the people were sitting round the room to witness the performance. Right in front, in the very best place, sat a stout butcher, with a great bull-dog by his side who seemed very much inclined to bite. He sat staring with all his eyes, and so indeed did every one else in the room.

And then the play began. It was a pretty piece, with a king and a queen in it, who sat on a beautiful throne and had gold crowns on their heads. The trains to their dresses were very long, according to the fashion; while the prettiest of wooden dolls, with glass eyes and large moustaches, stood at the doors and opened and shut them, that the fresh air might come into the room. It was a very pleasant play, not at all mournful; but just as the queen stood up and walked across the stage, the great bull-dog, who should have been held back by his master, made a spring forward and caught the queen in his teeth by the slender waist, so that it snapped in two.

This was a very dreadful disaster. The poor man, who was exhibiting the dolls, was much annoyed and quite sad about his queen; she was the prettiest doll he had, and the bull-dog had broken her head and shoulders off. But after all the people were gone away, the stranger, who came with John, said that he could soon set her to rights. And then he brought out his box and rubbed the doll with some of

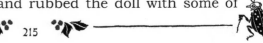

the salve with which he had cured the old woman when she broke her leg. As soon as this was done, the doll's back became quite right again; her head and shoulders were fixed on, and she could even move her limbs herself: there was now no occasion to pull the wires, for the doll acted just like a living creature, excepting that she could not speak. The man to whom the show belonged was quite delighted at having a doll who could dance of herself without being pulled by the wires; none of the other dolls could do this.

During the night, when all the people at the inn were gone to bed, some one was heard to sigh so deeply and painfully, and the sighing continued for so long a time, that everyone got up to see what could be the matter. The showman went at once to his little theatre and found that it proceeded from the dolls, who all lay on the floor sighing piteously and staring with their glass eyes; they all wanted to be rubbed with the ointment, so that, like the queen, they might be able to move of themselves. The queen threw herself on her knees, took off her beautiful crown, and, holding it in her hand, cried, "Take this from me, but do rub my husband and his courtiers."

The poor man who owned the theatre could scarcely refrain from weeping; he was so sorry that he could not help them. Then he immediately spoke to John's comrade, and promised him all the money he might receive at the next evening's performance if he would only rub the ointment on four or five of his dolls. But the fellow-traveller said he did not require anything in return, excepting the sword which the showman wore by his side. As soon as he received the sword, he anointed six of the dolls with the ointment, and they were able immediately to dance so gracefully that all the living girls in the room could not help joining in the dance. The coachman danced with the cook, and the waiters with the chambermaids, and all the strangers joined; even the tongs and the fire-shovel made an attempt, but they fell down after the first jump. So after all it was a very merry night.

The next morning John and his companion left the inn to continue their journey through the great pine-forests and over the high mountains. They arrived at last at such a great height that towns and villages lay beneath them and the church steeples looked like little specks between the green trees. They could see for miles round, far away to places they had never visited, and John saw more of the beautiful world than he had ever known before. The sun shone brightly in

the blue firmament above, and through the clear mountain air came the sound of the huntsman's horn, and the soft, sweet notes brought tears into his eyes, and he could not help exclaiming, "How good and loving God is to give us all this beauty and loveliness in the world to make us happy!"

His fellow-traveller stood by with folded hands, gazing on the dark wood and the towns bathed in the warm sunshine. At this moment there sounded over their heads sweet music. They looked up and discovered a large white swan hovering in the air and singing as never bird sang before. But the song soon became weaker and weaker, the bird's head drooped, and he sunk slowly down and lay dead at their feet.

"It is a beautiful bird," said the traveller, "and these large white wings are worth a great deal of money. I will take them with me. You see now that a sword will be very useful." So he cut off the wings of the dead swan with one blow, and carried them away with him.

They now continued their journey over the mountains for many miles, till they at length reached a large city containing hundreds of towers, which shone in the sunshine like silver. In the midst of the city stood a splendid marble palace, roofed with pure red gold, in which dwelt the king. John and his companion would not go into the town immediately; so they stopped at an inn outside the town, to change their clothes; for they wished to appear respectable as they walked through the streets. The landlord told them that the king was a very good man, who never injured anyone; but as to his daughter, "Heaven, defend us!"

She was indeed a wicked princess. She possessed beauty enough—nobody could be more elegant or prettier than she was; but what of that? for she was a wicked witch; and in consequence of her conduct many noble young princes had lost their lives. Anyone was at liberty to make her an offer; were he a prince or a beggar, it mattered not to her. She would ask him to guess three things which she had just thought of, and if he succeeded, he was to marry her and be king over all the land when her father died; but if he could not guess these three things, then she ordered him to be hanged or to have his head cut off.

The old king, her father, was very much grieved at her conduct, but he could not prevent her from being so wicked, because he once said he would have nothing more to do with her lovers; she might do as she pleased. Each prince who came and tried the three guesses, so that he might marry the princess, had been unable to find them out and had been hanged or beheaded. They had all been warned in time and might have left her alone if they would. The old king became at last so distressed at all these dreadful circumstances, that for a whole day every year he and his soldiers knelt and prayed that the princess might become good; but she continued as wicked as ever. The old women who drank brandy would colour it quite black before they drank it, to show how they mourned; and what more could they do?

"What a horrible princess!" said John; "she ought to be well flogged. If I were the old king, I would have her punished in some way."

Just then they heard the people outside shouting, "Hurrah!" and, looking out, they saw the princess passing by; and she was really so beautiful that everybody forgot her wickedness and shouted "Hurrah!" Twelve lovely maidens in white silk dresses, holding golden tulips in their hands, rode by her side on coal-black horses. The princess herself had a snow-white steed decked with diamonds and rubies. Her dress was of cloth of gold, and the whip she held in her hand looked like a sunbeam. The golden crown on her head glittered like the stars of heaven, and her mantle was formed of thousands of butterflies' wings sewn together. Yet she herself was more beautiful than all.

When John saw her, his face became as red as a drop of blood, and he could scarcely utter a word. The princess looked exactly like the beautiful lady with the golden crown, of whom he had dreamed on the night his father died. She appeared to him so lovely that he could not help loving her.

"It could not be true," he thought, "that she was really a wicked witch, who ordered people to be hanged or beheaded, if they could not guess her thoughts. Everyone has permission to go and ask her hand, even the poorest beggar. I shall pay a visit to the palace," he said; "I must go, for I cannot help myself."

Then they all advised him not to attempt it; for he would be sure to share the same fate as the rest. His fellow-traveller also tried to persuade him against it, but John seemed quite sure of success. He brushed his shoes and his coat, washed his face and his hands, combed his soft flaxen hair, and then went out alone into the town and walked to the palace.

"Come in," said the king, as John knocked at the door. John opened it, and the old king, in a dressing gown and

embroidered slippers, came towards him. He had the crown on his head, carried his sceptre in one hand, and the orb in the other. "Wait a bit," said he, and he placed the orb under his arm, so that he could offer the other hand to John; but when he found that John was another suitor, he began to weep so violently, that both the sceptre and the orb fell to the floor, and he was obliged to wipe his eyes with his dressing gown. Poor old king! "Let her alone," he said; "you will fare as badly as all the others. Come, I will show you." Then he led him out into the princess's pleasure gardens, and there he saw a frightful sight. On every tree hung three or four king's sons who had wooed the princess, but had not been able to guess the riddles she gave them. Their skeletons rattled in every breeze, so that the terrified birds never dared to venture into the garden. All the flowers were supported by human bones instead of sticks, and human skulls in the flower-pots grinned horribly. It was really a doleful garden for a princess. "Do you see all this?" said the old king; "your fate will be the same as those who are here, therefore do not attempt it. You really make me very unhappy,—I take these things to heart so very much."

John kissed the good old king's hand and said he was sure it would be all right, for he was quite enchanted with the beautiful princess. Then the princess herself came riding into the palace yard with all her ladies, and he wished her "Good morning." She looked wonderfully fair and lovely when she offered her hand to John, and he loved her more than ever. How could she be a wicked witch, as all the people asserted? He accompanied her into the hall, and the little pages offered them gingerbread nuts and sweetmeats, but the old king was so unhappy he could eat nothing, and besides, gingerbread nuts were too hard for him. It was decided that John should come to the palace the next day, when the judges and the whole of the counsellors would be present, to try if he could guess the first riddle. If he succeeded, he would have to come a second time; but if not, he would lose his life,—and no one had ever been able to guess even one. However, John was not at all anxious about the result of his trial; on the contrary, he was very merry. He thought only of the beautiful princess, and believed that in some way he should have help, but how he knew not and did not like to think about it; so he danced along the highroad as he went back to the inn, where he had left his fellow-traveller waiting for him.

John could not refrain from telling him how gracious the princess had been, and how beautiful she looked. He longed for the next day so much that he might go to the palace and try his luck at guessing the riddles. But his comrade shook his head and looked very mournful. "I do so wish you to do well," said he; "we might have continued together much longer, and now I am likely to lose you; you poor dear John! I could shed tears, but I will not make you unhappy on the last night we may be together. We will be merry, really merry this evening; tomorrow, after you are gone, I shall be able to weep undisturbed."

It was very quickly known among the inhabitants of the town that another suitor had arrived for the princess, and there was great sorrow in consequence. The theatre remained closed, the women who sold sweetmeats tied crape round the sugar-sticks, and the king and the priests were on their knees in the church. There was a great lamentation, for no one expected John to succeed better than those who had been suitors before.

In the evening John's comrade prepared a large bowl of punch and said, "Now let us be merry and drink to the health of the princess." But after drinking two glasses, John became so sleepy, that he could not keep his eyes open and fell fast asleep. Then his fellow-traveller lifted him gently out of his chair and laid him on the bed; and as soon as it was quite dark, he took the two large wings which he had cut from the dead swan and tied them firmly to his own shoulders. Then he put into his pocket the largest of the three rods which he had obtained from the old woman who had fallen and broken her leg. After this he opened the window, and flew away over the town, straight towards the palace, and seated himself in a corner, under the window which looked into the bedroom of the princess.

The town was perfectly still when the clocks struck a quarter to twelve. Presently the window opened, and the princess, who had large black wings to her shoulders and a long white mantle, flew away over the city towards a high mountain. The fellow-traveller, who had made himself invisible, so that she could not possibly see him, flew after her through the air and whipped the princess with his rod, so that the blood came whenever he struck her. Ah, it was a strange flight through the air! The wind caught her mantle, so that it spread out on all sides, like the large sail of a ship, and the moon shone through it. "How it hails, to be sure!" said the princess, at each blow she received from the rod; and it served her right to be whipped.

At last she reached the side of the mountain and knocked. The mountain opened with a noise like the roll of thunder, and the princess went in. The traveller followed her; no one could see him, as he had made himself invisible. They went through a long, wide passage. A thousand gleaming spiders ran here and there on the walls, causing them to glitter as if they were illuminated with fire. They next entered a large hall built of silver and gold. Large red and blue flowers shone on the walls, looking like sunflowers in size, but no one could dare to pluck them, for the stems were hideous poisonous snakes, and the flowers were flames of fire, darting out of their jaws. Shining glow-worms covered the ceiling, and sky-blue bats flapped their transparent wings. Altogether the place had a frightful appearance.

In the middle of the floor stood a throne supported by four skeleton horses, whose harness had been made by fiery-red spiders. The throne itself was made of milk-white glass, and the cushions were little black mice, each biting the other's tail. Over it hung a canopy of rose-colored spider's webs, spotted with the prettiest little green flies, which sparkled like precious stones.

On the throne sat an old magician with a crown on his ugly head and a sceptre in his hand. He kissed the princess on the forehead, seated her by his side on the splendid throne, and then the music commenced. Great black grasshoppers played the mouth organ, and the owl struck herself

on the body instead of a drum. It was altogether a ridiculous concert. Little black goblins with false lights in their caps danced about the hall; but no one could see the traveller, and he had placed himself just behind the throne where he could see and hear everything. The courtiers who came in afterwards looked noble and grand; but anyone with common sense could see what they really were, only broomsticks, with cabbages for heads.

The magician had given them life and dressed them in embroidered robes. It answered very well, as they were only wanted for show. After there had been a little dancing, the princess told the magician that she had a new suitor and asked him what she should think of for the suitor to guess when he came to the castle the next morning.

"Listen to what I say," said the magician, "you must choose something very easy, he is less likely to guess it then. Think of one of your shoes; he will never imagine it is that. Then cut his head off; and mind you do not forget to bring his eyes with you tomorrow night, that I may eat them."

The princess curtsied low, and said she would not forget the eyes.

The magician then opened the mountain, and she flew home again, but the traveller followed and flogged her so much with the rod, that she sighed quite deeply about the heavy hail-storm and made as much haste as she could to get back to her bedroom through the window. The traveller then returned to the inn where John still slept, took off his wings, and laid down on the bed, for he was very tired.

Early in the morning John awoke, and when his fellow-traveller got up, he said that he had had a very wonderful dream about the princess and her shoe; he therefore advised John to ask her if she had not thought of her shoe. Of course the traveller knew this from what the magician in the mountain had said.

"I may as well say that as anything else," said John. "Perhaps your dream may come true; still I will say farewell, for if I guess wrong, I shall never see you again."

Then they embraced each other, and John went into the town and walked to the palace. The great hall was full of people, and the judges sat in arm-chairs, with eider-down cushions to rest their heads upon, because they had so much to think of. The old king stood near, wiping his eyes with his white pocket-handkerchief. When the princess entered, she looked even more beautiful than she had appeared the day before, and greeted every one present most gracefully; but to John she gave her hand and said, "Good morning to you."

Now came the time for John to guess what she was thinking of; and oh, how kindly she looked at him as she spoke. But when he uttered the single word shoe, she turned as pale as a ghost; all her wisdom could not help her, for he

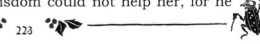

had guessed rightly. Oh, how pleased the old king was! It was quite amusing to see how he capered about. All the people clapped their hands, both on his account and John's, who had guessed rightly the first time. His fellow-traveller was glad also, when he heard how successful John had been. But John folded his hands and thanked God, who, he felt quite sure, would help him again; and he knew he had to guess twice more.

The evening passed pleasantly like the one preceding. While John slept, his companion flew behind the princess to the mountain and flogged her even harder than before; this time he had taken two rods with him. No one saw him go in with her, and he heard all that was said. The princess this time was to think of a glove, and he told John as if he had again heard it in a dream. The next day, therefore, he was able to guess correctly the second time, and it caused great rejoicing at the palace. The whole court jumped about as they had seen the king do the day before, but the princess lay on the sofa and would not say a single word.

All now depended upon John. If he only guessed rightly the third time, he would marry the princess, and reign over the kingdom after the death of the old king; but if he failed, he would lose his life, and the magician would have his beautiful blue eyes.

That evening John said his prayers and went to bed very early, and soon fell asleep calmly. But his companion tied on his wings to his shoulders, took three rods, and, with his sword at his side, flew to the palace. It was a very dark night and so stormy that the tiles flew from the roofs of the houses and the trees in the garden upon which the skeletons hung bent themselves like reeds before the wind.

The lightning flashed, and the thunder rolled in one long-continued peal all night. The window of the castle opened, and the princess flew out. She was pale as death, but she laughed at the storm as if it were not bad enough. Her white mantle fluttered in the wind like a large sail, and the traveller flogged her with the three rods till the blood trickled down, and at last she could scarcely fly; she contrived, however, to reach the mountain. "What a hail-storm!" she said, as she entered; "I have never been out in such weather as this."

"Yes, there may be too much of a good thing sometimes," said the magician.

Then the princess told him that John had guessed rightly the second time, and if he succeeded the next morning, he would win, and she could never come to the mountain again or practice magic as she had done, and therefore she was quite unhappy.

"I will find out something for you to think of which he will never guess, unless he is a greater conjuror than myself. But now let us be merry."

Then he took the princess by both hands, and they danced with all the little goblins and Jack-o'-lanterns in the room. The red spiders sprang here and there on the walls quite as merrily, and the flowers of fire appeared as if they were throwing out sparks. The owl beat the drum, the crickets whistled, and the grasshoppers played the mouth-organ. It was a very ridiculous ball.

After they had danced enough, the princess was obliged to go home, for fear she should be missed at the palace. The magician offered to go with her, so that they might be company to each other on the way. Then they flew away through the bad weather, and the traveller followed them, and broke his three rods across their shoulders. The magician had never been out in such a hail-storm as this. Just by the palace the magician stopped to wish the princess farewell and to whisper in her ear, "Tomorrow think of my head."

But the traveller heard it, and just as the princess slipped through the window into her bedroom and the magician turned round to fly back to the mountain, he seized him by the long black beard and with his sabre cut off the wicked conjuror's head just behind his shoulders, so that he could not even see who it was. He threw the body into the sea to the fishes, and after dipping the head into the water, he tied it up in a silk handkerchief, took it with him to the inn, and then went to bed.

The next morning he gave John the handkerchief and told him not to untie it till the princess asked him what she was thinking of. There were so many people in the great hall of the palace that they stood as thick as radishes tied together in a bundle. The council sat in their arm-chairs with the white cushions. The old king wore new robes, and the golden crown and sceptre had been polished up so that he looked quite smart. But the princess was very pale and wore a black dress as if she were going to a funeral.

"What have I thought of?" asked the princess of John. He immediately untied the handkerchief, and was himself quite frightened when he saw the head of the ugly magician. Everyone shuddered, for it was terrible to look at; but the princess sat like a statue and could not utter a single

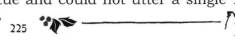

word. At length she rose and gave John her hand, for he had guessed rightly.

She looked at no one but sighed deeply and said, "You are my master now; this evening our marriage must take place."

"I am very pleased to hear it," said the old king. "It is just what I wish."

Then all the people shouted "Hurrah." The band played music in the street, the bells rang, and the cake-women took the black crape off the sugar-sticks. There was universal joy. Three oxen, stuffed with ducks and chickens, were roasted whole in the market-place, where everyone might help himself to a slice. The fountains spouted forth the most delicious wine, and whoever bought a penny loaf at the baker's received six large buns, full of raisins, as a present.

In the evening the whole town was illuminated. The soldiers fired off cannons, and the boys let off crackers. There was eating and drinking, dancing and jumping everywhere. In the palace, the high-born gentlemen and beautiful ladies danced with each other, and they could be heard at a great distance singing the following song:—

> "Here are maidens, young and fair,
> Dancing in the summer air;
> Like two spinning-wheels at play,
> Pretty maidens dance away—
> Dance the spring and summer through
> Till the sole falls from your shoe."

But the princess was still a witch, and she could not love John. His fellow-traveller had thought of that, so he gave John three feathers out of the swan's wings, and a little bottle with a few drops in it. He told him to place a large bath full of water by the princess's bed, and put the feathers and the drops into it. Then, at the moment she was about to get into bed, he must give her a little push, so that she might fall into the water, and then dip her three times. This would destroy the power of the magician, and she would love him very much.

John did all that his companion told him to do. The princess shrieked aloud when he dipped her under the water the first time, and struggled under his hands in the form of a great black swan with fiery eyes. As she rose the second time from the water, the swan had become white, with a black ring round its neck. John allowed the water to close once more over the bird, and at the same time it changed into a most beautiful princess. She was more lovely even than before and thanked him, while her eyes sparkled with tears, for having broken the spell of the magician. The next day, the king came with the whole court to offer their congratulations, and stayed till quite late. Last of all came the travelling companion; he had his staff in his hand and his knapsack on his back. John kissed him many times and told him he must not go, he must remain with him, for he was the cause of all his good fortune. But the traveller shook his head, and said gently and kindly, "No: my time is up now; I have only paid my debt to you. Do you remember the dead man whom the bad people wished to throw out of his coffin? You gave all you possessed that he might rest in his grave; I am that man." As he said this, he vanished.

The wedding festivities lasted a whole month. John and his princess loved each other dearly, and the old king lived to see many a happy day, when he took their little children on his knees and let them play with his sceptre. And John became king over the whole country.

The Emperor's New Clothes

MANY years ago there lived an emperor who was so fond of new clothes that he spent all his money on them in order to be beautifully dressed. He did not care about his soldiers, he did not care about the theatre; he only liked to go out walking to show off his new clothes. He had a coat for every hour of the day; and just as they say of a king, "He is in the council-chamber," they always said here, "The emperor is in the wardrobe."

In the great city in which he lived there was always something going on; every day many strangers came there. One day two impostors arrived, who gave themselves out as weavers, and said that they knew how to manufacture the most beautiful cloth imaginable. Not only were the texture and pattern uncommonly beautiful, but the clothes which were made of the stuff possessed the wonderful property that they were invisible to anyone who was unfit for his office or who was unpardonably stupid.

"Those must indeed be splendid clothes," thought the emperor. "If I had them on I could find out which men in my kingdom are unfit for the offices they hold. I could distinguish the wise from the stupid! Yes, this cloth must be wo-

ven for me at once." And he gave both the impostors much money, so that they might begin their work.

They placed two weaving-looms and began to do as if they were working, but they had not the least thing on the looms. They also demanded the finest silk and the best gold, which they put in their pockets, and worked at the empty looms till late into the night.

"I should like very much to know how far they have got on with the cloth," thought the emperor. But he remembered, when he thought about it, that whoever was stupid

or unfit for his office would not be able to see it. Now he certainly believed that he had nothing to fear for himself, but he wanted first to send somebody else in order to see how he stood with regard to his office. Everybody in the whole town knew what a wonderful power the cloth had, and they were all curious to see how bad or how stupid their neighbour was.

"I will send my old and honoured minister to the weavers," thought the emperor. "He can judge best what the cloth is like, for he has intellect, and no one understands his office better than he."

Now, the good old minister went into the hall where the two impostors sat working at the empty weaving-looms.

"Dear me!" thought the old minister, opening his eyes wide, "I can see nothing!" But he did not say so.

Both the impostors begged him to be so kind as to step closer and asked him if it were not a beautiful texture and lovely colours. They pointed to the empty loom, and the poor old minister went forward rubbing his eyes; but he could see nothing, for there was nothing there.

"Dear, dear!" thought he, "can I be stupid? I have never thought that, and nobody must know it! Can I be not fit for my office? No, I must certainly not say that I cannot see the cloth!"

"Have you nothing to say about it?" asked one of the men who was weaving.

"Oh, it is lovely, most lovely!" answered the old minister, looking through his spectacles. "What a texture! What colours! Yes, I will tell the emperor that it pleases me very much."

"Now we are delighted at that," said both the weavers, and thereupon they named the colours and explained the make of the texture.

The old minister paid great attention, so that he could tell the same to the emperor when he came back to him, which he did.

The impostors now wanted more money, more

silk, and more gold to use in their weaving. They put it all in their own pockets, and there came no threads on the loom, but they went on as they had done before, working at the empty loom.

The emperor soon sent another worthy statesman to see how the weaving was getting on and whether the cloth would soon be finished. It was the same with him as the first one; he looked and looked, but because there was nothing on the empty loom he could see nothing.

"Is it not a beautiful piece of cloth?" asked the two impostors, and they pointed to and described the splendid material which was not there.

"Stupid I am not," thought the man, "so it must be my good office for which I am not fitted. It is strange, certainly, but no one must be allowed to notice it." And so he praised the cloth which he did not see and expressed to them his delight at the beautiful colours and the splendid texture. "Yes, it is quite beautiful," he said to the emperor.

Everybody in the town was talking of the magnificent cloth.

Now the emperor wanted to see it himself while it was still on the loom. With a great crowd of select followers, among whom were both the worthy statesmen who had already been there before, he went to the cunning impostors, who were now weaving with all their might but without fibre or thread.

"Is it not splendid?" said both the old statesmen who had already been there. "See, Your Majesty, what a texture! What colours!" And then they pointed to the empty loom, for they believed that the others could see the cloth.

"What!" thought the emperor, "I can see nothing! This is indeed horrible! Am I stupid? Am I not fit to be emperor? That were the most dreadful thing that could happen to me."

"Oh! it is very beautiful!" he said. "It has my gracious approval." And then he nodded pleasantly and examined the empty loom, for he would not say that he could see nothing.

His whole court round him looked and looked and saw no more than the others, but they said like the emperor, "Oh! It is beautiful!" And they advised him to wear these new and magnificent clothes for the first time at the great procession which was soon to take place.

"Splendid! Lovely! Most beautiful!" went from mouth to mouth; everyone seemed delighted over them, and the emperor gave to the impostors the title of court weavers to the emperor.

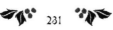

Throughout the whole of the night before the morning on which the procession was to take place, the impostors were up and were working by the light of over sixteen candles. The people could see that they were very busy making the emperor's new clothes ready. They pretended they were taking the cloth from the loom, cut with huge scissors in the air, sewed with needles without thread, and then said at last, "Now the clothes are finished!"

The emperor came himself with his most distinguished knights, and each impostor held up his arm just as if he were holding something and said, "See! Here are the breeches! Here is the coat! Here the cloak!" and so on.

"Spun clothes are so comfortable that one would imagine one had nothing on at all; but that is the beauty of it!"

"Yes," said all the knights, but they could see nothing, for there was nothing there.

"Will it please Your Majesty graciously to take off your clothes?" said the impostors; "then we will put on the new clothes here before the mirror."

The emperor took off all his clothes, and the impostors placed themselves before him as if they were putting on each part of his new clothes which was ready, and the emperor turned and bent himself in front of the mirror.

"How beautifully they fit! How well they sit!" said everybody. "What material! What colours! It is a gorgeous suit!"

"They are waiting outside with the canopy which your majesty is wont to have borne over you in the procession," announced the master of the ceremonies.

"Look, I am ready," said the emperor. "Doesn't it sit well?" And he turned himself again to the mirror to see if his finery was on all right.

The chamberlains who were used to carry the train put their hands near the floor as if they were lifting up the train; then they did as if they were holding something in the air. They would not have it noticed that they could see nothing.

So the emperor went along in the procession under the splendid canopy, and all the people in the streets and at the windows said, "How matchless are the emperor's new clothes! That train fastened to his dress, how beautifully it hangs!"

No one wished it to be noticed that he could see nothing, for then he would have been unfit for his office or else very stupid. None of the emperor's clothes had met with such approval as these had.

"But he has nothing on!" said a little child at last.

"Just listen to the innocent child!" said the father, and each one whispered to his neighbour what the child had said.

"But he has nothing on!" the people called out at last.

This struck the emperor, for it seemed to him as if they were right; but he thought to himself, "I must go on with the procession now." And the chamberlains walked along still more uprightly, holding up the train which was not there at all.

The Snow Man

"IT IS so delightfully cold," said the Snow Man, "that it makes my whole body crackle. This is just the kind of wind to blow life into one. How that great red thing up there is staring at me!" He meant the sun, who was just setting. "It shall not make me wink. I shall manage to keep the pieces."

He had two triangular pieces of tile in his head, instead of eyes; his mouth was made of an old broken rake, and was, of course, furnished with teeth. He had been brought into existence amidst the joyous shouts of boys, the jingling of sleigh-bells, and the slashing of whips. The sun went down, and the full moon rose, large, round, and clear, shining in the deep blue.

"There it comes again, from the other side," said the Snow Man, who supposed the sun was showing himself once more. "Ah, I have cured him of staring, though; now he may hang up there and shine, that I may see myself. If I only knew how to manage to move away from this place,—I should so like to move. If I could, I would slide along yonder on the ice, as I have seen the boys do; but I don't understand how; I don't even know how to run."

"Away, away," barked the old yard-dog. He was quite hoarse and could not pronounce "Bow wow" properly. He had once been an indoor dog and lay by the fire, and he had been hoarse ever since. "The sun will make you run some day. I saw him, last winter, make your predecessor run, and his predecessor before him. Away, away, they all have to go."

"I don't understand you, comrade," said the Snow Man. "Is that thing up yonder to teach me to run? I saw it running itself a little while ago, and now it has come creeping up from the other side."

"You know nothing at all," replied the yard-dog; "but then, you've only lately been patched up. What you see yonder is the moon, and the one before it was the sun. It will come again tomorrow and most likely teach you to run down into the ditch by the well; for I think the weather is going to change. I can feel such pricks and stabs in my left leg; I am sure there is going to be a change."

"I don't understand him," said the Snow Man to himself; "but I have a feeling that he is talking of something very disagreeable. The one who stared so just now and whom he calls the sun is not my friend; I can feel that too."

"Away, away," barked the yard-dog, and then he turned round three times and crept into his kennel to sleep.

There was really a change in the weather. Towards morning, a thick fog covered the whole country round, and a keen wind arose, so that the cold seemed to freeze one's bones; but when the sun rose, the sight was splendid. Trees and bushes were covered with hoar frost and looked like a forest of white coral; while on every twig glittered frozen dew-drops. The many delicate forms concealed in summer by luxuriant foliage were now clearly defined and looked like glittering lace-work. From every twig glistened a white radiance.

The birch, waving in the wind, looked full of life, like trees in summer; and its appearance was wondrously beautiful. And where the sun shone, how everything glittered and sparkled, as if diamond dust had been strewn about; while the snowy carpet of the earth appeared as if covered

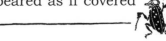

with diamonds, from which countless lights gleamed, whiter than even the snow itself.

"This is really beautiful," said a young girl, who had come into the garden with a young man; and they both stood still near the Snow Man and contemplated the glittering scene. "Summer cannot show a more beautiful sight," she exclaimed, while her eyes sparkled.

"And we can't have such a fellow as this in the summer time," replied the young man, pointing to the Snow Man; "he is capital."

The girl laughed, and nodded at the Snow Man, and then tripped away over the snow with her friend. The snow creaked and crackled beneath her feet, as if she had been treading on starch.

"Who are these two?" asked the Snow Man of the yard-dog. "You have been here longer than I have; do you know them?"

"Of course I know them," replied the yard-dog; "she has stroked my back many times, and he has given me a bone of meat. I never bite those two."

"But what are they?" asked the Snow Man.

"They are lovers," he replied; "they will go and live in the same kennel by-and-by, and gnaw at the same bone. Away, away!"

"Are they the same kind of beings as you and I?" asked the Snow Man.

"Well, they belong to the same master," retorted the yard-dog. "Certainly people who were only born yesterday know very little. I can see that in you. I have age and experience. I know everyone here in the house, and I know there was once a time when I did not lie out here in the cold, fastened to a chain. Away, away!"

"The cold is delightful," said the Snow Man; "but do tell me, tell me; only you must not clank your chain so; for it jars all through me when you do that."

"Away, away!" barked the yard-dog; "I'll tell you; they said I was a pretty little fellow once; then I used to lie in a velvet-covered chair, up at the master's house, and sit in the mistress's lap. They used to kiss my nose and wipe my paws with an embroidered handkerchief, and I was called 'Ami, dear Ami, sweet Ami.' But after a while I grew too big for them, and they sent me away to the housekeeper's room; so I came to live on the lower storey. You can look into the room from where you stand and see where I was master once; for I was indeed master to the housekeeper. It was certainly a smaller room than those upstairs; but I was more comfortable; for I was not being continually taken hold of and pulled about by the children as I had been. I received quite as good food, or even better. I had my own cushion, and there was a stove—it is the finest thing in the world at this season of the year. I used to go under the stove and lie down quite beneath it. Ah, I still dream of that stove. Away, away!"

"Does a stove look beautiful?" asked the Snow Man. "Is it at all like me?"

"It is just the reverse of you," said the dog; "it's as black as a crow, and has a long neck and a brass knob; it eats firewood, so that fire spurts out of its mouth. We should keep on one side or under it, to be comfortable. You can see it through the window, from where you stand."

Then the Snow Man looked and saw a bright polished thing with a brazen knob, and fire gleaming from the lower part of it. The Snow Man felt quite a strange sensation come over him; it was very odd, he knew not what it meant, and he could not account for it. But there are people who are not men of snow, who understand what it is.

"And why did you leave her?" asked the Snow Man, for it seemed to him that the stove must be of the female sex. "How could you give up such a comfortable place?"

"I was obliged," replied the yard-dog. "They turned me out of doors and chained me up here. I had bitten the youngest of my master's sons in the leg, because he kicked away the bone I was gnawing. 'Bone for bone,' I thought; but they were so angry, and from that time I have been fastened to a chain and lost my bone. Don't you hear how hoarse I am? Away, away! I can't talk any more like other dogs. Away, away, that is the end of it all."

But the Snow Man was no longer listening. He was looking into the housekeeper's room on the lower storey, where the stove stood on its four iron legs, looking about the same size as the Snow Man himself. "What a strange crackling I feel within me," he said. "Shall I ever get in there? It is an innocent wish, and innocent wishes are sure to be fulfilled. I must go in there and lean against her, even if I have to break the window."

"You must never go in there," said the yard-dog, "for if you approach the stove, you'll melt away, away."

"I might as well go," said the Snow Man, "for I think I am breaking up as it is."

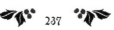

During the whole day the Snow Man stood looking in through the window, and in the twilight hour the room became still more inviting, for from the stove came a gentle glow, not like the sun or the moon; no, only the bright light which gleams from a stove when it has been well fed. When the door of the stove was opened, the flames darted out of its mouth; this is customary with all stoves. The light of the flames fell directly on the face and breast of the Snow Man with a ruddy gleam. "I can endure it no longer," said he; "how beautiful it looks when it stretches out its tongue!"

The night was long, but it did not appear so to the Snow Man, who stood there enjoying his own reflections and crackling with the cold. In the morning, the window-panes of the housekeeper's room were covered with ice. They were the most beautiful ice-flowers any Snow Man could desire, but they concealed the stove. These window-panes would not thaw, and he could see nothing of the stove, which he pictured to himself, as if it had been a lovely human being. The snow crackled and the wind whistled around him; it was just the kind of frosty weather a Snow Man might thoroughly enjoy. But he did not enjoy it; how, indeed, could he enjoy anything when he was "stove sick?"

"That is a terrible disease for a Snow Man," said the yard-dog; "I have suffered from it myself, but I got over it. Away, away," he barked and then he added, "the weather is going to change."

And the weather did change; it began to thaw. As the warmth increased, the Snow Man decreased. He said nothing and made no complaint, which is a sure sign. One morning he broke and sunk down altogether; and, behold, where he had stood, something like a broomstick remained sticking up in the ground. It was the pole round which the boys had built him up.

"Ah, now I understand why he had such a great longing for the stove," said the yard-dog. "Why, there's the shovel that is used for cleaning out the stove, fastened to the pole." The Snow Man had a stove scraper in his body; that was what moved him so. "But it's all over now. Away, away." And soon the winter passed. "Away, away," barked the hoarse yard-dog. But the girls in the house sang,

"Come from your fragrant home, green thyme;
Stretch your soft branches, willow-tree;
The months are bringing the sweet spring-time,

When the lark in the sky sings joyfully.
Come gentle sun, while the cuckoo sings,
And I'll mock his note in my wanderings."

And nobody thought any more of the Snow Man.

Contents

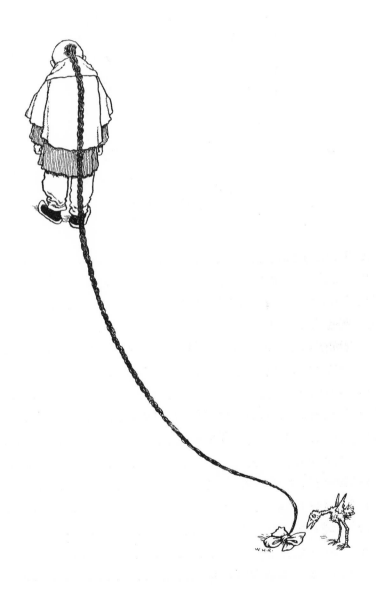

Manufactured by Amazon.ca
Bolton, ON